HIGH WAGES

Persephone Book N° 85
Published by Persephone Books Ltd 2009
Reprinted 2016

First published in 1930 by John Murray Ltd

Endpapers taken from 'Farm Scene', a 1930 dress
fabric by Crysède Ltd
© V & A Images, Victoria and Albert Museum

Prelim pages typeset in ITC Baskerville by
Keystroke, Tettenhall, Wolverhampton

Printed and bound in Germany by
GGP Media GmbH, Poessneck

ISBN 9781903155752

Persephone Books Ltd
59 Lamb's Conduit Street
London WC1N 3NB
020 7242 9292

www.persephonebooks.co.uk

Tracy

HIGH WAGES

by

DOROTHY WHIPPLE

✳✳✳✳✳✳✳

with a new preface by

JANE BROCKET

PERSEPHONE BOOKS
LONDON

PREFACE

✳✳✳✳✳✳✳✳

'What possessed me to write about a girl in a shop? I know nothing about it,' wrote Dorothy Whipple in her journal on the day she finished and posted *High Wages* to the publisher which had brought out her first novel *Young Anne* in 1927. When Jonathan Cape refused the new novel, believing it would not be a 'commercial success', Dorothy was downcast but not discouraged. She sent it to John Murray, who accepted it. Her post-script, written in *Random Commentary* (a selection of extracts from her note-books and journals published in 1966), happily points out that the book 'afterwards sold thousands of copies and is now in . . . its tenth edition.'

The truth is that, like many women and thousands of delighted readers, Dorothy Whipple knew a great deal about girls in shops, especially those in dress-shops. Indeed, she unconsciously reveals her keen interest in the subject of clothing on the very next page of *Random Commentary* when, à propos the invitation of Lord Gorell, a director of John Murray, to meet in London to discuss *High Wages*, she writes with relief, 'Thank goodness I've got my new coat.'

Despite her misgivings about her subject matter, Dorothy Whipple is undoubtedly at home in *High Wages*. Although she later came to be associated with the Midlands (*They Knew Mr Knight, They Were Sisters* and *The Priory* are all set in that part of England) this novel is set in her beloved home county of Lancashire ('that grand poetic landscape' she called it) which she observes with deep interest and portrays with affection, humour and pride. It is a celebration of the Lancastrian values of hard work and stubbornness, and there could be no finer setting for a shop-girl-made-good story than the county in which cotton was king, muck was turned into brass on a daily basis, judges of cotton staple are revered on the Exchange, and the nearby cities of Manchester and Liverpool were world-renowned centres of progress and industrial energy. It might have been satanic and hellish in some respects (there are echoes of Dickens's *Hard Times* in the description of the mills Jane sees from the train as she travels to and from Manchester) but Dorothy Whipple recognised that it was nevertheless pulsatingly alive, and full of opportunity for an ambitious young girl.

When *High Wages* was published in 1930, readers in the North West must have experienced thrills of recognition as they read about the places and character-types they knew: the prosperous businessmen with spats and flamboyant button-holes and furriers with diamond shirt-studs, the dishes of sheep's head and tripe, parkin, jumbles and Bury Simnel cake, the cleverly noted, pettily snobbish class distinctions between St Anne's and Blackpool. (Just as I did, in fact, when I first read the novel several years ago and found myself recalling bus-trips in the 1960s with my grandmother to the shops of Manchester, the steamy confines of the basement Kardomah café in St Ann's Square, the smell of tripe emanating from the UCP shop and, above all, the plushness, poshness and glamour of Kendal's on Deansgate.) The story is given extra Northern flavour with a sprinkling of Alan Bennett-style observations; Dorothy Whipple enjoyed listening to other people's conversations and wrote down many gems overheard on buses, in Turkish Baths, golf clubs, hotels and restaurants. So Jane speculates about Mr Briggs' 'dropped stomach', Maggie calls eau de cologne 'odyclone', and the wonderfully comic exchange between Mrs Briggs and her Blackpool landlady is worthy of anything performed by Thora Hird or Victoria Wood.

As well as being a marvellously engrossing and deeply caring novel, *High Wages* has tremendous historical value – although, as ever with Dorothy Whipple, the reader never feels she is being browbeaten about social issues. Unlike many of her contemporary, often male, writers such as HG Wells and Arnold Bennett who dealt with similar subjects of shopgirls and dressmakers but with the clear objective of pressing home their arguments for social change, Mrs Whipple's non-judgmental style leaves the reader free to draw her own conclusions. And, because of the author's light touch, her enjoyment of the subject matter and her desire to tell a good story rather than lecture the reader, *High Wages* is as relevant today as it was when it was published in 1930 and contains many parallels with contemporary issues. The book chimes in with serious present-day discussions of our consumer culture, concepts of 'retail therapy' and 'shopaholism', debates about women's clothing and shoes, and indeed the question of whether intelligent, educated women should even be interested in something as frivolous as fashion.

It was very clever of Mrs Whipple to begin the story in 1912, just as shops, clothing, and women's lives were on the cusp of change. Gordon Selfridge may have opened his magnificent, glittering department store on Oxford Street in London in 1909, but his revolutionary new ideas about elegant merchandising and wooing the customer had not yet percolated down to the resolutely old-fashioned provincial market-squares of places like Tidsley, where Mr Chadwick's window is crammed and stuffed with merchandise ('stalactites of eiderdowns' and a Christmas display that uncannily resembles the dead birds in the window of the neighbouring poulterer). Mr Chadwick is typical of most drapers of the time in refusing to countenance innovation. In 1912 ready-made clothes were still virtually unheard-of in the provinces, and drapers still sold 'piece-goods' or lengths of fabric which were then sent, with a pattern and any trimmings, to customers' private dressmakers; in much the same way the ladies of *Cranford*, a century earlier, fuss over buying their muslins and silks and send for dress patterns from the cities. So Chadwick's remains a period piece forever preserved in aspic, the kind of thing we might now see in a heritage museum, something that makes it all the more fascinating for any modern reader interested in the history of dressmaking and clothes.

Like many young girls entering the trade at that time, Jane begins as a junior assistant in haberdashery, the section that will soon come to be associated with all that is old-fashioned and unchanging about drapers' shops. With the little drawers, fiddly packets and ribbon-cards, the careful counting out, wrapping up and putting back, and the vast range of products (a supplier's list of the period contains, amongst many things, 10 types of elastic, 16 'mendings', 21 sorts of pins, and 26 braids each in a range of colours), the goods took a disproportionately large amount of time to serve and all for very low returns and thus negligible commission. This is one reason why the unfortunate junior girls were stationed in 'haby', usually by the front door where the cold draughts brought in imperious customers who ignored them, in the manner of the 'better-end' Mrs Greenwood in the novel. Yet it is here that Jane quickly picks up her arcane but invaluable trade knowledge of fabrics (sateen, alpaca, aeolian, foulard, flannel, unbleached twill, gabardine) and trimmings (braids, 'galons', 'ciré', ribbons, feathers, Peter Pan collars) that sets her up to compete in the man's world of women's clothing.

Unlike her parochial, short-sighted boss who is in thrall to the local bigwigs, the outward- and forward-looking Jane (who blithely steps all over her 'elders and betters' in the *Tidsley Telegraph* in her bare feet when taking her bath) soon realises that 'ready-mades' are on their way. Her trip to Manchester to see the stylish windows of Kendal's and to pick up ideas reflects the immense interest at the time in the recently built department stores in cities such as Liverpool, Manchester and Newcastle.

Like the manufacturers themselves, these retailers were beginning to see that there was big money to be made in clothing the masses. As a result of the market for ready-mades taking off, not only did department stores spring up, but also small independent dress-shops opened in towns and cities up and down the country. Often owned by women, they were known in the trade as 'madam' shops and at their peak in the 1920s they had cornered almost half of the women's clothing market. Jane's little enterprise is part of this trend towards eponymous shops which offered a personalised service, an intimate knowledge of the clients and, crucially, tact and good taste. Like many skilled saleswomen of the period, she is at the forefront of a new culture of shopping in which women are, for the first time, powerful consumers. With the advent of department stores in the 1890s, shopping had become the new leisure activity, a diversion for bored women like Sylvia in the novel, and a pleasure rather than a household duty (as Sylvia's mother, Mrs Greenwood, views it).

When Jane opens her shop it is the antithesis of the pre-war, Edwardian style, and Dorothy Whipple demonstrates that she is very much the daughter of an architect with an acute eye for contemporary design. With its simple, imaginative, creative and carefully edited window displays ('poems' as Wilfrid calls them), bright electric lights, and fresh greens, yellows, whites and French grey (Dorothy Whipple's favourite, spring-like colours – she has a deep distrust of pink, a colour she uses to denote over-pampered, over-heated taste and interiors), it is an ultra-modern riposte to the heavy maroons, blues, dark woods and marble stuffiness and excess of the town's pre-war retailers and house-owners.

The goods that Jane sells are very different, too, from those of the traditional draper. She happily relinquishes haberdashery to Mr Chadwick and moves on to new clothes for new women who have been recently liberated by world events from closeted, restricted lives, clothes that are soft and fluid, that allow them freedom of movement, to play sport, to work and to walk. The casting-off of imprisoning corsets and rigid undergarments is a powerful metaphor for the new attitudes towards women's roles and activities, and the liberation of the female form was as important as anything else in the fight for women's rights.

However, the deep significance of what a person wears concerns everyone, not just women, in Tidsley. Although she never labours the point, Dorothy Whipple is fascinated by the meaning of clothes, the social coding and signals they carry, and uses to devastatingly accurate effect the telling detail of a hat or an accessory to reveal the personality and the status, the fancies and the foibles of the wearer. She is acutely sensitive to the fears and anxieties of socially unconfident characters who live in an agony of torture about the 'correct' way to dress; a Hospital Ball can be blighted by the wrong stud and a shop-owner can be considered bold and danger-ously self-important to go about in the market square without a hat.

At this time, clothes were far more of a social signifier than they are now, long after 'ready-mades' swept away forever many of the subtle demarcations between classes and social groups and largely democratised the world of fashion. As Catherine Horwood writes in her fascinating study *Keeping Up Appearances: Fashion and Class between the Wars* (2005), 'Clothes have always been a key component in that most British of rituals, maintaining class distinctions' in what was then a 'minutely stratified' society. Men and women dressed to reflect status and to demonstrate correctness, respectability, dignity – and they expected others to live up to their 'positions', too. Mr Chadwick has no respect for Mrs Briggs who lives in one of the posh houses and yet clings to her humble origins and wears sateen petticoats, but is full of admiration for Tidsley's self-crowned monarch, the Queen Mary-style Mrs Greenwood, who promenades in regal fashion up the Road, a majestically stiff and corseted figure in a fine mauve dress and a toque.

It is this proudly traditional Northern town in which everyone is expected to know their place and to doff their hats at the right time to the right people that is the backdrop of Dorothy Whipple's version of the 'shop-girl' story. But what did she know of girls in shops, as she herself asked? Well, one only has to look in social history books, histories of shops and shopping, and accounts of working in shops to see that *High Wages* is one of the most complete descriptions of the early twentieth-century world of women's dress-shops and clothing available to the modern reader. By the time Dorothy Whipple was writing in the late 1920s, the theme of the shop-girl was already a well-worn one in romantic novels and musicals. She had entered popular culture via the theatre in two very successful musical comedies, *The Shop Girl* (1894) and *Our Miss Gibbs* (1909), and then appeared in countless romantic novels and 'girl comedies'. She is usually a pretty, alluring, novel-reading, empty-headed heroine who captures the attention of a male to win a wealthy husband and returns to the shop as a customer.

****

But it was not all pretty props and objects of desire, and writers of grittier social realism were determined to portray the flip side of the shop-girl's existence as a vulnerable, exploited worker. (In fact Jane reads several of these novels during the course of the book, as if reading different versions of her own story.) The shop-girl is an important late-Victorian and Edwardian social and cultural type who represents the growing number of women going into new sectors and places of work. From the 1890s, working in a shop was one of the few ways a young girl or woman of independent means could breach the gap between the family and the marital homes without having to go into domestic service or the mill, and by 1918 the retail trade was established as a major employer of women who dominated the sector. But as writers such as George Gissing, Arnold Bennett and HG Wells showed, the reality of the shop-girl's life was often far removed from the image presented on the stage and in popular literature, and she soon became the focal point of reports into, and debates about, women's labour, particularly in reviews carried out by socialists and feminists such as those published in the war years in *The Women's Industrial News* that highlighted the poor working conditions and long working hours.

Jane discovers on her first day at the shop, after being woken at 5.30 am by the sounds of the women mill-workers' clogs and going back to sleep with relief until 7am, that her so-called freedom comes at a price, and she is quickly intro-duced to the harshness and privations of the living-in system. In 1912 the practice of living-in as Maggie and Jane do was falling out of favour in the big cities; in a radical move,

****

Gordon Selfridge dispensed with it altogether, giving over the whole of his shop space to selling, and instead built hostels nearby to accommodate single employees. Nevertheless, in places such as Tidsley (said to be based on Preston, but quite possibly an amalgam of several Lancashire mill-towns), it was still the norm to live in, in return for a large cut of the wages which were kept by the employer for board and lodging, a system that was widely referred to as 'wage-slavery'. Young girls often worked twelve-hour days, with only Sunday and one half-day off, and as late as 10pm twice a week (Dorothy Whipple is not exaggerating when she describes how Jane falls wearily into bed after 11pm on Christmas Eve). They lived in dismal shared rooms which were often cold, dirty and dingy, and were given poor and inadequate amounts of food on which to subsist (in the novel Mrs Chadwick prides herself on her mean 3d per head suppers for Jane and Maggie).

The theme of hunger in *High Wages* strikes the modern reader forcibly – Jane spends all her years at Chadwick's in a permanent state of hunger – and it was this exploitative, autocratic treatment of underfed, underpaid and overworked shop-girls that enraged the campaigners for women's labour rights and feminist writers such as Cicely Hamilton (author of *William – an Englishman*, Persephone Book No. 1) who wrote her brutally frank but witty and therefore popular play *Diana of Dobson's* in 1908 in an attempt to make audiences aware of what was happening. When Jane is cheated of 9d commission by Mr Chadwick she knows she is not in a position to complain or threaten action because she would be out on the street in a trice. This very vulnerability in, and

****

complete dependence on, a situation provided by a man (as a daughter, wife, servant or employee) is what accelerated legislation in the 1910s to protect young working girls and to improve their rights and working conditions.

Jane is a shop-girl, but one who bucks trends and stereotypes to become a shopkeeper without the help of any man and in doing so she challenges all the male hierarchies of the town. She is most definitely a New Woman, but she is a self-made new-style woman who relies on her own skills, judgment and hard work. She does it all in an admirably non-militant style, non-campaigning style and all without a whisper of suffragism or feminism (this is not a criticism, more an observation of style). And yet Dorothy Whipple is without doubt a feminist writer. In the midst of a delightful book full of details of clothes and furnishings, bust-bodices and gloves, she creates a powerful argument for the need for women to work, not for political or primary economic reasons, but for self-fulfilment and for the realisation of talent and potential. She writes in *Random Commentary* that she used the life of a 'Miss S.' as inspiration; sadly we shall probably never know who Miss S. was, but clearly she was a marvellous role-model and demonstrated a quite different escape route from drudgery than the clichéd shop-girl-as-buyable-commodity story.

High Wages is a gem of a novel, 'a perfect thing, clear and simple' (as Jane describes *Marie-Claire* by Marguerite Audoux, a 1911 novel written by a former seamstress) with a very special, endearing Northern character and charm. I like to think that my grandmother

****

who was a great reader may have taken it out of her local Free Library in Manchester and enjoyed it just as I do, and indeed as much as my mother for whom it brought back memories of a Saturday job in the 1940s in Affleck and Brown, another Manchester shopping landmark. It is a tribute to Dorothy Whipple's writing skills that she can weave a thread through generations of women to bring them together, in the same way that dressmaking and clothes-shopping always have done.

Jane Brocket
Windsor, 2009

CHAPTER ONE

I

JANE CARTER had come to Tidsley on her half-
day off to look at the shops, but she looked mostly
at the sky. She had seen skies for seventeen years,
but never one, she was sure, like this before.

The whole expanse of heaven was covered with
minute clouds, little abrupt things, kicking up their
heels, flying off into nothing. They were so madly
inconsequent that Jane laughed. And then, as if
someone had said to them, 'Come now! Quietly!
Quietly!' they stopped rioting and settled down
together in the rosy glow. They were merged and
gradually were lost to sight. A majestic gold arose
and suffused the sky, leaving a pool of green in the
east.

Jane lowered her beauty-dazed eyes to Tidsley
market-place. Beneath that canopy, it was transfigured. The peaky roofs of shops and houses stood
up darkly in the January air, the windows reflected
a green-blue like the shell of a bird's egg. The
lamplighter was going round, and now behind him
shone a string of jewels, emeralds pale and effulgent.
There was almost no one about. It was a moment.
Jane sometimes had these moments. She stood still
in them.

As she stood on the cobbles of the empty market-place, a beam of light struck suddenly from the right to her very feet. She looked up and saw that an obscuring eiderdown hanging in Chadwick's shop window had been pushed aside and that a small man had stepped into the window and was affixing a piece of paper low down in the right-hand corner of the pane. Then, stepping carefully round the tea-cosies and peaked napkins, he retired and replaced the eiderdown. Tidsley market-place was as before.

Jane Carter left her moment and walked across to Chadwick's shop. In the confused light she could just make out what was written on the paper in a fine, spidery hand and signed with a flourish of initials :

> ' Wanted : a young lady to assist in the shop. Apply within.
>
> ' W. H. C.'

Jane's heart beat faster. She straightened up.
' Well . . .' she breathed.
She bent down and read again.
' Well . . . I never . . .'
She straightened up and pressed down the fingers of her gloves one after the other in agitation.

These gloves were the most noticeable thing about Jane. She wore an insignificant black coat and an insignificant black hat, but her gloves were dazzlingly white, fluffy, enormous. In the dusk now Jane could hardly be seen at all ; only her gloves. They had been marked one-eleven-three in Commins', drapers, where she worked in Elton, Tidsley's small neighbour, but to her they had been one-and-seven, nearly half a week's wages.

She fiddled with her precious gloves, her mind

working rapidly. She read the notice again, saying it over under her breath :

> 'Wanted : a young lady to assist in the shop. Apply within.
>
> 'W. H. C.'

What a queer thing this should happen on the very day she came to Tidsley ! She hadn't been for weeks ; and then, just this very day, Chadwick's wanted a girl.

It would be a fine thing for her to get into Chad-wick's. It was the best draper's shop in Tidsley. Cars drew up at its door ; she had even seen Lady Farborough go in once. It was solid and respectable and sold good stuff. That eiderdown now ; it was satin on one side. Chadwick's was no gimcrack, mixed-up place like Commins'. She was sick to death of Commins' ; and of Elton ; and of living with her stepmother and those children. It would be a fine thing if she could get into Chadwick's.

She looked once more at the notice ; then skipped round the corner into the side alley. She fumbled with her encumbering gloves in her handbag until she found a mirror. It was so small that she had to move it about to capture first a half-curve of her cheek, then the two flakes of dark hair over her ears, then up to her blue-grey eyes already dilated with excitement at the thought of applying for a situation. She thrust the mirror away and adjusted her shabby coat.

'Oh, my goodness . . . all over bits ! These gloves . . .'

She picked wildly at the fluff on her coat, adding to rather than removing it.

' Oh, drat the things . . . ! '

She gave them up as a bad job. Someone might be getting into Chadwick's before her, if she fiddled any longer. She took a long breath, emerged from the alley and walked into Chadwick's.

It was dim on the immediate threshold, the lights being shrouded by stalactites of eiderdowns, curtains and other draperies dependent from brass rods. Jane was conscious of a smell of cotton and woollen stuffs, of a counter to right and a counter to left, a small oil-stove giving out smell without heat, and a headless dummy exhibiting a pink ripple-cloth dressing-gown on its incredible bosom. At the far end of the shop, the light shining on his two small scallops of hair, Mr. Chadwick wrote at his desk. Half-way down one counter, a substantial young woman was measuring off braid. She came forward with an inquiring bend of the head, for Jane had an elegant air from a distance and was mistaken for a customer.

Jane advanced diffidently to the counter.

' I've come about the place,' she said huskily, and muffled a nervous cough in her glove.

' Oh,' said the young woman. ' Have you ? ' Her eyes said plainly : ' What d'you mean—making me come forward like that ? '

She sauntered along the counter and stood by Mr. Chadwick's desk. She did not speak until he looked up ; he had evidently trained her to that.

' There's a girl come about the place,' she said at last, jerking her head in Jane's direction.

Mr. Chadwick peered down the shop.

' Very well, Miss Pye.'

He continued to write, with flourishes both on and off the paper, as if to make it clear that he was not going to disturb himself for a girl who had come about the place. He also liked writing ; you could tell that. When his dignity was appeased, he put down the pen and called :

'Come forward, please.'

Jane advanced into the glare of the electric lamp. He saw that she was pale and young and thin.

'Ladylike appearance,' was his inward comment. It was also his highest praise ; but he wasn't going to rush at her for all that. Everything must be done in order.

'The notice of the vacancy has not been in the window more than five minutes,' he announced.

'I know. I saw you put it in,' said Jane, smiling diffidently at him.

He frowned. She mustn't smile too soon. You couldn't smile your way into Chadwick's, he would have her know.

'What's your name ? ' he asked, taking up the pen again.

'Jane Carter.'

She wished, for the hundredth time, that her name was Gladys.

'Address ? '

'21, St. John Street, Elton.'

'Any experience ? '

'I've worked in Commins' for two and a half years.'

William Henry Chadwick made a grimace of disapproval. He didn't think anything of Commins'.

'How old are you ? '

'Eighteen in March.'

He noticed that she spoke well. Slightly aggrieved, he noticed that she spoke better than he did.

'What's your father?'

'My father's dead. He was a reporter for the *Elton Post*.'

'Oh!' That's where she got it from, was it? Reporters were, in Mr. Chadwick's estimation, a cut above the ordinary.

'Have you a mother?'

'A stepmother.'

'Ah!' That said a lot. A stepmother.

He noticed that Miss Pye was edging nearer to the conversation.

'Have you finished that braid, Miss Pye?' he asked.

She started, looking foolish.

'Yes, Mr. Chadwick. Twelve and an eighth, Mr. Chadwick.'

'Get some more from upstairs, then.'

'Yes, Mr. Chadwick.' She patted her fuzzy hair and disappeared.

Mr. Chadwick resumed his cross-examination of Jane, making extensive and unnecessary notes with the fine pen.

'Well,' he said at last, looking her over again and stroking his chin. 'It all seems fairly satisfactory.'

Seeing an eagerness in Jane's face, he quickly put an end to it. It wasn't so easy as that, after all.

'I will inform you of my decision,' he said. 'You can go now.'

The light went out of Jane's eyes.

'Thank you!' she said, turning away. 'Good afternoon.'

Mr. Chadwick got out of his chair to follow her to the door. He felt some anxiety in case she should try for a place elsewhere.

'I must see the other applicants first, you understand. There will be a great many, of course. We have a reputation, Miss Carter. A reputation.'

He clasped his hands under the tails of the frock-coat he always wore in the shop and rose on the toes of his buttoned boots.

'I know,' said Jane with sincerity. 'That's why I want to get here.'

'Well, we shall see,' said Mr. Chadwick. 'Good afternoon. *Good* afternoon.'

There were, as he foretold, many applicants for the post, but it was Jane who received the intimation that she was appointed as assistant at five shillings a week, to 'live in.'

II

Ten days later, Jane presented herself at Chadwick's accompanied by a small Japanese basket-hamper considerably the worse for wear.

The back door was opened to her by a young woman in a rough apron, who stared through an obscurance of wispy hair.

'I'm the new assistant,' volunteered Jane.

'Oh,' said the young woman, looking helplessly behind her.

'Well . . .' she began again. 'I suppose you'd better come in. Master didn't say anything, like, but I'll go and tell 'im, shall I ? '

'Step intert kitchen,' she said, with more resolution in her tone. 'That's it. Step inside. 'Appen Master 'ull be in t' shop. I can 'ave a look, can't I ? '

She cautiously lifted one corner of a short green curtain and peered under it.

'Yes, 'e's there, and there's nobody in t' shop. I'se just tell 'im you're 'ere, shall I?'

'Yes, please,' said Jane.

The young woman tiptoed into the dark passage and called in a hoarse whisper :

'Mr. Chadwick! Mr. Chadwick! A young lady's come wi' 'er things. She says she's the new assistant. What shall I do?'

Mr. Chadwick came to the kitchen door and looked at Jane.

'Good afternoon, Miss Carter,' he said importantly. 'Lily will take you upstairs to the bedroom you will share with Miss Pye, and then I shall be obliged if you will come down into the shop. You are in your black, I presume?'

'Yes,' said Jane.

'Very good.' He pinched in his lips and went back into the shop.

Lily grasped the strap of the basket-hamper.

'This way. Can yer see? Black as pitch, isn't it?'

Jane fumbled her way up the stairs at Lily's heels and came out into daylight in a small back bedroom. The unbalanced furniture was painted a bilious yellow and had glass knobs on it. The lace curtains were sticky with soot and the floor covering was a cold and glassy oilcloth of a presumptive white. But Jane did not notice this. She only noticed that there were two beds. She had been so afraid she would have to sleep with Miss Pye.

'It's a nice room, isn't it?' said Lily. 'Bonny wallpaper.'

She put out a hand and lovingly touched the criss-cross of magenta roses.

' I always think I'll 'ave my room at 'ome beautified like this when I can afford,' she said wistfully.

'Don't you live in?' asked Jane, taking off her hat.

' Eh, no, I'm married,' said Lily with astonishment. ' I work 'ere by the day. Mrs. Blackledge my name is, but they call me Lily. Eh, yes, I'm married. Bob, 'e's called. I've 'ad a lot of trouble. Beautiful little 'ome I 'ad, false blinds and everything you could think of; but 'e drank it all away. We live with 'is mother now; just one room, we 'ave.'

' Oh dear,' said Jane with sympathy.

'Yes, I 'ad a lovely 'ome. Two velvet chairs in t' front room, and a pair of them painted china vawses I got at t' Pot Fair, and a plush tablecloth wi' bobs on, and a brass bedstead in mi bedroom . . .'

Jane stirred uneasily.

' I'd better go down,' she said.

'Yes,' agreed Lily, and continued in a whisper down the stairs :

' And a lovely toilet set, blue it was with a lovely pink rose on each article. Eh, it did look well! But it all went; 'e drank it all away.'

' Oh dear,' said Jane over her shoulder as she went forward into the shop.

Mr. Chadwick called her to his desk for the homily he made to each new assistant. She listened, anticipating his meanings rather in the manner of a young dog.

In her desire to please, she presented a very different Jane from the one who had banged her stepmother's door that morning with a grim :

' Thank goodness I'm out of that ! '

She had been fervently thankful to leave her stepmother and those children. Alice and Eddy were pallid and large-headed and their noses ran unduly.

Jane and her stepmother did not ' get on.' The second Mrs. Carter did not like Jane. Jane might have asked herself why any woman, with children of her own, should like a stepdaughter of thirteen. But Jane did not think of that side of the question. She felt her stepmother ought to have liked her, and she herself continued to be aghast that her father should have married her. A man with a sense of humour and a zest for life to marry a woman like that ; all the same colour, hair, skin, eyes, eyelashes, clothes—all drab. And her only interests those children and ' the Pictures ' !

The whole thing had been a catastrophe. After two years of uncomfortable living, he died abruptly from pneumonia. His meagre affairs proved to be in complete chaos, and after his wife had drawn ' the insurance,' there was nothing left for Jane but the fifty-two pounds her own mother, a Scotswoman, had left for her in the Savings Bank.

When her father died, she had to leave the Park View School.

' You'll have to set about earning your own living,' her stepmother told her.

Jane was bewildered. She didn't know how to begin. Park View School had given her some sort of genteel education, but had in no way fitted her for an emergency of this kind. Her stepmother could not help her to find work ; she could only say :

' This is what comes of going to your fancy schools. I kept telling your father. You should have gone to an elementary school like other folks and then you'd have known something.'

Jane tried looking after people's children. She pushed a heavy old man about in a wheeled-chair. But employment of this kind was spasmodic and she had to spend too much time at home, where she disagreed violently and continually with the other occupants. She was too young at this time to feel anything but injury and indignation at her altered position there. Although her stepmother warned her daily :

'You'd better be careful, my lady ! You haven't got your father behind you now, remember ! '

She could not realize it. It was not until she had come to anchor in Commins', the draper's, and the years went slowly by, that she came to admit that, after all, her stepmother had been rather decent not to turn her out altogether.

She realized that no one was under any obligation to house her. Neither her father's relations nor her mother's only brother in Scotland had shown any desire to occupy themselves with her. She was bound to acknowledge that her stepmother had done more than these, and she tempered her behaviour accordingly. She was, none the less, extremely glad to get away from her. She meant to stay away, too.

So she listened to Mr. Chadwick and took his words to heart. And when he had finished, she went to her place at the counter, filled with a desire to do her best.

Mr. Chadwick saw that he had made an impression and looked round for an opportunity to make another.

Fortunately a customer came into the shop and gave him a chance to show off his salesmanship. He bustled forward.

'Ah, good afternoon, Mrs. Barton, Madam. Will

B

you be so kind as to take a chair? What can I do
for you?'

He inclined his ear over his folded hands.

'Certainly. Miss Pye, please; just assist me.
The sateens.'

He thumped the rolls on the counter, and selecting
one, spun it deftly undone.

'One-and-three-halfpence the yard. Excellent
value, Mrs. Barton, Madam. Thirty-nine inches
wide.' He ran the material between his finger and
thumb, and shot a glance to the side to see if Jane
was watching his methods with intelligent interest.
She was.

'Or I have a heavier cloth here at one-and-four
the yard. Slightly heavier in weight. You prefer the
cheaper? Very good. Two yards? Thank you.'

With an ear-splitting tear, Mr. Chadwick had the
two yards off the roll, folded into neat compass, par-
celled, pinned. He made out the bill with a flourish
and bowed the customer out of the shop with a few
discreet remarks on the coldness of the day.

'Put those sateens back, please, Miss Carter.'

He switched on the electric light, and by the same
movement the shadows of Jane's lashes on her cheek.
He took a startled look at her. He hoped she wasn't
going to turn out to be one of those pretty girls. They
were a nuisance. Flighty. Thoughts never on the
business.

He wondered what his customers would think of
her. What Mrs. Greenwood would think of her.
Mrs. Greenwood was the autocrat of Tidsley and his
most esteemed customer.

CHAPTER TWO

I

THE market clock struck half-past eight. On the last stroke, Mr. Chadwick got down from his stool and bolted the shop door. He put his books into his desk, locked it, and, after a final look round, went upstairs to Mrs. Chadwick and supper.

'Come on !' called Miss Pye to Jane. 'Give us a hand with this dust-sheet.'

They ran from end to end of the counter, shrouding it.

'Now the other !' said Miss Pye.

'And the old dummy. Night-night, love ! That's it. Now lights out, thank the Lord, and let's get to our supper ! What's she given us ?'

On the kitchen dresser were two kippers, a loaf, margarine, and tea measured out in a teapot.

'Not so bad,' remarked Miss Pye.

Shop assistants did not expect a great deal in nineteen-hundred-and-twelve.

'She's damped the fire down again,' said Miss Pye. 'But let me get at it. I'll make it burn in spite of her.'

She carefully inserted the poker here and there in the mass of cinders and induced small flames out of it.

'Now you set the table while I cook the kippers.

We get our own supper, you know. Pots in that cupboard. How d'you think you'll like?'

'Here? Oh, it seems all right,' said Jane.

Miss Pye seemed all right, too. She was cheerful and friendly, at any rate. She had red cheeks and light blue eyes and a fuzz of fair hair. She looked as if she had been made the right size and then hit on the head with a mallet, thought Jane. The effect was rather stumpy, but strong.

'Brew the tea, will you?' she called from the scullery. 'I'm coming with the kippers.'

She shut the kitchen door firmly and drew the table as close to the fire as possible.

'There! Now we can have ourselves to ourselves a bit. D'you mind if I undo the top hook of my corsets? It's been running into me all day. Let me get a drink of tea, for mercy's sake!'

They lingered luxuriously over their supper, pursuing the last vestiges of kipper among the fastnesses of bones. Maggie squeezed three cups of tea apiece out of the teapot. She talked a lot. Jane let her. It was Jane's unconscious habit to give the other person first innings. She kept quiet, listened, took in; then by and by her own personality stirred, stretched itself and began to stalk about. The other person gradually became aware of Jane.

'Are you walking out?' asked Maggie Pye.

'No. Are you?'

'Aren't you? Well, I should have thought you'd got a boy by now. Oh yes, I am,' she bridled complacently. 'Wilfrid Thompson his name is. A very nice boy. He works at the Free Library. He's very clever; keeps passing examinations at night school. I should have been out with him to-night, but he

goes to French class on Tuesdays. I don't grudge it
him, only it seems a funny way of enjoying yourself
to me.'

Maggie laughed comfortably into her empty cup.
She scooped the sugar out of the bottom of it with
her spoon.

'He's a funny boy, is Wilfrid,' she went on. 'You
wouldn't believe what bother I had to get him to
talk a bit when I went to change Mrs. Chadwick's
books. He never looked up at first, just used to
stamp them and push them back over the counter.
But I got him to looking at me in the end. And then
he got to leaning on the counter a bit, and then I knew
he was coming on. And now we're walking out.
And walking's the word, let me tell you ! Eh, he is a
one for walking ! On Sunday afternoons he walks me
for miles, all over Tidsley moors, and up over Barker
Brow, and Ennersley and goodness knows where. I
come in fagged out. My shoes are all wore through,
and I get that out of breath. But if I don't go with
him, someone else will, and that's a fact.

'He's always got a book in his pocket and keeps
nipping it out and reading. Well, you can't be very
lively with a chap like that, can you ? I wish he'd
take me to Barton's dances on a Thursday night, you
know, and things like that. We could have a lot of
fun. Shall you and me go sometime ? Eh, I love a
dance. I love the Veleta and the Doris Waltz—don't
you ? '

The kitchen door opened and Mrs. Chadwick came
in with a tray of pots. She looked at Jane with
curiosity as she went into the scullery and again as
she came out. She said 'Good night' and went
upstairs again.

Mrs. Chadwick was taller than her husband. She wore curlers and an overall in the mornings and worked with Lily upstairs. In the afternoons she did her hair, taking care not to comb out the crimp, over a high pad in front. She wore striped flannel blouses with high collars, and a gold watch pinned by a gold lover's knot over where her bosom should have been, but was not. She sometimes went down into the shop in the afternoons, but more often she sat in the upstairs sitting-room, her hands crossed on her hard front, looking out on the market-place and giving now and then a loud contemplative suck of the teeth.

Mrs. Chadwick was rather mean. Not excessively so ; but just mean enough to add interest to her days. She enjoyed exerting her ingenuity in the provision, for the girls, of suppers that did not cost more than threepence a head. She was adept at ringing the changes on cheap food. It was nice to think, too, that the tasty little suppers she took with Mr. Chadwick upstairs were justified by the economies she practised downstairs.

At ten o'clock Mr. Chadwick came down to turn out the lights and see that everything was secure for the night.

Jane and Maggie went up to the cold bedroom. They began to undress ; Jane rather shyly, Maggie with large, untrammelled gestures.

' D'you wear a bust-bodice ? ' Maggie inquired.

' No,' murmured Jane.

' Well, it's not much good wearing a bust-bodice if you haven't got a bust, I must say. I have to ; though speaking for myself, I like a bit of figure.'

She shook down a little fall of hair to her shoulders,

and brought a handful of what looked like tortured worms out of the dressing-table drawer.

'Don't you wave your hair?' she asked Jane.

'No. It doesn't suit me waved.'

'Eh, I like a wave, I must say.' Maggie looked in surprise at this waveless, bustless creature.

She seized a rather soiled comb and, dipping it into the common washing jug of water, began to damp her hair before rolling it up in the wavers.

At this Jane revolted.

'If she thinks I'm going to wash in that water after she's dipped her comb in it, she's wrong, that's all.'

She stood shivering in her petticoat, wondering what to do. It said in *Home Chat* that the evening toilet was most important and must never be missed. Behind Maggie's back she seized a towel.

'I'm just going down to the kitchen,' she murmured inaudibly, and before Maggie could question her, was feeling her way down the staircase.

The scullery sink showed conveniently in the last glow of the fire, and there, her clothes slipping downwards on her slender hips, with many a nervous glance backwards in case anyone should come, Jane washed. As she dried on the harsh towel, she gave a series of leaps into the air. She was exhilarated by her new beginning in life.

When she returned to the bedroom, Maggie Pye, grotesque in curlers, a flannel bed-jacket and woollen bed-socks, was in the act of getting into bed.

'Whatever have you been doing? Have you been washing you downstairs? Didn't you want me to see you? Goodness me, we're all made alike, aren't we? You are a queer one. I'm not washing me to-night. Too blooming cold.'

Jane took the bolster from her bed. It said in *Home Chat* that you must sleep low if you wanted to be beautiful. Jane passionately wanted to be beautiful.

She turned off the light.

' Ta-ta till seven to-morrow morning,' murmured Maggie. ' Eh, I wish I'd never got to get up ! Not in winter, anyway.'

Her breathing became heavy and regular in an incredibly short time. The slight, chill January wind moved the blind now and then, letting in an upward shining from the pale green lamplight that filled the market-place like a pool.

Jane lay in the strange bed. She held first one foot and then the other in her hands to warm them. Her mind was filled with the events and figures of the day : the Chadwicks, Maggie Pye, the shelf where the silks were kept, the gloves dangling on wires on the glass door . . . all these delayed sleep. At last, when she was warm, she drifted off into oblivion.

II

She awoke to blackness filled with the clatter of clogs. She lay startled for a second or two, then got up to look out of the window. Dark shapes streamed across the market-place ; clatter, clatter, clatter. Not a word seemed to pass their lips. Hundreds of men and women, but all silent.

' Thank goodness I don't go to the mill,' breathed Jane, plunging back into bed. ' I couldn't get up at half-past five.'

It was bad enough at seven. Black cold still. She struggled into a few clothes and fled to the scullery sink where the water was still slightly warm. Maggie, yawning but resigned, joined her. She put the kettle on the gas-stove, and they tiptoed back to do their hair. By the time the kettle was boiling they were down again.

Oh, the comfort of that first cup of tea ! The warmth and life it put into you ! They held their hands round the cups to warm them and their eyes looked less heavily on the bleak kitchen.

' What do we do now ? ' asked Jane.

' We have another cup of tea,' said Maggie, ' and then we sweep and dust the shop, and get it tidy while Lily's lighting the fire. She'll be here soon. And then while we're having our breakfast, she scrubs the floor and does the step. Come on, you take that brush and begin behind the silk counter. Brush down towards me. See ? '

They worked together, warming to it. Maggie unlocked the shop door, and Jane pursued the collection of dust minutely to the gutter. She looked round the market-place, grey and cold this morning, and round at the shops where economical lights burned for the cleaners : the Victoria Café on the other side of the square ; Bland's, the grocer's, at the corner ; Foster's, the boot shop ; Fenwick's, the furrier's ; strange and bleak they all looked. She hurried in again.

Lily arrived. She whimpered as she lit the fire, and as Jane reappeared at intervals in the kitchen, she told her Bob wasn't like a husband at all.

' Aren't you going to love me a bit I says to 'im this morning, and 'e says with such a nasty look, " To 'ell with you and your love." Just like that.'

And when she tried to kiss him good-bye, he'd thrown a plate at her.

'Whatever do you want to kiss him for?' asked Jane, squeezing out the wash-leather for the shop-door glass. 'Throw a plate back at him, my goodness.'

She thought she herself would make short work of such a husband.

'No . . .' Lily shook her head as she dipped the bald brush into the blacklead. 'I couldn't do that. Bad as 'e is, I love 'im. Besides, it's me as 'as to pay for the plates.'

'Ah,' said Jane, 'then there's nothing to be done.'

She would have liked to say something about the combination of love and economy. But she couldn't get it right in time. She often wanted to say things like that; get things neat; but they evaded her, until she was alone, in bed mostly, and then it was too late.

She hurried off with the wash-leather.

By nine o'clock Jane and Maggie were in their black frocks behind the shining counters.

The oil-stove was lighted, and the dummy robed afresh. Lorries rumbled by piled high with bales of cotton, coal-carts sauntered up and down. Men crossed the market-place on the way to offices; mill-owners went by in their cars. There was a quietness in the streets for an hour or so, and then the women of Tidsley began to appear. A little welcome bustle began in the waiting shops.

The market clock had just struck the quarter after eleven, when a large and glossy car drew up outside Chadwick's. The occupant thereof talked so loudly on the pavement that her voice penetrated the closed door of the shop. Mr. Chadwick threw down his pen and hurried forward.

'Miss Carter, a piece of paper on the floor! Quick!' he hissed.

He opened the door with a flourish, and immediately the shop was filled with noise. The very gloves seemed to vibrate on the wires.

'We'll go and see Mr. Hind then, dear, when I have finished here. He ought to be in, I think. Quarter-past eleven. Yes, I think he ought to be in. . . .'

She was evidently addressing her daughter, who followed her, but she could have been heard by the man cleaning the face of the market clock.

'Good morning, Mrs. Greenwood, Madam, and good morning, Miss Sylvia,' murmured Mr. Chadwick. 'Very cold, is it not? It is, indeed.'

He lifted two chairs into the air and set them down again, as if to remind the ladies that they were there, waiting to be sat on, as he was, at their good pleasure.

'Although I think he often goes out in the middle of the morning to the Borough Club. I am not sure. However, we shall see. Good morning.'

She did then deign to notice Mr. Chadwick and take a chair.

'I want some twill sheets for the maids' beds. Something strong,' she vociferated. 'Have you any unbleached twill sheets or sheeting? Let me see both.'

'It's just as if she were telephoning,' thought Jane.

Mr. Chadwick and Maggie Pye hurried to the linen shelves, and Jane, conscious that Mr. Chadwick would wish the whole shop to be devoted to Mrs. Greenwood's service, hurried after them, and, like the clown at a circus, gave a hand here and a hand there, without

doing anything to help.   When she got a chance, she
looked at the ladies.

She observed Mrs. Greenwood's toque, her maroon
coat and skirt, her violets, her complexion, somewhat
empurpled by the cold.   They all matched, thought
Jane.

She looked at her haughty mouth, her sables, her
tight, light gloves.

' Rich and proud,' thought Jane, ' and everything
about her stiff and firm.   Even the violets pinned
tight.   She wouldn't let even a violet nod.'

It was not until Mrs. Greenwood had settled down
to criticizing the sheeting and making it perfectly clear
to Mr. Chadwick that she always got her best linen
and anything else of importance in London, that Jane
dare look at Sylvia Greenwood.

Ah, here surely was all the beauty she read about
in *Home Chat* !   Here was the perfect skin, the faint
lovely flush, the straight nose, the red mouth.

Sylvia was bored with the sheeting.   She lifted her
head and looked indifferently at Jane.   She looked
with the same indifference at Maggie Pye, and Maggie
made a large foolish smile at Sylvia.   Jane winced at
that smile ;   it was too humble.   But it evoked no
response whatever from Sylvia.   She walked on her
high heels to the oil-stove ;   but getting neither
interest nor heat from that, she walked to the shop-
door and looked out through the gloves.   Her attitude,
as she held an expensive fur coat round her slender
body, expressed extreme boredom.

Suddenly she became alert.   She opened the door.

' There's Noel,' she called backwards to her mother.
She went out of Chadwick's, leaving the door open to
the bitter wind.

'You can shut the door,' shouted Mrs. Greenwood to Jane. She pivoted round to do this. 'Miss Greenwood may be some time.'

Jane hastened to the door. Sylvia Greenwood was outside talking to a tall young man. Before Jane could get the door latched, it was snatched out of her hand and her ears cracked under a further bellow from Mrs. Greenwood.

'Good morning, Noel. How are you? And how is Mother? Sylvia and I are going to have coffee at Cooper's in a moment. Will you take her on there? It's so cold for her here. And if you will stay for coffee with us, we shall be delighted. I will join you in a moment.'

Jane, closing the door at last, saw them walk away together, and thought what a handsome young pair they made.

'It must be fine to wear a coat like that and have coffee with young men in the mornings,' she said to herself.

But the slight mist of envy was dispelled by the arrival of a customer wanting suspenders. As Mr. Chadwick and Maggie Pye were still devoting themselves to Mrs. Greenwood and the sheeting, Jane attended to the suspenders. It was her first real customer; and she was elated to serve her and to be on the way to earn commission. At twopence in the pound, the commission on one-and-eleven was almost incalculable. Still, she was on her way to earning it.

CHAPTER THREE

I

'I'VE to go and change Mrs. Chadwick's books at the Free Library to-night,' said Maggie. 'Come with me, and then you'll see Wilfrid.'

Jane assented. She always had a healthy curiosity to see anyone who had been talked about.

They went to see what was for supper. A piece of red polony waited on the dresser.

'My goodness!' said Maggie. 'I could eat it all in one bite. But come on! We'll not be long.'

They put on their shabby coats and went out into the raw night. The Free Library was not five minutes away. Maggie hurried through into the Lending Department and poked her head round the frontage of metal numbers in a glass case.

'Wilfrid!' she whispered loudly. 'Wilfrid!'

A study in black and white appeared; a thin young man with dark hollows of eye and cheek in a white face and long black hair falling over his forehead.

'How's your cold, Wilfrid?' inquired Maggie, leaning on the counter.

'Not much better. What does she want this time? More tripe, I suppose.'

'Now go on!' admonished Maggie. 'She doesn't. She wants something of Marie Corelli's, she says. She doesn't like this *Three Muscatelles*.'

'Good Lord!' exclaimed Wilfrid, looking up for the first time. 'Have you never heard of the *Three Musketeers* before?'

'No, I haven't,' said Maggie good-humouredly. 'Why should I have?'

Wilfrid made a terse noise and went away with the books.

'What d'you think of him?' Maggie asked immediately.

'I can't tell yet.' Jane looked round at the sightless and dusty busts on the window-ledges. 'I wonder who those are supposed to be.'

'Oh, come off it!' said Maggie. 'Don't bother with them old dead men. What d'you think of Wilfrid?'

'I think he's very nice,' said Jane conventionally. 'But he's very pale.'

'Oh, he always looks like that. Always has done. He doesn't ail anything. Well, Wilfrid, are we going for a walk on Sunday?'

'I am.'

'Well, I am, then,' said Maggie. 'This is Miss Carter, our new girl at the shop. Eh, it should have been the other way round, shouldn't it? Well, Mr. Wilfrid Thompson, Miss Jane Carter. There!'

They shook hands across the counter, and Wilfrid murmured, 'Pleased to meet you!' But he did not look at her.

'She wants to know who that old gent is,' pointed Maggie.

'Oh, that?' Wilfrid's nostrils distended with a little pride, as if there was some sort of reflected glory in even mentioning the name. 'That is Themistocles.'

He made it rhyme with ' cockles,' but Jane was none
the less impressed.

' Oh,' she said, with interest. ' What did he do ? '

With some pawing at the piece of hair that fell over
his brow, he told her.

' Here ! ' interrupted Maggie. ' Supper's calling
me. I'm off. What time Sunday, Wilfrid ? '

' Half-past eleven I want to go.'

' Oh, Wilfrid, I can't miss my Sunday dinner,' said
Maggie piteously. ' We get a cut from the joint and
pudding and everything on Sunday.'

' Don't miss it, then. Stay and eat it. I'm going
at half-past eleven.'

' Oh, Wilfrid, y'are mean.'

' Don't come this time,' suggested Wilfrid.

' Go on, of course I'm coming.'

Wilfrid glanced at Jane, then became absorbed in
the date stamp in his hand ; twisting it round rapidly
from Jan : to Jun : Jul : Aug : .

' What about your friend, then ? Er—does she like
walking ? Have you ever been up Bover Fells, Miss
Carter ? '

' No, I haven't,' faltered Jane. ' But . . .'

She wasn't going to spoil Maggie's walk.

' Eh, come if you like,' said Maggie. ' And welcome.'

Jane looked uncertainly from one to the other.

' You'd better come, Miss Carter,' said Wilfrid. ' A
good walk is what we need at the week-end ; we're
cooped up all week.'

' Oh, I would like to, if you don't mind,' cried
Jane. ' And I tell you what, Maggie. We could
ask her to cut our meat off and we'll have it for
supper.'

' Yes, but it's not the same, is it ? ' said Maggie mournfully. ' But never mind. Half-past eleven, then, Wilfrid. Usual place.'

II

Mr. and Mrs. Chadwick went to church on Sunday morning ; Mr. Chadwick in his morning-coat, his two scallops of hair showing like the wings of a bird that had got imprisoned under his bowler hat ; Mrs. Chadwick in a toque like a humble relation of Mrs. Greenwood's ; she carried before her a round muff like a hedgehog, and another strip of hedgehog bristled round her flat, creased face. They looked worried.

They went to St. James's Church. They had to go to church somewhere, and they chose St. James's because it was good for business ; the Conservatives went there, the people with money. Mrs. Greenwood herself attended St. James's. The Chadwicks had a ' sitting ' some way behind her. Hitherto they had wished to be nearer her, but now they were glad they were not.

The new vicar had requested, in the Parish Magazine, that the congregation should stand when he entered with the choir. Mrs. Greenwood was affronted. She refused to stand. She sat firmly, pressing into the red pew-cushions, and she made Sylvia sit too.

Mr. Chadwick knew that she would expect him to follow her in this matter ; but he felt acutely that it was unbecoming in him to sit while his customers and betters stood around him. He decided anew every Sunday morning to stand, but not quite upright, leaning on the rail ; a compromise of a position out of

c

which he could slip into a seat if Mrs. Greenwood
should look round. He was always extremely worried
until the vicar had settled himself in his stall.

When the Chadwicks had gone, Maggie conducted
Jane on a tour of the house. When that was concluded, Maggie gossiped with Lily, while Jane washed
out a few Peter Pan collars. Lily promised to iron
them for her during the morning. Jane's gloves were
already washed and fluffed up for the walk.

At half-past eleven Wilfrid, wearing a waterproof but
no hat, appeared under the market clock, and the girls
joined him. They went through the empty streets to
the Bover tramcar, and were borne for two miles and
more between rows of houses all alike ; almost all
showing an aspidistra in a glazed pot in the parlour
window. Some were so fond of the aspidistra that
they had to have one in the bedroom window too ;
sleep with it.

By and by the houses began to thin. Pieces of waste
ground appeared ; then a few trees. The car was
empty, except for the three of them. Jane, feeling
lively, imitated Mrs. Greenwood. Maggie laughed
hugely, calling her a ' caution ' and a ' one.' Wilfrid
laughed too, showing his teeth in a constrained
fashion. The conductor stood with his hands on his
hips, smiling. Jane knew she was showing off ; but it
didn't matter. She was in a soaring mood.

They alighted at the terminus, and set off at a good
pace up the stony road to the fells. The air was like
cold water. Jane drew in great breaths ; her pale
cheeks began to glow, her eyes to shine. She didn't
want to chatter now in the face of these moors, black
and wild, crossed by low, ruined walls. She walked a
little ahead of the others, missing nothing ; the squelch-

ing moss, the light, terrified eyes of a sheep, the black
pools in the bog.

Maggie dragged a little, and Wilfrid kept making
excuses to feel in his pockets or look over a wall, to get
rid of her arm, which weighed on him like a heavy
parcel. He was a little aggrieved that Jane walked
on in front, when it was he who had arranged for her
to come.

After a time Maggie clamoured for food, and they
sat on a wall to eat. Bread and cheese was good in
that air. When they came to apples, Wilfrid pulled
out a book.

' Have you ever heard this? '

Maggie nudged Jane and giggled.

> ' Helen, thy beauty is to me
> Like those Nicean barks of yore . . .'

Jane stopped eating her apple.

' What lovely words ! What lovely, lovely words
. . .'

' Oh, read it again ! ' she begged him.

He read it again. But this time his reading irked
her. It got between her and the poem.

' Let me read it to myself,' she begged.

He gave her the book. Again he felt aggrieved.
He didn't like being baulked of reading aloud. Wilfrid was one of those people who like to read aloud,
who feel, unconsciously, that everything they read is
improved by being read aloud by them. He sat nursing his resentment, until Jane lowered the book and
looked over the fells before her. Then his resentment
faded as if it had never been, and he held his breath.
Here was the look he had waited in vain to see in the
eyes of another ; a look that was aware of beauty, a

look that saw—what ? Ah, no one could tell ; it was a secret of each soul and not to be formulated. Perhaps she saw, as he did, the splendour of the past reaching out to cover the present ; perhaps she saw the continuity of beauty, of experience, the thickness of life ; perhaps she saw—oh, what was it ? What was it that sometimes filled him with ecstasy, that made him a king—a spirit ?

Gazing at her brooding eyes and parted lips, he knew that she saw a vision equal to his own. And suddenly she became part of his vision ; entering into it, concentrating it on herself.

And there they were. Jane with the book in her hand, her breath visible in the cold air, sitting on the wall motionless ; Wilfrid on a stone below her, his black hair streaked on his forehead, gazing with luminous cyes at Jane ; and Maggie, totally unaware of what was going on, biting noisily into her apple and spitting bits of skin around her with gusto. Behind them, a cluster of little stunted thorn-bushes, and before them the black moor and the winter sky.

Maggie broke the spell.

She jumped up suddenly.

'Here, come on ! The damp's striking through.'

She twisted round to look at where she sat.

'Yes, I thought as much. My coat's all damp. Now let's get a move on. I don't want a cold. Mr. Chadwick stops your wages if you're off ill, let me tell you, Jane Carter.'

Wilfrid and Jane got down from the wall with reluctance.

'Where can I get a book like that ? ' asked Jane. She felt that all her meagre wages should go to the buying of it if necessary.

'You'd better take a ticket for the Free Library.
It's only tuppence, and I'd pick your books for you.
I'd like to.'

'Oh, don't start her off reading,' grumbled Maggie.
'You're bad enough. I can't put up with two of
you.'

'You need warming up,' said Wilfrid. 'You're
getting cross. Run!'

He seized her hand, and Maggie, enlivened by a
little notice, bounced down the stony path, shouting
with laughter, and came to a panting halt at the foot
of the hill, with a colour like the winter sun itself.

'Come on, Jane!' she called out. 'Wilfrid's going
to treat us to tea when we get to Bover.'

They walked on. Wilfrid let Maggie hold his arm
without protest. He didn't mind Maggie holding his
arm so long as she let him talk to Jane. And talk
they did. About how Jane's father used to read to
her when she was little. *Alice in Wonderland* she remembered, and *David Copperfield* and *Oliver Twist*. And
the *Heroes* she had had for Christmas once; and lots
of those little *Books for the Bairns*. One about Pandora
and her box, there was. But since her father died,
she had been too taken up in earning her own living.
Now Wilfrid should show her what to read. He
waxed eloquent about what waited for her.

They came in the dusk to Bover village; a mere
thickening of the moor road by a row of little stone
houses on each side. Wilfrid knew where to ask for
tea; he had often tramped this country. They had
tea in a cottage kitchen by the red glow of a fire; the
housewife gave them each a piece of pasty-cake for
love and sat down with only the white patch of her
apron to show where she was.

They went out again into the cold air ; the moor road stretched away dim and lonely, but they turned away from it.

' Not far now to go to the tram,' encouraged Wilfrid. He felt somehow strong and capable ; a protector, a provider. He threw out his chest, and eased Maggie's arm on his a little.

They went back to Tidsley on the tramcar. They were silent and pleasantly tired. Jane's cheeks were flushed and her eyes sleepy. Wilfrid left them at the door in Chadwick's alley and started his steep climb to No. 110, Varley Street, where he lived with his mother and his sister Isabel.

The Nottingham lace curtains of the windows of No. 110 were looped back with yellow satin bows, and when you opened the front door, you were confronted by another pair of lace curtains with body-belts of crimson plush about them. These curtains veiled the stairs, as if stairs ascending to where people undressed and slept were indecent.

Wilfrid's mother liked lace curtains and bows and padded handkerchief sachets. She had a fancy mind. She was thin and sallow, with dark eye sockets. She wore a band of black velvet round her neck and played Chaminade on a piano with a fluted silk front. She was a strange creature, whose inward passion seemed to be able to express itself only in these ways, but she perhaps accounted for Wilfrid. Perhaps his mother's enthusiasm for *St. Elmo* and *Ben Hur* accounted for Wilfrid's determination to get among the books in the Free Library rather than go as a clerk to the Rate Office, where his father had been employed.

The Thompsons were poor. In addition to the earnings of Wilfrid and Isabel, Mrs. Thompson had an income of forty-five pounds a year, and three hundred shares in the Dacre Mills, Ltd., of which Mr. Greenwood was chairman. Her husband had great expectations of these shares ; but they had not been realized in his lifetime.

Wilfrid Thompson's life was, to all outward seeming, as ordinary as could be. He ate his breakfast every morning at eight o'clock, put on his mackintosh —it rained a great deal in Tidsley—but no hat, and walked down Queen's Road, reaching the Free Library at a quarter to nine. There he sorted, catalogued, arranged, changed, stamped books ; made out tickets, renewed tickets, listed and numbered tickets, went backwards and forwards hundreds of times a day across the black-and-white tiled spaces of the Library, was aware of the chaff of Robinson and Dodd, who scuttered when they heard the librarian coming and got together to snigger again about their girls when he had gone. He went home to dinner, and was aware of his mother's mild concern with his eating and drinking, and of his sister's absorption in her young man, Percy. He went back to the Library and back home at six ; three evenings a week he returned to the Library until ten o'clock, when the reading and reference rooms closed.

All this was as ordinary as could be, but Wilfrid did not notice it. The real, the thrilling life he found in the books he read in all intervals, standing at his desk, one foot over the other, a small figure in a lofty room.

When he heard the clatter of footsteps over the tiles and saw without looking that someone had come to stand at the counter, his body left the book, but his mind was still with it as he took the slip and mounted the steps for a G. A. Henty or a Charles Garvice. He served out books with patience, but went back to his own at the first opportunity.

And so during the day his life was lifted out of the rut by books, and at night he went for long walks by himself, the wind whipping his hair and often the rain streaming down his face. Sometimes a fierce ecstasy would seize him and he ran like a madman in the dark. When his mother saw his wild eyes and flushed cheeks, her own heart bounded in response ; but she did not tell him so. She only brought him a few fancy biscuits arranged on a billowing lace d'oyley as an addition to his supper cocoa.

For some time before the appearance of Maggie at the Library counter, Wilfrid had been yearning for some sort of contact with another human being. Maggie provided herself. She took no interest in the things he did, but neither did anyone else that he knew of, so that did not disappoint him in her. She was cheerful and generous and somehow comforting to him. She kissed him a great deal more than he kissed her, but he did not mind much. There had been no kissing in his life until now, and it had its attractions.

CHAPTER FOUR

I

THROUGH the rain-obscured windows of the drawing-room at Stanfield, Sylvia Greenwood watched her father get into the car and be driven away over the crunching gravel by Schofield. She settled herself more comfortably in the pink arm-chair.

It was always a relief to her when her father went back to his mills after lunch. His presence somehow brought a tinge of discomfort into the house. She couldn't have said why. She didn't inquire into things ; she just felt glad when he was out of the house.

She turned over the pages of the latest *Vogue* with interest, and then picked up *The Tatler*. The drawing-room was warm and quiet. There was no sound except the faint scratch of Mrs. Greenwood's pen as she wrote at the gilded desk in the corner.

Sylvia came to the end of the illustrated papers. She yawned and looked out of the windows. There was nothing to look at there but the garden she had looked at for nineteen years. She yawned again until the tears came into her eyes. The comfortable feeling she had experienced when her father went had been swamped by a creeping boredom.

Her mother wrote on, her firm back erect.

The ornate clock supported by a simpering shepherd pair struck three. It struck lightly and cheerfully, but Sylvia sighed at it. Three o'clock, when you have nothing to do, is the dull herald of a still duller hour.

She sighed again, and more loudly. Her mother heard.

'Play something. Play " Songe d'Automne," dear, will you?' she said, without turning round.

Sylvia did not respond immediately. But in a moment she let the papers slip from her knee to the floor and went slowly to the piano. She sagged on the stool and gazed out of the wet windows. She put her inadequate hands on the keys and played until she came to the part that was more difficult and had no tune in it, and then her hands slid from the piano to her lap.

Mrs. Greenwood put down her pen. Something must be done.

'Well, darling,' she said briskly. 'What would you like to do?'

No answer from Sylvia.

'Would you like to ring up Madge and ask her to come over for tea?'

'No,' said Sylvia.

'Wouldn't you like to finish that camisole you're making? You know, the pretty pink one.'

'No.'

Mrs. Greenwood thought again.

'Should we go to Chadwick's for that navy blue gaberdine? It is really time Miss Bowen took it in hand.'

At last she was rewarded by a dawn of interest in Sylvia's eyes.

But she would not be gracious ; she kept her boredom up after it was over.

'I suppose we might as well,' she said. 'There doesn't seem to be anything better to do.'

'Run along and get ready,' said Mrs. Greenwood, closing the desk. 'I'll order the car. We will have tea at Cooper's afterwards.'

Sylvia took an interest in dress. She had not many other interests. She was one of those unfortunate people who seem to be incapable of doing anything well. Although beautiful and well-formed, she could not play tennis or golf, or even dance very well. She had begun to ride, but because riding jerked her hat to the back of her head and made her face too red, she would not go on with it.

She had no real friends. She was not a lively companion and no one sought her out. Her mother gave lavish parties for her, but just as, when she was a child, her guests forgot they were invited for her amusement and amused themselves while she sulked in the nursery, so now, when she was grown up, they continued to dance and flirt together without taking more than a polite notice of their hostess. She remained, always, on the edge of things. In a dim sort of way she was conscious of this. Sometimes, at other people's parties, the feeling of being quite out of it would become unbearable and she would leave abruptly, amid astonished protests, and go home, where she was sure of notice and admiration.

'Let's go to the new girl for the gaberdine,' said Sylvia, as the car drew up at Chadwick's shop. 'She seems to have more idea about things than anybody else.'

Jane was at the right-hand counter and Maggie at

the left. There was, by tacit agreement between them, no rushing forward to secure customers and commission. They waited where they happened to be in the shop and let the customer choose. But more and more, people chose Jane.

Mrs. Greenwood made for Jane now, but Mr. Chadwick intercepted her. She bought three and a half yards of gaberdine without much ado, but began then to worry loudly about trimming.

'I cannot conceive how you can have it trimmed, darling. I cannot conceive . . . What about a gilt braid, Miss Carter? Have you a discreet gilt braid— a "galon," if you know what I mean? I suppose you don't. Oh dear me, no! Nothing like that at all. Have you a tinsel braid, with colours, then? Let me see something of that kind.'

Jane brought out every length of tinsel braid in the shop and laid them, one after the other, against the blue cloth. They were received with loud outcries from Mrs. Greenwood and fretful murmurs from Sylvia.

'We must go to Manchester, Mother. It's quite hopeless to try to get anything in Tidsley.'

'I'm afraid you're right, my darling,' agreed Mrs. Greenwood. 'Haven't you *anything*, Mr. Chadwick?'

The fervour of her contempt for Tidsley and his shop threw Mr. Chadwick into a panic. He scrabbled among the braids like an agitated hen, throwing some of them on to the floor in his desperate anxiety to find something—anything—for his revered customer.

'One moment, Madam!' he begged. 'We really have some very nice braids here.'

Sylvia turned on her heel and made for the door.

Jane ran to the ribbon drawer. She had an idea.

She brought out a card of narrow black waxed ribbon ;
' ciré ' the travellers called it.

' How would this do ? ' she asked, deftly arranging
three rows of the ribbon against the cloth.

' Why, of course ! ' cried Sylvia, coming back from
the door. ' The very thing. Why ever couldn't you
show us this before ? '

' It would have saved a great deal of trouble,'
remarked Mrs. Greenwood, ' if you had shown us this
before.'

' I've only just thought of it,' said Jane. ' I just
remembered a photograph of a frock a French actress
was wearing I saw the other day. It was cloth,
trimmed with rows of ciré ribbon. Like that. . . .'

Mr. Chadwick frowned. This talk of French
actresses to Mrs. Greenwood ! This suggestion that
Miss Sylvia should wear a frock like the frock of a
French actress ! Miss Carter was forgetting herself.

But Mrs. Greenwood and her daughter did not
seem to be aware of it. They were pleased with the
idea.

' And if you thought of having one of the new cloaks,
Madam, of the same cloth, you could repeat the ribbon
in rows on the cloak. It would make a very nice
costume,' suggested Jane.

' Ah,' said Mrs. Greenwood. ' What do you think
of that, Sylvia ? Would you like a cloak, darling ? '

' Yes, I would.' Sylvia was quite animated. ' But
don't tell anybody else about it, Miss Carter. Don't
give the idea away to anybody else, will you ? '

' Certainly not, Miss Sylvia,' Mr. Chadwick hastened
to assure her.

' In that case, Miss Carter, we will have another
three yards of the gaberdine, and as for the ribbon,

you can send the piece up to Miss Bowen and she will use from it and send the remainder back to you. About two inches apart you meant the rows to be, did you say ? I see.'

She nodded her toque quite graciously to Jane and left the shop.

Jane put the despised braids away, her hands twinkling rapidly as she wound. She had made a good sale and a good impression. She felt the gratification of a business woman.

Mr. Chadwick returned to his desk with mixed feelings. He was relieved at the turn things had taken ; but he was a little alarmed of the possibilities revealed by his assistant. He stole a glance at her ; but she looked so young and harmless that he was reassured.

II

Weeks later, Mrs. Greenwood came into the shop to pay her bill.

Jane, high on the steps among the curtains, burst into a silent ditty :

> ' Hurray ! Hurray !
> She's come to pay !
> And I shall get some money ! '

Mr. Chadwick did not allow commission until the bill in question was paid. It was often a long time to wait. But now she would get a precious extra ninepence on the week's wages. She had planned what to do with it. It should not go prosaically to getting her shoes soled. She would buy a new collar. Jane took a pride and joy in her collars ; and Lily ironed them secretly and carefully for her.

She descended the steps with a happy scutter of her

slender legs and said 'Good morning' to Mrs. Greenwood with the amiability due to the bringer of that
ninepence.

On Friday night, tired from the long day, but looking forward to holding her wages in her hand, she went
to Mr. Chadwick's desk. She had reckoned it up ; it
would be five shillings wages, plus sixpence commission on cash sales, plus ninepence from Mrs. Greenwood's bill. Six-and-threepence.

Mr. Chadwick handed her five-and-sixpence.

She counted it as she turned away.

'Five-and-sixpence?' She was puzzled.

He had forgotten the ninepence from Mrs. Green-
wood's bill. She turned again and regarded him
diffidently. How was she going to remind him?
Remind him she must. Suddenly she saw his eyes
slide sideways, and she knew he had not forgotten.
Not forgotten at all. The omission was calculated.
Her heart began to beat thickly with nervousness.
She stood by the desk, trembling a little.

'Mr. Chadwick . . .' Her voice was husky. 'I
. . . I think . . . isn't there some commission due to
me on the sale of that ribbon and extra gaberdine to
Mrs. Greenwood?'

What a long sentence it seemed ! She had to take
breath in the middle of it.

Mr. Chadwick lifted his face. It showed meanly in
the bald light.

'You have had all the commission due to you, Miss
Carter.'

He bent his head again and made the usual pre-
liminaries to writing ; but in his secret agitation he
got no further than that.

'I don't understand,' said Jane more clearly. 'I

made the sale of ribbon and extra gaberdine, if you
remember.'

'I am busy, Miss Carter,' said Mr. Chadwick, still
making hieroglyphics in the air. He was upset.
Assistants never questioned him about commission.
They took what he gave them, and were glad to get
it.

'What is your commission, then?' asked Jane.
She came nearer. Her nervousness was gone, and her
eyes were steady with anger.

'Twopence in the pound. Twopence in the pound,
as I said.'

'Then you owe me . . .' began Jane.

'Nothing of the sort. Nothing of the sort,' blustered
the draper. 'The sale was mine. I attended to Mrs.
Greenwood myself.'

A wild and exhilarating anger caught Jane and
swept her up into the air. She opened her mouth to
give it vent.

But standing there, hot with anger, she suddenly
froze. She remembered her position. Ah, what a
burden is a position—inferior or superior—what a
handicap, what a clog! Jane remembered hers. She
remembered that Mr. Chadwick had the power to
turn her away at a day's notice, without wages. She
remembered that she would have great difficulty in
getting another job in Tidsley, if she left for such a
reason as this. She remembered that she had nowhere
to go—but her stepmother's house.

She swallowed with difficulty, and chinked the coins
softly one upon the other in her hand. But she did not
see them. Tears filled her eyes.

Mr. Chadwick looked up. He had expected a
storm. But it had not come. He saw that she was

beaten and his spirits rose. She was only a girl, after all. Whatever had come over him to make him afraid? Yes, he could admit it now. He had been afraid that he was going to have to give her that commission, after all.

He gathered his tattered dignity about him.

'I repeat, Miss Carter, that I am busy.'

Jane turned away and walked slowly out of the shop into the kitchen.

'I'm stewing this tripe,' said Maggie, 'to make it a bit tastier. Whatever's up?'

Jane shook her head warningly. She found it hard to speak. Her jaw was stiff with repressed emotion.

She went to stand by Maggie, and gained, as Wilfrid did sometimes, a sort of comfort from Maggie's very substance.

'Smells good, doesn't it?' said Maggie. 'You'll be better when you've had your supper. I always am myself.'

She doled out the tripe stew into the plates she had made hot in the ashes.

'There y'are. Now sit you down and get that inside you, and then you can tell me about it.'

They ate almost in silence. Mr. Chadwick was still in the shop.

'Wish he'd get upstairs,' whispered Maggie. 'You never get a bit of peace here.'

At last they heard him go up to the sitting-room where Mrs. Chadwick waited for him with roast pigeons and Australian burgundy, which he took with hot water and sugar.

'Now then,' inquired Maggie, pushing aside her burnished plate. 'What's up?'

D

'You know that sale I made to Mrs. Greenwood?
That ciré ribbon and gaberdine?' began Jane.

'Well, what about it?'

'It was my sale. It was me who suggested she
should have a cloak and trim it with ribbon . . .'

'You don't need to go on,' interrupted Maggie. 'I
know what you're going to say. You're going to say
that the little devil hasn't given you commission on it,
aren't you? Well, I could have told you that before.
He got the braids out of the drawer, or he passed you
the cloth or something. That's enough. The sale
goes through his book. It's his sale.'

Jane gaped at her.

'Eh, bless you !' went on Maggie, enjoying herself.
'You don't know what he is. When you're making a
sale, you want to keep a mile off him, and never ask
him where nothing is. Not so much as a pin. Else
he'll send the sale through his own book.'

'The mean little sneak !' said Jane huskily. 'Mean,
mean little sneak. . . .'

''Course he is,' agreed Maggie comfortably. She
drained her teacup.

'Fancy cheating a girl out of ninepence !' cried
Jane. 'And him with hundreds of pounds ! He
knows we can't fight. He knows we've got to put up
with whatever he does—all his dirty little sneaking
ways !'

'And he's a fool to himself, too !' she burst out
again. 'Cramping his own trade ! He cheats us out
of ninepence and stops us from earning pounds more
for him. Who's going to bring out any ideas when he
treats you like that? It doesn't pay to have ideas
here.'

'Speaking for myself,' said Maggie, 'I haven't got

any as I know of. But cheer up, love. You're not
dead yet. What d'you say to going to the Pictures?
Pictures is very good for the hump. And I just feel
like them. We're not very late for the second house.
Come on.'

Heavily, Jane put on her hat and coat and accompanied Maggie to the Star Picture Palace. They paid
fourpence for a seat in the side balcony. Maggie
liked to sit where she could observe, in the intervals,
the people in the two-shilling seats in the front balcony. The fourpenny seats were so full when they
got there, that they were pushed up almost against
the screen. The figures thereon were gigantic and
distorted. The life they portrayed was all leisure and
luxury, and Jane felt a bitter resentment against it.

Why did some people—Sylvia Greenwood, for instance—have so much? Parents, money, a grand
house, a grand car, grand clothes. It wasn't fair.
Not that she wanted all that. She wanted her due.
She wanted that ninepence.

Why did some people have so much? And yet,
compared with Lily, she herself must seem almost rich.
Was it all like this? Did every one look with envy at
the one above? Funny. And funny, too, that the
thought of someone else being worse off than you were
yourself should make you feel more cheerful. Jane
smiled grimly in the dark.

When the lights went up, Maggie nudged Jane.

'There's Noel,' she said.

Maggie took a lively interest in the young bloods of
Tidsley. She called them by their Christian names
among her friends.

'You know who I mean,' she said to Jane. 'Noel
Yarde, Sylvia Greenwood's young man. Well, I

don't know as she's got him yet, but I dare say she will. He is swanky, my word. Dick Elliott's with him. He's a one, he is ! You should hear what Lizzie Stevens says about him. He takes her out reg'lar."

Jane looked at the two young men with interest. They were elegant creatures ; the creases of their trousers were admirable ; the way they smoked fascinated her. She liked the way Noel Yarde turned his head to look with concentration at Dick Elliott and then dismissed what he had said with a vigorous ' Rot ! '

Jane had a secret test which she applied to men. She looked at travellers when they came to the shop, at men in trains and tramcars and in the street, and though she would never have dared to confess it, she said to herself :

' Should I like that man for a lover ? '

It was astonishing how often she had to say ' No.' Men, she found, were very largely unlovable and unloverlike. Very few passed her secret test.

But this time, looking at Dick Elliott and Noel Yarde, she asked herself :

' Should I ? '

She said ' No ' to Dick Elliott, but to Noel Yarde she said :

' Mmm.'

Jane, as a child, often wished the front of a row of houses would fall down and allow her to see what was going on in all the rooms at once. But how much more exciting, and possibly more catastrophic, it would be if we could look into the minds of the people around us ! How startled the audience of the Tidsley Star Picture Palace would have been if they could have witnessed the love passages that were going on in

Jane's mind between herself and the good-looking young man in the front row of the two-shilling seats ! Jane was trying him out in every sort of rôle.

' Have a Liquorice All Sort,' urged Maggie.

' No, thanks.'

' Yes, do. You like them plain square ones with liquorice in between, don't you ? Well, I'll just see if I can find you one.'

She just had time to get one out of the bag before the Star Picture Palace was again plunged into darkness.

Jane, her thoughts diverted, turned her attention to the elongated figures flickering on the screen.

CHAPTER FIVE

I

THE shop door stood wide open to the June morning. Outside there was sunshine and the cheerful noise of the Saturday market in full swing ; but the interior of the shop was dim, and for the moment empty of customers.

Mr. Chadwick took the opportunity to go upstairs for his mid-morning tea. As soon as his back was turned, Maggie left her moorings at the counter and went to the window to look at the people crowding the pavements. Jane put her hand behind the velveteen shelf and brought out *Ann Veronica*. She turned the pages eagerly. Her eyes would not move quickly enough along the lines for her. Oh, if only she had some time ! Time to read it now ; this minute.

Since Wilfrid had introduced her to H. G. Wells, Jane's life had been different. Her horizons had widened and extended incredibly. H. G. Wells was like wind blowing through her mind. She felt strong and exhilarated after reading him. It didn't matter whether she agreed with him or not. She wasn't sure that he ever pointed out any road that she could follow. It didn't matter. He made her want to get up and fight and go on. . . .

There was a step on the wooden floor. Jane hurriedly dropped *Ann Veronica* behind the velveteens.

' Good morning,' she said to a small figure standing uncertainly in the middle of the shop ; a little middle-aged woman looking like Mrs. Noah out of a child's Ark.

' Good morning, Mrs. Briggs,' said Maggie, returning to her counter.

Mrs. Briggs advanced to Jane.

' I want some sateen, if you please,' she began. ' It'll have to be black.'

' Yes, Madam,' said Jane.

' It's for a petticoat,' whispered Mrs. Briggs.

' Will you take a chair ? ' Jane bent over the counter to bring the papier-mâché chair to Mrs. Briggs's notice.

Mrs. Briggs sat down and coughed gently. All her movements and expressions were diffident and shy.

She bought three yards of sateen, and while Jane was wrapping it up, she began again :

' I thought of having something for a dress. But I don't know what to get . . .' Her voice trailed away. ' Have you any alpaca ? '

' Yes,' said Jane, stooping to the low shelf where the alpaca lay in gloom. She didn't like alpaca. She had many likes and dislikes. She displayed the alpaca before Mrs. Briggs, but could not bring herself to say a word in its favour.

' I don't know . . .' said Mrs. Briggs, bending over it helplessly. ' I wish I knew what to get. I had alpaca last time ; it lasted three years. I'd like a change now, if I could think of one.'

Jane pushed the alpaca away with delight.

' What about eolian ? ' she asked briskly, bringing
up a soft, gentle stuff.

Mrs. Briggs looked at her as if fearing to hurt her
feelings.

' If you don't mind,' she said, ' I won't have that.
It's very pretty, but it'll fall to me too much, if you
know what I mean. I need to be stood out round
now.'

' Something stiffer ? ' considered Jane. ' What about
a foulard ?   Here's a pretty one.'

She draped it and held it at arm's length. Mrs.
Briggs gazed at it. She looked wistfully at Jane
again.

' D'you think I could carry it off ? ' she asked.

' 'Course you could,' said Jane warmly. She felt
a sudden liking for this little woman so devoid of
self-confidence. ' You could have it made with a
plain tucked bodice ; not very waisted. All those
bones and linings and hooks and eyes are going out,
aren't they ? '

' Eh, are they ? ' Mrs. Briggs was despairing at
their defection. ' But what's going to take their
place ?   I wish I had someone to advise me.'

Jane hesitated.

' Would you like me to look out a style for you ? '
she ventured at last. ' I think I know what you
would like. I saw something in a paper in the
Library last night.'

' Now, thank you ! ' ejaculated Mrs. Briggs with
fervour. ' That's right-down kind of you. I shall
be very much obliged if you would. Very. I
shall indeed. I haven't much idea myself, you
know.'

' Don't buy any material to-day, then,' advised

Jane. ' If you could come in to-morrow, I'll have something for you to choose from.'

' It's very kind of you,' said Mrs. Briggs, getting down from the chair. ' And I'm very much obliged. Will you—do you mind telling me your name? I don't think you've served me before, have you? I don't often come in. I'm not much of a shopper.'

' Jane Carter, my name is.'

' Good morning, then, Miss Carter.'

' Good morning,' said Jane smilingly.

' Good morning,' said Mrs. Briggs, smiling back. ' Good morning,' she said again, turning before she went out at the door.

' Good morning,' said Jane.

' Oh, stop it ! ' whispered Maggie. ' You're making me dizzy the two of you playing catchers with your good morning like that ! '

' Couldn't help it,' said Jane, throwing an india-rubber at her. ' I had to answer. Besides, I like her.'

' What did Mrs. Briggs want ? ' asked Mr. Chadwick, coming into the shop.

The girls exchanged glances. He'd been spying again.

' Sateen ? ' went on Mr. Chadwick. ' I might have known. That, Miss Carter, is the wife of Mr. Briggs of Greenwood & Briggs. A very different lady from the other partner's wife. I mean our Mrs. Greenwood, you know.' He rummaged in his desk, but went on with a subject he evidently felt very strongly about : ' Mrs. Briggs doesn't live up to her position. It must be very trying for a gentleman like Mr. Briggs to have a wife who can't rise with him. Sateen petticoats and living in a house like Glenroyd ! '

He sniffed, and went out of the shop again.

Maggie darted to the window again.

' There's that Evelyn Wood and Mary Barton going past again. That's the tenth time, about, this morning. Hope they'll catch something soon. If you and me walked about the streets like that, Jane, they'd call us a couple of tarts. . . .

' There's Sylvia Greenwood. Oh, mercy, what a lovely frock ! Come and have a look at her, Jane ! She's just getting into the car. Lucky beggar ! '

Mrs. Greenwood stood on the pavement taking a loud farewell of her daughter. A middle-aged man stood by her, hat in hand. He wore a white flower in his button-hole, white linen spats, and very yellow chamois-leather gloves.

' Is that Mr. Greenwood ? ' asked Jane with interest.

' No, that's Mr. Briggs. You know, the husband of Mrs. Briggs as has just been in. Mrs. Greenwood often parades him up the Road on Saturday mornings. Sylvia goes home in the car ; I suppose it wouldn't do for her to walk up the Road. Use up her legs, or something.'

Sylvia was borne away in the maroon car, the envy of onlookers, and Mrs. Greenwood and Albert Briggs began their walk up the Road.

Queen's Road was always called ' the Road '. The small, insignificant streets, Elton Street, George Street, Barley Street, Exchange Street, that ran into the Square, poured out at the upper end, unified and dignified, as the Road. This highway ran for a little while past more shops, grew wider and wider as it flowed past the Park, clearing its banks little by little of doctors' houses and schools and churches, until it stretched out broad and strong and unimpeded all the way to the sea. It was a good road, and a beautiful road when, as now, it was hung over with hawthorn and laburnum blossom from the gardens, and the sky was blue above it.

Mrs. Greenwood and Albert Briggs often walked up the Road on Saturday morning. A somewhat heavy and extremely respectable flirtation was maintained between them. Mrs. Greenwood talked with loud archness to Albert, and Albert responded with gallantry. Gallantry had not come easily to him, but, with Mrs. Greenwood's help, he was improving. He carried her parcels. He skirmished round her with his stick to see that no one jostled her. He admired her well-fitting dress of mauve cloth, her stately gait, her loud voice. She was his idea of a lady.

Fragments of conversation drifted on the balmy air.

'You are a man of the world, Mr. Briggs, and you know that one cannot ignore one's social obligations. One has, after all, some slight penalty to pay for wealth and position. . . .'

She articulated slowly and with great pleasure. And Albert Briggs listened, continually taking off his hat as his companion bowed, like a royal personage, to tram-conductors and postmen, policemen and scavengers. He hardly ever knew whom he was supposed to be saluting, and had much ado to get his hat off in time.

When he passed any of his old friends, men still in the humble station he himself used to occupy, he was filled with satisfaction and thought: 'By gum, I wonder what they think of me now!' He still thought in terms of 'By gum,' but he never spoke like that now. By infinite pains, he had managed to pluck the Lancashire accent from his speech; that stubborn thing as hard to get rid of as willow-herb from a garden.

They continued their leisurely progress up the Road. They passed the Park and came to the stretch of road arched over by giant elms. The sunlight dappled Mrs. Greenwood's mauve dress and Mr. Briggs's grey suit. It was very pleasant. Mrs. Greenwood confided to her friend that she did not much like Barker, the cashier at the mill.

'No, I can't agree with you,' said Mr. Briggs. 'I can't agree with you there.' His tone implied that he could and would agree with her on any other matter. 'Barker's not a bad chap at all.'

Albert Briggs still looked on Barker as some sort of god dispensing money; more money than he had ever dreamed of handling. Albert Briggs had been a half-timer in Greenwood's mills; he had risen to overlooker and then to manager. He achieved a sort of fame in Tidsley as a judge of cotton staple. He had, it appeared, the almost legendary 'cotton touch.' When Amos Belton offered him a job at two thousand a year, Charles Greenwood countered by offering him a partnership, and Albert Briggs accepted with a surprised gratitude that had not worn off yet.

The partnership was, to all appearances, a good one. Charles Greenwood disliked the Manchester end of the business; he disliked going on 'Change; he knew little about cotton, or his mills, or his work-

people. He liked making money, more and more
money, pulling strings, forming companies, buying
people up and selling them out again.

Albert Briggs was therefore very useful to him.
Briggs knew cotton from A to Z, he knew the inside
working of the mills, he knew the work-people. He
liked going to Manchester in a first-class carriage ;
he liked his fellows,—a good, hearty lot he thought
them. He was quite content to leave the financial
side of the business in Greenwood's hands, where it
had been before he was made a partner. In fact, he
would have thought it presumption on his part to
ask to look at the books. Twenty per cent. had been
allotted him on his partnership, but he, as he put it,
left it to Greenwood, and drew out money from
Barker when he wanted it ; amounts being credited
and debited to him accordingly.

It was a grand thing to have money on tap like
that, he thought. He had just drawn out three
thousand pounds to buy Glenroyd. That was a fine
house for you ! What stables ! You didn't use
stables now, but stables gave tone to a house. Made
people think you'd lived in it a long time ; before
the time when horses went out and cars came in.
He was proud of his empty stables ; he was proud
of the house. If only Martha would do more credit
to it !

He sighed. Martha was a trial. She would not
live up to her position. He sometimes told Mrs.
Greenwood what a trial Martha was, and she, with
great enjoyment, gave him advice. But although
he followed it, nothing changed Martha. She
remained exactly what she had been in Sarah
Ellen Street. She had never even risen to 9, Arthur

Avenue, so it was useless to expect her to live up to Glenroyd.

II

You could tell it was Sunday as soon as you awoke. It was so quiet. No mill-folks, no clogs, no carts— just peace. Although there was no tree nearer than the Park half a mile away, a bird sang. Birds sang even in back-yards.

It was a fine morning. The paper blind had a shining edge of sunlight.

Jane, lying in her low bed, had a sudden desire to be very clean ; to be newly washed in cold water. Mrs. Chadwick only allowed one bath a week in the bathroom. Maggie's night was Tuesday, Jane's Wednesday, and Mr. Chadwick 'got in' after Mrs. Chadwick had finished with the water on Friday. Jane dared not think of having a Sunday bath, even cold, in the bathroom ; but there was, under the scullery sink, the tub in which Lily did the washing. She could bathe in that.

She leaped out of bed, put on the mackintosh which did double duty and was also a dressing-gown ; she took towel, soap and her clothes and went down the stairs. You had to go down the stairs with flat feet because they were so narrow.

She closed all the doors and got out the tub. It was big, and smelled cool and clean. She spread sheets of the *Tidsley Telegraph* on the floor to take up any spillings, and with great caution she poured cold water from the tap into the tub by means of the washing-up tin.

'That's enough,' she said, peering into the dark depths.

HIGH WAGES   63

She took off mackintosh and night-gown and stepped
into the tub.

' Oh, goodness ! Oh, I say ! Oooh . . .'

She disappeared into the tub and re-emerged,
startled and shining with water.

' Uh ! ' she gulped.

She disappeared again.

' It's grand ! ' she glowed.

She seized the loofah and the Castile soap recom-
mended by *Home Chat*. She scrubbed earnestly. She
plopped up and down in the tub, rinsing. Her body
glowed rosy and full of health. She had got what
she wanted. She had triumphed over circumstance
and Mrs. Chadwick. She stepped out of the tub
on to the *Tidsley Telegraph*, and dried briskly.

When she was dry, a solemn elation seized her.
She stood still, her hands clasped over her small,
firm breasts. In the back-yard the bird still sang.
She threw back her head, and contemplated the
cracked ceiling.

' Oh, God,' she said fervently, ' let me live ! Let
me know all of life ! '

A strange prayer, and not at all like those Mr. and
Mrs. Chadwick would be making later on at the
church of St. James.

Jane returned to herself.

Goodness ! Lily will be here before I know where
I am.'

She dressed ; her clothes slid deliciously against
her cool skin.

She opened the scullery door and looked out.
Over the tiled back of the Free Library the sky was
a serene blue with a few clouds tossed light and white
and high. She was going with Maggie and Wilfred

to Enderby Woods to-day, and she had *Old Wives'
Tale* to read. Life was good.

She put the kettle on the gas-stove, and carefully
removed all traces of her surreptitious ablutions.
No sooner had she finished than the latch of the
alley door lifted and steps came over the flagged
yard.

'Hello, Lily,' said Jane.

Lily only murmured in reply. Jane turned at
that and found her standing on the doormat waiting
to make an effect with mourning habiliments.

'We've 'ad a death in the family,' she said with
appropriate gloom.

'Yes, I know.' Jane felt she couldn't go into all
that again. 'But your husband's great-uncle was
eighty-six and you'd only seen him twice. You can't
be so fearfully bereaved about it, Lily, really. . . .'

'We buried 'im yesterday,' said Lily with dignity.

'Oh,' said Jane with resignation. It was no use
trying to do Lily out of her tale.

'Our Emma lent me this 'at,' continued Lily.
'She 'as two, you see. One for Sundays and one for
days. This is the one for days. Do I suit it?'

Jane took her head out of the kitchen cupboard
to say, 'Very nicely.'

'And 'ow d'you like me boa?' asked Lily, brightening. She fluffed up a small piece of marabout round
her neck. It looked wet, though no rain had fallen.

'Very much.'

'This is the blouse you gave me. I dyed it. I
think I looked as well as anybody at the grave.'

'I'm sure you did,' agreed Jane. 'But what about
getting their breakfast? It's half-past eight. I wish
Maggie would come down.'

Lily removed Emma's hat and carefully hung the boa over the back of a chair.

'Eh, it was sad,' she went on, refilling the kettle at the scullery tap. 'We all sat in t' parlour waiting for the 'earse. And Bob's sister took on something awful. Well . . .' Lily rolled her eyes round at Jane. 'I 'ad to cry with 'er. I'm very touchous like that,' she said deprecatingly.

'Maggie,' called Jane in a loud whisper up the stairs. 'I've brewed the tea. Yes?' she said encouragingly to Lily.

'Oooh, and when the carridges come and they called out for "Mr. and Mrs. Robert Blackledge"— that's me and Bob, you know—I come over that funny I could 'ardly stagger to the coach.'

'Dear me,' said Jane.

'Bob 'ad to 'elp me. He was very good yesterday, was Bob. Never touched a drop. I felt very proud of 'im. He looked a proper gentleman in 'is black gloves. Excuse me if I reaches past you for a tray-cloth. Thank you. They drove very solemn to the simmeterry. But they drove quite fast back to Forresseses.' Lily could never manage her 'sts'. 'And we all sat down to a grand tea; cold 'am and trifle. Eh, it was good!' Lily beamed; then remembering herself, she lengthened her face and added: 'But it was very sad.'

Jane had finished her breakfast by this time and went upstairs to make her bed. Maggie went down, yawning, and Jane heard Lily begin again:

'We've 'ad a death in the family.'

Jane smiled. Funerals and murders were to Lily what cold baths and summer skies were to her.

The day kept its fair promise, and Enderby Woods

were at their loveliest. Jane and Wilfrid settled into their books and Maggie disposed herself for sleep. The earth resisted her, pushing up three generous curves of shoulder, hip and leg. Her straw hat was over her face and she drew comfortable breaths through the rather soiled lining.

Jane's eyes kept wandering to the beauty around her. By and by she put out a hand and touched Wilfrid.

'Look!' said her eyes.

On the root of a tree near by a field-mouse sat on its haunches making its toilet. It passed its incredibly tiny front paws over and over its face, and minutely attended to its whiskers. Having completed all to its satisfaction, it made a little scurry to the left, a little scurry to the right, and disappeared.

'Wasn't that pretty?' asked Jane.

'What was it?' inquired Maggie idly from under her hat.

'Only a mouse.'

'A what?' shrieked Maggie, leaping up. 'Where? Where is it?'

'Gone, silly. And it was only a field-mouse.'

'What's the difference?' asked Maggie, looking uneasily round. 'Any mouse is a mouse, isn't it?'

She arranged herself once more.

Jane and Wilfrid fell into desultory talk. They talked about all sorts of things. Spiritualism.

'Think of sitting alone at night. In the dead vast and middle of the night,' said Wilfrid, 'trying to get into touch with—what?'

Jane's eyes grew wide and dark. They were caught up together into what Maggie called one of their 'potty moods.'

'Trying to *compel* an answer,' said Jane. 'And getting no answer. Oh, Wilfrid. No answer. It's so much more awful than any answer could be.'

'Oh, good heavens above,' groaned Maggie, shuffling on the ground. 'Can't you be a bit more cheerful on a Sunday afternoon? It's no P.S.A. with you two, let me tell you.'

' "'Tis the voice of the sluggard," ' said Jane, lifting Maggie's hat from her face. 'Fancy! I thought she'd gone off long ago.'

Maggie slapped the hat back into place.

'Go on with you!' she admonished good-naturedly.

Wilfrid was still in an exalted mood. He drew another little book out of his pocket and began to read aloud.

Jane would rather have gone on with *Old Wives' Tale*, but she listened to please him. She liked Wilfrid. He had brought a lot into her life : walks, books, himself. He was a friend. What was he reading now?

'Never seek to tell thy love,
Love that never told can be ;
For the gentle wind doth move
Silently, invisibly.

'I told my love, I told my love,
I told her all my heart,
Trembling, cold, in ghastly fears :—
Ah ! She did depart.

'Soon after she was gone from me
A traveller came by,
Silently, invisibly :
He took her with a sigh.'

He raised his eyes and there she sat before him ; abstracted, playing with a piece of moss ; not hearing the words that suddenly seemed ominous to him.

CHAPTER SIX

M R. CHADWICK put down the telephone into which he had spoken with great civility.

'Miss Carter, get out some corsets, please; Outsize, C.B., and Worcester and any others we have there, and take them up to Stanfield. Mrs. Greenwood wishes them to be fitted on.'

He bustled round to where Jane was already busy with the boxes.

'This is the first time Mrs. Greenwood has bought corsets from us,' he said, rubbing his hands together and emitting a dry crackling sound therefrom. 'She usually has them fitted in London. So I need hardly impress upon you, Miss Carter, the necessity of fitting them correctly and—er—with proper politeness, and—er—all that.'

'Yes,' said Jane, feeling nervous.

'Here is threepence for your tram fares.' Mr. Chadwick brought the coppers out of an old-maidish purse.

Jane made up the parcels, two long, bulky ones, and went up to the back bedroom to get ready. It would be good to get out into the blowy October afternoon, she reflected, arranging her best hat on her head. She had bought the hat for two-and-eleven in the Market House; but no one would guess that. It was transformed according to *Vogue*.

Her coat was furbished up, too, for the winter, by a little imitation fur on the collar.

Mr. Chadwick saw her off with more fussy instructions. The wind was very high. Jane, a parcel hanging at the length of each arm, tried to keep her hat on by her eyebrows, raising them to incredible heights. But catching sight of herself in Fenwick's window mirror, she giggled and restored them to their natural level.

She noted with interest that Fenwick's had two ready-made fur-trimmed coats in their window. They were evidently starting on ready-mades. She must warn Mr. Chadwick. That would cut into his business.

Thus reflecting, she turned into Exchange Street and immediately her hat soared from her head and flew away like a bird. Blinded by hair and hampered by parcels, Jane set off in difficult pursuit.

'Oh, my hat!' she called out despairingly. 'Oh, my hat! . . .'

'Oh!' she cried loudly, dropping the parcels and coming to a paralysed halt. The hat had precipitated itself in the path of an advancing cart-wheel. 'It's done for,' moaned Jane.

In the very nick of time the hat was saved. A young man stepped out and snatched it from ruin. He looked round for its owner. Jane, from afar, saw that it was Noel Yarde. For one fleeting second she entertained the wild idea of leaving the hat in his hands and disappearing up Carrington Street. But she came to her senses without visible pause, and advanced towards this splendid male creature who had such glossy hair and took Miss Greenwood out to coffee in the mornings.

'Thank you very much,' she said, looking up through

the hair whipping her nose and temples. 'Thank you very much indeed.'

Close to, how good-looking he was ! And shy. She did not expect that. Whatever had such as he to be shy about ? But shy he was. He grimaced slightly as he raised his hat.

'I was only just in time,' he said.

'I know,' said Jane. 'And I'm so glad, because it's its first time out.'

'Oh, good egg !' said the young man, raising his hat again and continuing his way down Exchange Street.

Jane stood with the parcels wedged between her ankles and returned the hat to her head. She tucked in all the wild ends of hair, broodingly.

The conversation with the young man had left her strangely depressed. Why had she said, 'It's its first time out'? Awful. 'It's its first time out.' Why mention it at all ? No lady would have done. But if mentioned, why 'it's its'?

His reply seemed to her unintelligible, but elegant. She said it over to herself in the car.

'Good egg.' Some saying of the smart, no doubt.

She alighted at the terminus, and, the parcels colliding first with her shins and then with her calves, climbed the hill towards Stanfield.

This was the residential part of Tidsley ; it was known among the shopkeepers as the 'better' or 'west' end. Stanfield was quite the best end ; almost in the country. Not the county ; there could not be said to be any county round Tidsley. Noel Yarde lived on Hill Rise too ; in a house called Greystones.

Jane turned into the gravelled drive. This was the first big house she had ever visited. She looked round at everything. The drive was bordered by rhododendrons and laurels with spotted leaves ; it was the sort of garden, she thought, that would be laid out later with those india-rubber rosettes of plants.

She came into view of the house ; it was built of yellow stone and had small pointed windows.

' It's like a chapel,' she said with disappointment.

She did not know whether to go to the front door or round to the back. A dreadful dilemma ! She ought to have asked Mr. Chadwick. She hovered uncertainly round the house, until she spied a side door, which she hailed as the happy medium.

A maid with streamers to her cap admitted her. Jane took a seat, as she was told, in the hall. She sat next to a large mantelpiece. Marble, she supposed, but it looked like congealed brawn, complete with white of egg. The hall and staircase were panelled in pitch-pine. To the right of the front door was a conservatory, but there did not seem to be anything pretty in it ; just greenery punctured by something in the shape of raw rat-tails, and a few orchids with flowers like intestines. Through an open door, to the left, she could see Sylvia Greenwood playing on a grand piano.

Jane felt a little humble and wistful. It must be fine, she thought, to play on a grand piano in the afternoons, after having been out with young men to coffee in the mornings. She visualized Sylvia Greenwood's life as being all like that ; all leisured ; all elegant.

The maid returned.

' This way,' she said, drawing her streamers through her hand at the back.

Jane followed her up the staircase, carpeted in red and blue. The house seemed to her like some rich, dark plum-pudding ; it even smelled rather like it.

The maid knocked on a door, and Mrs. Greenwood's familiar bellow told her to come in. Jane entered a vast bedroom with a vast upholstered bed in it. A girlish white night-dress case disposed thereon struck her as incongruous and forlorn.

Mrs. Greenwood sat by the fire. She wore a purple dressing-gown which fitted her familiarly, her curves being identically those of the dummy it had once adorned in Mr. Chadwick's shop.

'Ah,' shouted Mrs. Greenwood. 'I expected you earlier.'

'I'm sorry. I came as soon as I could,' said Jane, beginning to undo the parcels.

'You had better warm your hands,' said Mrs. Greenwood. 'There is nothing I dislike more than coming into contact with cold hands.'

Jane approached the blaze with nervous trepidation. She felt overcome by a sense of her own inadequacy; she did not know how she was to get through this trying-on business.

'Come on!' she admonished herself. 'This isn't the way to get on.'

This reminder enabled her to rise to almost any occasion.

Mrs. Greenwood was as completely at ease while being fitted with stays as she was in more dignified situations. It was a test, and she came through it triumphantly. Jane felt something like respect for her. She herself would have died to have been so bulky, so resilient, and to have given such trouble with laces and hooks.

The fire was very hot, as she knelt before it half buried in the thick skin rug. It was, of course, out of the question to ask Mrs. Greenwood to move. It was all very difficult. As fast as she got the lady buckled in one place, she emerged in another. Jane began weakly and secretly to giggle.

Sylvia came in and sat down by the fire. Mother and daughter talked ; mostly about going to London in good time for Sylvia's dress for the Hospital Ball.

Although they were careful not to include Jane in their conversation in any way, it seemed to her that they were not as unconscious of her as they pretended.

'Ring for tea, darling,' said Mrs. Greenwood. 'We'll have it here. I'm not yet satisfied that I am going to be able to get anything to fit me.'

Tea was brought, and a mild panic seized Jane. They might offer her a cup of tea ; no bread-and-butter or anything—but possibly a cup of tea. Sometimes she seemed to make a loud noise when she swallowed. She prayed that she wouldn't do that to-day. Her prayer was answered. They did not offer her any tea to swallow.

She busied herself, while they ate and drank, in folding up the stays already tried on and arranging others. Her awkwardness had gone. A cold competence possessed her. They didn't think her good enough to be offered a cup of tea. All right. She didn't care what they thought. She disliked them. She would serve them to earn her daily bread. But she herself stood off, unimpressed.

She decided suddenly that she would ask for a rise in wages. Mrs. Greenwood and Sylvia were remotely responsible for this. The more you trod on Jane, the more she wasn't squashed.

With cool determination, she laced Mrs. Greenwood into stays that received her grudging approval, and took her leave.

She went down Hill Rise to wait for the tramcar.
At the terminus Mrs. Briggs waited too. But she was
for the moment too occupied to notice Jane. She was
waving her hands to three children coming down the
hill with their mother. But none of the little party
took much notice. The girl pushed a doll's perambu-
lator, the boy jumped on and off the pavement, and
the baby lurched at the end of his mother's hand. The
mother wore a moleskin shoulder cape over her mackintosh, and made its silken fringe dance as she walked.

The car appeared in the distance and Mrs. Briggs
waved more vigorously. She called out :

'See, children ! It's grandma !'

But that did not move them to further speed ; they
came on as indifferently as before. Mrs. Briggs took a
few hasty steps towards them, but the car arrived at
the terminus and she was obliged to return.

'I can't wait, Lizzie,' she called again. 'I'm going
to the doctor's.'

'Right-ho,' said the daughter-in-law negligently.
She was annoyed at being called Lizzie so publicly.
Since they had moved into the big house, she called
herself Elizabeth.

'Bye-bye, children. Bye-bye, Baby !' cried Mrs.
Briggs, twisting round to look at them again as she
got on the car, flustered by the conductor's repeated
bell-clanging.

But the children and their mother had already turned
down the road in the opposite direction, and did not
look round. Mrs. Briggs gazed after them from the
platform of the car, before going inside to take her seat.

When she saw Jane, she smiled and went to sit by
her.

'Good afternoon. I didn't see you before. You

must excuse me. That was Willy's wife and the
children. The car came so quick I never got a proper
look at them. Bonny little children, aren't they?'
she said, with a mixture of pride and wistfulness.

Jane smiled with sympathy. The incident had
touched her.

'I see you've been out,' said Mrs. Briggs.

'Yes,' said Jane.

'Somewhere up our way,' Mrs. Briggs remarked
with innocent curiosity.

'To Mrs. Greenwood's.'

'Oh, have you?' Mrs. Briggs was interested and a
little awed. 'She's the senior partner's wife, you know,
of our firm Greenwood & Briggs; perhaps you've
heard of it. She's a very clever lady, isn't she? Not
but what,'—Mrs. Briggs's face puckered with a mischief
Jane had not expected in her,—'not but what I
wouldn't rather it was you going to Mrs. Greenwood's
than me. She frightens me a bit. She does really.
Aren't I soft?'

She laughed at herself and looked out of the window
to see if she was approaching the doctor's. Then she
twisted back to Jane and said hurriedly :

'You must excuse me, but I've taken a fancy to you.
Ever since you was so kind about that dress. You
don't mind me telling you, do you? What I mean to
say is—could you come and 'ave a cup of tea with me
on your afternoon off? I won't ask you on a Sunday,
because th' Mester's about then,' said Mrs. Briggs,
wrinkling up her nose a little and looking to Jane for
understanding. 'And it's never the same when there's
a man in the 'ouse, is it? Could you come next Thursday? I'd be right glad to see you. About half-past
four. Would that suit you?'

' Oh,' cried Jane, ' I'd love to come. Thank you very much.'

' I must get off now,' said Mrs. Briggs beamingly. ' Good-bye till Thursday, then. Good-bye.'

Jane went back to the shop, delighted at the unusual prospect of going out to tea. But the kindlier feelings towards the world in general, inspired by Mrs. Briggs, did not prevent her from asking Mr. Chadwick for a rise in wages. Mr. Chadwick was grudging and astonished, but Jane flung so many arguments, culled from H. G. Wells, at him that he was driven, in the end, to put up the screen of an extra half a crown a week between himself and this determined young woman.

CHAPTER SEVEN

I

WILFRID waited in the alley ; he leaned against the wall and watched Chadwick's back door. When a striped cat stalked with marvellous grace along the top of the wall, he followed it with his eyes ; then fixed them again upon the door.

'Soon. Soon,' he told himself.

He had not seen her on Sunday because she had a cold. And because he could not bear a week without a sight of her, he had managed to change his half-day holiday to coincide with hers.

Steps in the back-yard at last. Colour flooded Wilfrid's sallow cheeks. The door-latch lifted. He stepped forward, his eyes alight. But Maggie alone emerged.

'Jane's not coming to-day,' she announced, buttoning up her collar against the bitter wind. 'A customer asked her out to tea. Took a fancy to her and asked her out to tea. Getting on, isn't she?'

The colour left Wilfrid's face as swiftly as it had come.

'Not coming?' he said. He couldn't believe it. He couldn't believe he wasn't going to see her. Not going to see her again.

Maggie, the unobservant, noticed his strange look.

'What's up, Wilfrid?' she asked, coming close so

78

that the cheap scent she used on her days off enveloped him like a saccharine cloud. 'Not sick, are you?'

'A bit,' he said with truth, averting his head.

Not coming. And he had counted every minute of this damned day.

'When did it come on, dear?' Maggie asked solicitously.

'Oh, I don't know.'

He made a move to go, and Maggie put a hand under his arm.

'Shall I get you a drink of water?'

'No, come on . . .' said Wilfrid flatly. 'It's all right.'

He looked up at the bedroom window, but there was no sight of her. He went away with Maggie. He was void; dissolved into unhappiness.

Meanwhile Jane, dressing to go to Mrs. Briggs's, was congratulating herself on being able to leave Wilfrid and Maggie alone together. Although they insisted that she should make a third on all excursions, she still felt that two ought to be company, even if it was not.

She had, from time to time, come across a case of love that astonished by its mildness, and she supposed this must be such another. Maggie seemed to want no more than to take Wilfrid's arm on the walks, and to sit by him in tramcars. Wilfrid seemed to want nothing at all. However, it was their own affair, she concluded, going, in her turn, out of the back door.

But it wasn't her idea of love.

Jane, of course, thought quite a good deal about love. If she had not been so busy all day, and so tired at night, she might have thought more. She had made several false starts towards it.

There was that boy, Mitchell, she met at Barton's Thursday night dancing class. She had reached a pitch of pleasurable excitement about him, and with brilliant cheeks and eyes, had led him on considerably. But when she discovered that he was following her home —his footsteps echoing behind hers in the empty streets —her interest suddenly died away and she shut the back door firmly in his face.

'I can't be bothered with him,' she said to Maggie.

There was Harding, the traveller from Spenser's. She flirted with him for several weeks, and when he asked her to go to the Pictures, having informed her that he was staying in Tidsley for the express purpose of taking her, she went. She thought she was beginning to like him, and stole many glances at his handsome profile in the half-dark. But during one passionate screened episode, she felt his hand creeping up her arm, predatory, furtive, and the virginal Jane took fright and thrust him off abruptly. When the lights went up, she left him.

She turned these things over in her mind as she walked.

There was no life in the town on early-closing day. The market-place was a grey waste ; the Market House, shuttered and silent, exhaling a strong smell of fish in its sleep. Exchange Street was empty ; the old Exchange, now the Star Picture Palace, stood there, its dark dignity woefully affronted by the bright red paint lining the Cinema proprietors had given to its Gothic porch. The effect, thought Jane, was startling ; as if you got a sudden view into a raw stomach. She laughed at the idea, and looked at it again. It was exactly like that.

She laughed easily to-day, because she was happy about several things. Going out to tea. Her extra half-crown a week. The book she was reading : *Marie Claire*—a perfect thing, clear and simple.

She turned into the Park. The great beech trees in their bareness reminded her by their grey, their massive limbs, of elephants ; huge elephants moving through a forest. What a crashing, what a thunder they would make ! If only she could witness such gigantic happenings !

She said over to herself the poem that Wilfrid had copied out for her :

> ' Tiger, tiger burning bright
> In the silence of the night. . . .'

She loved it ; it shattered the commonplace.

She reached Hill Rise and Mrs. Briggs's house. She rang the bell at the imposing front door and was admitted by a maid. Mrs. Briggs was hovering behind to take the chill off the welcome.

' Come in ! ' she said, bustling forward. ' I've been watching for you. Would you like to take your hat off ? I know it's not the thing to ask people to do, but you and me don't need to bother about that, do we ? Take your hat off and make yourself at home. You'd better come up to my bedroom. They don't have hat-stands in these houses, you see,' she whispered. ' In-convenient, isn't it ? '

She led the way up the staircase, turning round incessantly to smile and talk to Jane. She was like an elderly child having a friend to tea.

The staircase was much nicer than the Greenwoods', thought Jane. Mrs. Briggs's bedroom was very well done, too.

F

' Before we settle,' said Mrs. Briggs, ' I dare say you'd like to look over the house.'

She led the way from room to room ; each beautifully furnished and unused.

' It's all lovely,' breathed Jane.

' Yes, it's very grand,' agreed Mrs. Briggs, closing the last door behind her. ' Veering & Armstead did it all. I 'ad no say in it. I didn't want none. I shouldn't have liked the responsibility of furnishing a place like this. I never sit in any of these rooms ; except on a Sunday sometimes when the Mester's about. I don't feel at home in them, somehow. This is my room.'

She opened a door and bustled in.

' Now then,' she said in a voice that was suddenly bright and motherly, ' come in and make yourself at home.'

Jane could have laughed aloud at Mrs. Briggs's room. They had kept her down all over the house, but here she had broken out with determination. A blue and red carpet, plush furniture, brass fire-irons, a rocking chair, a sewing machine, and, yes—sure enough, an aspidistra in a glazed pot with a crocheted mat beneath it on a table in the window.

' Draw up,' said Mrs. Briggs. ' I'll mash the tea. I always mash it myself, you know, because I can't trust them girls. The stuff they send in on a Sunday ! You wouldn't believe.' She bustled happily with caddy and kettle, her cheeks faintly pink.

If Jane had expected afternoon-tea such as she read about in the fashion papers, she was not to experience it at Glenroyd. But it was more heartening to see luscious tinned peaches decorated with turrets of whipped cream, and plates of all kinds of bread :

white, brown and currant bread ; and all kinds of
home-made cakes : rock-buns, jumbles, parkin.
' I had a bit of a bake this morning,' explained Mrs.
Briggs. ' They don't like me being in the kitchen, but
I was determined to give you a proper tea, because I
don't suppose you get overmuch to eat where you are.
Mrs. Chadwick looks as if she'd skimp you a bit.'

A dish of sausages, accompanied by bread-sauce, was
here brought in, and Jane began on a meal such as she
had not eaten for many a year.

' Now you must make a good tea,' said her hostess,
creaking over to push one loaded plate after another
towards Jane.

' Oh, I shall,' said Jane, her young teeth making a
vigorous crescent in a piece of oven-bottom cake.

She was happy, warm and comfortable, and so was
Mrs. Briggs. As the meal progressed, they became
communicative. Jane told Mrs. Briggs all about herself, her dead parents, her stepmother, Alice and Eddy,
how she came to Chadwick's, about Maggie and Wilfrid, and Mrs. Briggs was just in the middle of her
account of Albert, Willy and Lizzie and Peggy, and
Michael and Baby, when the door opened. Mrs.
Briggs looked up and her face changed. All its comfort fell away.

' Oh, Albert . . .' she faltered. ' Have you come
home ? You're early, aren't you ? '

Mr. Briggs ignored her and stared at Jane. He did
not remember his wife having anybody to tea before.

' You'd better introduce me, Martha,' he said,
heavily gallant.

' It's Miss Carter, Albert. From Mr. Chadwick's,
the draper's.'

' How d'you do ? ' said Albert, nodding. A shop-girl.

Funny how they managed to make themselves look like ladies nowadays.

He walked to the fire and watched them from the hearthrug.

Mrs. Briggs and Jane made a pretence of going on with tea. Mrs. Briggs moved things aimlessly about and nibbled at her bread-and-butter. Jane could not avoid a view of Mr. Briggs from her place. His fingers were like pale sausages, she thought ; and she thought he must suffer from what she had heard of, but never before seen :

' A dropped stomach,' she said to herself, getting through her piece of parkin under his eye. ' A dropped stomach, obviously. And no manners,' she added, beginning to blush.

She was moved to this criticism because he embarrassed her, and because she felt that Mrs. Briggs was afraid of him. Perhaps not afraid, but anxious and embarrassed, too, in his presence.

' You'll be wanting your tea, Albert,' said Mrs. Briggs. ' I'll just get Lucy to see to it.'

' Ring the bell, then,' said Albert testily. ' You've no need to go into the kitchen about it.'

' No,' said Mrs. Briggs, ringing the bell obediently. ' It won't be long. I dare say it's laid ready in the dining-room. You see, I didn't expect you home yet,' she apologized.

Her face was wistful. Her little entertainment of her new friend was spoiled. She looked round in bewilderment. What could they do, now he had made a third ?

' I must be going,' said Jane.

Mrs. Briggs seemed to think it would be best.

' You must come again,' she whispered on the way

upstairs. ' He isn't home as early as this not once in
six months. It's a pity it just happened like that to-day.
But I 'ave enjoyed our chat,' she said, brightening.
' You will come again, won't you ? '

She went to the front door with her guest, looking
round with some anxiety in case Albert caught her
usurping the office of the parlourmaid.

' Good-bye, love. That is a pretty hat. You look
like—eh, I don't know what ! But just what I should
'ave liked my girl to look like, if she'd lived. I've only
Willy now, you know, and he's married and doing very
well, so I don't see much of him. Good-bye, and you
will come again, won't you ? '

On a sudden impulse, Jane proffered her lips to
Mrs. Briggs. They kissed. They were, inexplicably,
friends ; warm friends.

Jane went down the drive, winking away a slight,
and, she sternly judged, absurd mist of tears. Poor
Mrs. Briggs ! The house was too grand for her ; the
husband and the son, too grand. It was obvious that
Mrs. Briggs did not take kindly to grandeur. She
suffered in it.

II

Wilfrid was disappointed again the following Thursday ; because Jane went to Manchester. Her ambit
had extended. Once she had gone from Elton to
Tidsley on her half-day off ; now she was going on a
three-shilling excursion to Manchester. Some day she
might reach out to Liverpool. Her thoughts dared as
far as London. But she did not think she would ever be
able to follow them.

She looked persistently out of the dirty window so
that the other passengers should not guess from the

excitement in her eyes that she was going to Manchester
for the first time.

Trains passed in the opposite direction, taking back
the cotton princes to Tidsley, Elton, Burrows, and
further on to Southport, Blackpool, St. Anne's. She
could see the occupants of the first-class carriages playing cards, or fallen into unlovely sleep. They did well
to avert their eyes from the landscape they had made.
They had made it ; but they could not, like God, look
and see that it was good. Monstrous slag-heaps, like
ranges in a burnt-out hell ; stretches of waste land
rubbed bare to the gritty earth ; parallel rows of
back-to-back dwellings ; great blocks of mill buildings,
the chimneys belching smoke as thick and black as
eternal night itself ; upstanding skeletons of wheels and
pulleys. Mills and mines ; mills and mines all the
way to Manchester, and the brick, the stone, the grass,
the very air deadened down to a general drab by the
insidious filter of soot.

But Jane, Lancashire born and bred, did not find it
depressing. It was no feeble, trickling ugliness, but a
strong, salient hideousness that was almost exhilarating.
She would, however, have found almost anything exhilarating in her present mood.

She felt she was again going to smile at the prospect
of going to Manchester. She drew in the corners of
her lips and opened her worn handbag to give herself
countenance. There was her trip ticket quite safe, and
the little old purse with five-and-fourpence in it. It
would be more than enough ; she could not afford to
spend it on anything.

After premature uprisings at Bolton and Salford, she
arrived at Victoria Station. The dirty wooden platform surprised her. Really . . . for Manchester !

Manchester, however, maintained the family likeness to
Tidsley, Burrows, Elton and other Lancashire towns
further than the platform. It was the same colour, but
deeper. It was almost black, almost all black. That
church now—was it the cathedral?—was the blackest
building she had ever seen or ever would see. The
pavements were covered with a thin, sticky mist of
soot ; she noticed that she lifted it up on the soles of
her shoes, leaving a defined print behind.

But it didn't matter ; the soot, the general blackness,
the ugly streets, even the fine mizzle of rain that now
began to fall. It was Manchester. It stood for something.

She went to Deansgate on a tramcar, because Mr.
Chadwick had told her Deansgate was the hub of
Manchester. She stood bewildered and excited on the
pavement. There were the most wonderful shops on
all sides. Where should she begin ?

With a skip, she made for the biggest : ' Kendal,
Milne and Company,' she read. So this was Kendal's.
A name uttered with respect by Mr. Chadwick as being
the very acme of a draper's establishment. This was
Kendal's. It had been a name and now it was a
reality.

' My goodness ! ' breathed Jane.

She darted from window to window ; all round.

' It's huge. Ready-mades, silks, cottons, linens,
shoes, men's department. . . .'

She came round to her starting-point, and with a
sigh of pleasurable anticipation, began a lengthy exam-
ination of every window in turn.

' It's not,' she reflected at the window where household linens were displayed,—' it's not that the
quality is any better than ours, or that the things are

really different in any way. It's the way they're set out. Now if Mr. Chadwick would only . . .'

She took it all in, leaning against the pane in the darkling afternoon light.

'All that pink together, now. You'd come across the road to see what it was making such a lovely glow. A pink lampshade, a pink silk eiderdown, a fluffy pink blanket—a *pink* blanket—a crêpe-de-Chine night-gown —and a little net cap with pink ribbons even—and pink bedroom slippers. It makes you feel luxurious and extravagant. As if you could spend all your money and never care. Goodness, I wish I could buy that little cap. But it wouldn't go with the bedroom at Chadwick's, and no one would see me in it, and I should never have time to wear it. But it is a darling.'

She even opened her purse to finger her money, but snapped it shut again and laughed.

'That's a clever window!'

She passed on and discovered King Street. Oh, the discreet little shops! Fancy having nothing but one hat in a whole window ; one hat against a backcloth of buff velvet and one pearl bracelet laid negligently afar off!

Up one side of the street and down the other she went.

'If I had a shop, should I go in for quality or quantity?'

Her instinct was for quality, but she thought quantity would pay best. The speculation was interesting. She hugged her bag closer, and thought of many things.

The furniture shops entranced her.

'If I had a house . . .'

Ah! If she had a shop! If she had a house! She

had nothing but five-and-fourpence in her bag and
fifty-two pounds in the Tidsley Savings Bank.

She liked St. Ann's Passage ; the little low, brilliant
shops ; jewellery, cakes, coloured wools and silks.
She came out into St. Ann's Square, and just as she
was gazing into Parker's windows, Noel Yarde went
into tea with Dick Elliott. It was not surprising that
she should see him there ; Manchester was full of
Tidsley people. She watched them go into the warmth
and the light ; tall with an elegant suggestion of
waist, wash-leather gloves and bowler hats. Very
grand they were, and completely out of her orbit. She
felt their attraction and sighed as she turned away.

' I'd like some tea,' she thought. ' But not here.'

She found a shop where the absence of tablecloths
proclaimed it the place for her, and a large cup of tea
and a Bury Simnel cake restored her to complete cheerfulness for fourpence.

She hurried out again to look at more shops before
train-time. Manchester was all alight now, and more
cheerful than by day. Emboldened by tea, Jane
walked into and about Kendal's. No one noticed her,
and that was a great relief.

She went back to Victoria Station, impressions, ideas
and schemes crowded together in her head. As the
train sped through the night, the mills were palaces
of light with myriad blazing windows, and rivers of
fire ran down the slag-heaps ; it was wonderful.

III

The next morning, as soon as Mr. Chadwick had
settled himself at his desk, it being as yet too early for
customers, Jane advanced and asked permission to dress
a window in a one-colour scheme.

Mr. Chadwick squeezed his lips white in a way he had.

'The windows do very well, Miss Carter,' he said with dignity. 'I have dressed them myself for twenty years, and I don't think you can teach me anything about window-dressing.'

'It's only that I saw some new ways yesterday,' said Jane. 'And I wondered if we could try them for a change. If you didn't like it, we could go back to the old way.'

'This business, Miss Carter,' said Mr. Chadwick, still speaking from a very high horse, ' has gone on very nicely for many years. It went on very nicely before you came to it, and I dare say it will go on very nicely when you have left it.' That sounded very well. He could afford to be a little more explicit now. ' Besides, these new-fangled notions do not suit an old-established and highly respectable business.'

'But the new ways aren't at all loud or cheap.' Jane was not to be put off so easily. ' Mr. Fenwick is trying them, I can see.'

Was it chance or intention that she brought in Fenwick's name? Mr. Chadwick looked up with suspicion, but Jane's face was innocent as she looked back at him with candid eyes.

Fenwick loomed large in William Henry Chadwick's secret thoughts. He admired, feared, hated and envied Fenwick above all men. His attitude when he met Fenwick at the Chamber of Commerce and up and down the town alternated between a cringe and a swagger. Fenwick was his Ideal Tradesman, if the truth were to be told. Fenwick kept a shop ; furs. He served in the shop, and when he was so inclined, he walked about casually outside the shop, and about the front of other

shops. Without a hat. Actually without a hat. Mr.
Chadwick had tried it, but he had scuttled back to his
shop when he got as far as the Victoria Café. He felt
indecent and conspicuous without a hat. He had not
Fenwick's nerve.

Fenwick drove a car ; a large Daimler. It stood
for hours before Fenwick's shop, making Mr. Chadwick
writhe with envy. He himself had enough money to
buy as good a car as Fenwick's ; but he didn't feel he
would be able to drive it, and had visions of running
amok in the market-place and ruining his dignity and
his trade.

Fenwick mixed unconcernedly in Tidsley society ; on
a par with the best. It was extraordinary. He played
golf. He went to dances with his wife and daughters,
the strange, bold man ! He even went to the peak
and pinnacle of Tidsley functions—the Hospital Ball.
However he got tickets for that, Mr. Chadwick simply
couldn't think.

So that when Miss Carter said that Fenwick was
adopting the new ways of window-dressing, he immediately felt he must adopt them too, although he did
not know in the least what they were. But he mustn't
give in too quickly.

' What exactly do you mean when you say Fenwick
is trying them, Miss Carter ? '

' Well,' said Jane. ' You know how he used to have
his window full of skins and furs ? Tailed furs in rows
on the floor, and muffs and stoles all over the place, and
fur coats on dummies, and fur rugs hanging over the
rail at the back. When I went past the other day, he
had one coat spread against a low stand, one ready-
made cloth coat trimmed with the same fur over
another, and a bag and umbrella very carefully chosen

laid to one side. Nothing else ; except a water-lily floating in a bowl.'

'A water-lily floating in a bowl ? ' exclaimed Mr. Chadwick. ' Good gracious me ! '

'That's the new way,' said Jane triumphantly. ' But you know, Mr. Chadwick, those ready-made coats in Fenwick's frighten me. If you don't look out, Fenwick's will capture all the ready-made trade in dresses and blouses that's coming to this town. Because it is coming. I'm sure. The day of the private dressmaker is over.'

Mr. Chadwick stared at her.

' Miss Bowen is as old-established as I am,' he said.

' Well, her day's over, I'm afraid.'

' Nonsense, Miss Carter ! As if a lady like Mrs. Greenwood will ever wear ready-made clothes, or Miss Sylvia either. Nonsense, I say. And what do you know about it ? '

Jane went back to her counter, considerably irritated.

' He's hopeless. Hopeless,' she said to herself.

Nevertheless, he called out to her later in a grudging voice :

' You can try a window, Miss Carter. But remember, if I don't like it, you'll have to undo it again.'

' Oh, thank you ! ' cried Jane delightedly.

It was when she had almost finished the window and was gazing critically at it from the pavement outside, that Mrs. Briggs came hurrying up.

' Well, I am glad to catch you like this,' she exclaimed. ' I've been wondering how I was going to get at you without buying anything and I couldn't think of anything as I wanted. Oh, what a lovely setout you've made ! Well, I never did see anything so pretty ! But see, love,'—she fumbled in her handbag, and Jane thought she was going to bring out one of the packets of sweets she was fond of buying for her,— ' Mrs. Greenwood's made me buy three tickets for the Hospital Ball. She flusters me into buying tickets for everything as goes on. The 'ouse is cluttered up with tickets for things we never go to. If there's anything I 'ate it's tickets. So will you take these 'ere, and go if you can, but if you can't, take 'em, anyway. Because if th' Mester see them, 'e'll 'appen be reminded 'e wants to go, and speaking for meself, I'd rather go to the Hospital itself than the Hospital Ball.'

She thrust the tickets into the hands of the astonished Jane.

' Now don't stand out here in the cold, love. Run along in, and don't forget to come to your tea on Thursday. Good-bye.'

' But, Mrs. Briggs,' cried Jane, ' I couldn't possibly take these. I could never go to the Hospital Ball. . . .'

Mrs. Briggs firmly repulsed the tickets.

' Never mind. Take 'em to please me. I'll be rid of them, anyway. Good-bye, love. Run along in.'

She went off smiling and nodding, and Jane went into the shop like one in a dream.

' You've been a long time outside, Miss Carter,' complained Mr. Chadwick. ' What did Mrs. Briggs want ? What's that you've got ? '

He clambered down from his stool and came towards her, pen in hand.

' What's that you've got, Miss Carter ? ' he repeated, peering.

' Tickets for the Hospital Ball,' said Jane, still staring at the pasteboards in her hand.

' What ? ' cried Mr. Chadwick, seizing them.

' Tickets for the Hospital Ball,' he repeated, as

if he could not believe either his ears or his eyes. He turned the tickets round and looked at their backs. That seemed in some mysterious way to convince him.

'Good gracious me!' he exclaimed.

'Did Mrs. Briggs give them you?' he asked.

'Good gracious me!' he said again. It was the first time he had held such tickets in his hand. Why, they were the entry to the very best that Tidsley had to offer! And only two days ago Fenwick had said he was going.

'Are you going to use them?' he asked Jane.

'How could I?'

They stood in silence, with the tickets between them.

'It's a pity to have those tickets and not use them. It is a pity,' Mr. Chadwick mused, rasping his chin with his forefinger. 'And three of them, too.'

'It'll be a very grand do,' he went on. 'All the best people for miles round and Hanner's catering, and a band from some London hotel. Miss Carter!' he burst out. 'What do you say if we go?'

'Go!' Jane had never been so astounded in her life. She thought he had gone out of his mind.

'Mmmm,' said Mr. Chadwick. A sheepish smile came over his face, making him look for a moment like a little old-fashioned boy.

'How could we go?' asked Jane.

'Me and Mrs. Chadwick could take you.'

'Goodness!' ejaculated Jane, looking again at the tickets. They already looked different; as if they meant something now.

'If Fenwick goes,' said Mr. Chadwick, warming to it, 'why shouldn't I? I'm as good as he is, I hope. This business was established ten years before he came to Tidsley with his rabbit-skins. If he can go to the Hospital Ball, I can, and that's flat.'

' But I've no frock,' said Jane.

' Make one, then,' said Mr. Chadwick, reflecting cheerfully that he himself had the necessary dress-suit. He used, years ago, to sing at the St. Cæcilia. ' You've made many a frock before, and I dare say I can find a bit of crêpe-de-Chine I can let you have cheap.'

' Goodness,' thought Jane. ' He does want to go if he'll let me have something cheap.'

But her eyes widened with excitement.

' Oh—dare we go ? D'you think we really dare, Mr. Chadwick ? ' she cried, clasping the tickets.

' There's no dare about it,' said Mr. Chadwick with sudden hauteur. ' I'm as good as Fenwick any day, and you'll be all right with me.'

A customer entered, and Jane had to come down from her dizzy heights to get out the flannelette.

CHAPTER EIGHT

ALL over the town, lights shone from upper windows. Tidsley society was dressing for the Hospital Ball.

Sylvia Greenwood had rested all afternoon in her pink and white bedroom. At half-past six Mr. Harris, the hairdresser, came to wave her hair, and when that was done, she began a leisurely and elaborate toilet with two maids in attendance and her mother rustling in and out.

The daughter of the Greenwoods was in a capricious mood. She changed her mind a dozen times on every matter. Should she wear the Russian headband or not? Or pearls? Or simply a fillet of turquoise ribbon in her hair? The tired maids changed their weight from one hip to the other and stifled their sighs.

'What do you think, Mason? Like this? Or—wait a minute—like that? Collins, what do you say?'

Their advice, thus solicited, was then rejected.

'Oh, don't be silly, Collins. The headband is much the nicest, really. You are absurd. Go and fetch your mistress.'

At last she was ready. The maids withdrew, and she stood alone in the warm scented room, staring at her reflection in the four mirrors. She smiled with delight at her own beauty. Surely she was beautiful enough to get her programme booked up completely.

Nothing humiliated Sylvia more than an unbooked dance, a gap on her programme. When such a thing occurred, her mother had to get the Town Clerk or somebody like that to fill it, and then Sylvia could pretend that it was a duty dance ; that she had to dance with such people occasionally because she was her father's daughter.

Across the gardens, stiff in the winter night, Noel Yarde was tying and re-tying white ties. He also gazed at himself in the glass, but he did not smile. He wondered rather heavily why the devil he went to these affairs. At twenty-five they were beginning to pall on him. Noel Yarde suffered a little from too much ease. His father had been the senior partner of an old-established firm of lawyers. At his death Noel Yarde stepped into his place ; but the law did not interest him much, and old Ramsworth, the remaining partner, and Varley, the chief clerk, did most of the work.

Once a week Noel Yarde came to life. On Saturday afternoons he played Rugby in a field exposed to all the winds of heaven. There he shoved and butted and collared, and was shoved and butted and collared in return. And when the wind whipped his wet shorts and he was totally unrecognizable from blood and mud, and when he bit into his acid quarter of lemon at half-time—ah, then he lived ! And afterwards in his hot bath, and at dinner with the rest at the George, and in his stall in the front row at the Empire—he still lived. But Sunday morning found him back among soft chairs and quiet gardens and gentle women, and Monday morning back again at the office.

' I wish there was some blood in the job,' he said, throwing down a distorted tie. ' The very place smells of mummies. But what in hell can I do ? I've got

G

to stick it for Mother and Mary ; even if I do no more than draw the cash. Mary ! ' he shouted with sudden despair. ' Mary ! I can't tie my tie ! '

His sister, all ready in pink, came at his call.

' Helpless creature,' she said, secretly delighted. ' Hold up your chin.'

He held up his chin and looked gloomily at her over his cheekbones.

' Now what's the matter ? ' she asked with pretended sternness. ' Why are you depressed, you spoilt thing ? You're taking your mother and sister to the best dance of the year ; you'll get a good supper, and you've got that pretty Sylvia Greenwood to dance with ; you look very grand yourself. What more do you want ? '

' I don't know,' he groaned. ' That's it.'

' You're young,' said his sister. ' That's what's the matter. It's most uncomfortable. I'm only just getting over it. But cheer up ! It will pass ! '

' Good God ! What a horrible idea ! ' He gazed at her in alarm.

' Come along. Nothing to worry about. Get your coat on. What about that elegant scarf I knitted for you ? Best silk. You never really thanked me enough for it. I do like to be thanked. Thank me every time you put it on, will you ? I say, it's half-past. Do hurry.'

Jane, in the bleak bedroom, was also dressing in a fever of haste and excitement. Mrs. Chadwick, seeing that the tickets were Jane's, had allowed her to take a hurried dip in the mottled bath. She drew on her first pair of silk stockings, and in a passion of delight kissed her own knees. She put on the dress she had made herself of palest water-green, and surveyed her thin young arms and modest oval of neck with some concern. She felt rather unclothed. She arranged her hair with care. Then with a sigh of pleasure at coming to it at last, she removed from its paper wrappings the crown and finish of her toilet—a little ostrich feather about two and a half inches long. This she affixed to a string of artificial pearls and bound it round her brow. She gazed into the spotted mirror.

That feather, she thought, just made all the difference. It took the home-made look from her dress. It struck a festive note, and was yet discreet. A very good little idea, that feather! Her spirits soared to dizzy heights. She snatched up her coat, the white shawl she had been wrapped in as a baby, the calico bag to bear her slippers across the market-place, and, after one more excited glance into the mirror, she went downstairs to be looked at. Maggie and Lily, who had come specially from York Street, waited in the kitchen, and Wilfrid was posted in the back-yard to look through the window.

Jane stood under the light and smiled self-consciously.

'Eh, well . . .' said Lily gravely. 'You do look lovely. A proper lady.'

'I only hope,' said Maggie, 'as you get somebody to dance with you. It would be a pity to have laid all that out unless.'

Wilfrid, his hands gripping the rough stone of the window-sill, moved his head restlessly to peer through the interstices of the Nottingham lace curtain.

'Oh, Jane . . . Jane . . .' he breathed.

She was always escaping him. Going out to tea, going to Manchester, and now going to a ball, where someone would be sure to fall in love with her. Men would put their arms round her to-night. Put their arms round her ! While he, in his wildest dreams, never got beyond cooling his eyelids in the palms of her hands !

His breath obscured the cold pane. He rubbed the haze away with his sleeve, but when he saw again, she was gone.

Mr. Chadwick had called to say they were ready. Jane went out to find Mrs. Chadwick's head draped in a woollen fascinator, with blue and white bobs round her face. Under Mr. Chadwick's greatcoat she could see genuine dress trousers concertinaed over patent-leather pumps with bows on. They were all doing the thing properly. It was splendid. With her heart beating high from excitement, she followed them across the market-place, threading her way through the skeleton stalls set up in readiness for the next day's market.

The Town Hall doors were thrown wide, letting out a flood of light. The steps were carpeted in red felt. Mr. and Mrs. Chadwick and Jane ascended. Jane suddenly wanted to laugh. It was like the pantomime. She half expected Mr. Chadwick to slither backwards from top to bottom of the steps like the funny man.

In the entrance hall the trio broke up. Mr. Chadwick went off, his eyebrows raised nonchalantly, to the gentlemen's cloak-room on the left, and Mrs. Chadwick and Jane to the right. There was no one in the ladies' cloak-room, except two aproned attendants. Mrs. Chadwick took off the fascinator, and, producing a hatpin surprisingly from somewhere, lightly ran it into her coiffure here and there, lifting it. Jane put on the satin slippers and adjusted the feather with great nicety. She and Mrs. Chadwick congratulated each other on success of costume.

' Shall we join Mr. Chadwick ? ' asked Mrs. Chadwick in refined accents.

' Certainly,' said Jane, also refined.

Mr. Chadwick, very small in the vast hall, was waiting. He bowed at their approach, and gallantly gave his arm to his wife. He made conversation in his best shop manner as they went up the stone staircase to the ball-room.

At the sight of the great shining empty room, a sudden nervousness assailed them all. They stood in the strong draught from the door, and tried to appear at ease. Jane's arms turned to gooseflesh and her teeth chattered lightly.

At last people began to arrive. Mr. Chadwick whispered their names to his wife and Jane out of the corner of his mouth.

' Mrs. Taylor, my love. She didn't get that trimming from *us*. I am surprised. I shouldn't have thought it of her. The Miss Robertsons . . . you remember the yellow brocade, Miss Carter ? '

The staircase was now thronged. Jane was beginning to forget her nervousness. The frocks were so interesting. And the men ! She had never seen men in evening dress before.

' Fenwick ! ' hissed Mr. Chadwick suddenly. ' Well . . . good heavens ! A diamond stud ! And I'll be bound it's real.'

He looked down with rage at the stud that punctured his own front ; it had been in the shirt when he bought it. He looked at every stud after that, and not one was like his. He beat his hands together under his coat-tails, and felt his evening was spoilt before it was begun.

Everybody was booking dances. Mr. Chadwick,

with a valiant effort, threw off the obsession of the
stud, and went in search of programmes. He wrote
himself down with a flourish for two waltzes on Jane's.

'We'll see how we go on,' he said.

The Greenwood party arrived. Jane gasped at the
sight of Sylvia radiant in white tulle.

'Is that Mr. Greenwood?' she asked in a whisper.

'Yes,' said Mr. Chadwick importantly. 'Clever-
looking gentleman, isn't he?'

Charles Greenwood, his hands twitching at the end
of his sleeves, was bowing rapidly to right and left.

'What a strange man,' thought Jane. 'Not at ease
at all.'

He made what he took for affable gestures, but there
was no sincerity in them, or in the smile that stretched
his lips.

'Bad nerves, I should think,' said Jane.

Mr. Briggs came up to his partner, and Jane looked
hopefully round for Mrs. Briggs. What a difference
it would make if she could see that homely little figure!
But there was no sign of her. She had successfully
avoided the ball.

Albert Briggs, a gardenia blooming near his loose
chin, was hearty. He chatted to his partner, looking
about him and hailing his friends. Greenwood bent
his head to listen, but Jane could see his eyes moving
rapidly under his eyebrows.

'Strange man!' she thought again, and felt a thrill
of interest.

People were strange; all of them. All these here
with secret lives of their own. She felt as if she had
stepped suddenly into the tide of life. And just at that
moment the band struck up and filled her with the
most pleasurable excitement she had ever known.

The clotted groups broke, dissolved into pairs and drifted away from Jane. She found herself alone. She looked round in bewilderment. Even Mr. and Mrs. Chadwick had joined the dance. She hastily took refuge among the chairs and sat with her hands folded on her knee, the ostrich feather very erect on her young brow. Her eyes ran delightedly over the coloured throng. It presented the gayest, most splendid spectacle she had ever beheld.

There was Sylvia Greenwood dancing with Noel Yarde. Jane admired them wholeheartedly. Mrs. Greenwood, one heavy hand on the shoulder of Mr. Briggs, pushed her feet before her with slow dignity. Mr. and Mrs. Chadwick revolved in the middle of the room. Mrs. Chadwick's high coiffure had slipped a little backwards, giving her a strangely Oriental air ; her skirts swept the floor in oval swirls. Mr. Chadwick was intensely earnest, even grim, about the face and surprisingly skittish about the legs. Jane longed for Maggie to be there to see their employer in this guise.

She noticed suddenly that she was alone on her side of the room, with a long stretch of empty chairs to the right and a long stretch to the left. She was dreadfully alone ; cut off. Her cheeks burned. She had a sudden sense of nightmare ; the blare of the band, the revolving figures, a thousand staring eyes.

And then it was over. The music ceased, the figures drifted from the floor, Mr. and Mrs. Chadwick gave her the comfort of their presence. Jane relaxed.

They sat through two dances, looking on with interest. Then Mr. Chadwick said :

' Ours, I think.'

Mr. Chadwick had, in his day, been accounted a good dancer. He strove now to live up to that reputation. He spun Jane up until she felt like a humming-top of which nothing is seen but the vibration ; and then he unspun her with equal speed and equally disastrous sensation. She knew the feather had fallen over her eyes, but dared not remove a hand from Mr. Chadwick to put it to rights. As it was, clinging with both hands, she feared that she would fly off across the floor, knocking the legs of the dancers from under them and bringing the whole Hospital Ball to chaos about her. It was a dreadful thought, and she clung the tighter to the little draper. Through a dizzy haze, she saw his pale, wet face.

' I wouldn't have thought,' she gasped to herself, ' that he had it in him.'

At last the band stopped, and she somehow got to her seat. The room gradually resumed the horizontal. She recovered her breath and adjusted the feather with careful hands.

' Mrs. Greenwood is coming towards us,' whispered Mr. Chadwick. ' How kind . . .'

Jane looked up and saw the approach of Mrs. Greenwood and her husband, with Sylvia and Noel Yarde behind. She fluttered a little in sympathy with Mr. Chadwick. But the party was brought to a dead halt by Mrs. Greenwood within two yards of them. Mrs. Greenwood raised her eyeglass and gazed through it. She held it aside as if she could better trust the testimony of her own eyes. Mr. Chadwick meanwhile had risen and seemed about to offer her a chair, as if he were still in the shop. He remembered in time, however, and merely stood humbly before her.

She stared at him, at Mrs. Chadwick, at Jane, in outraged astonishment. But when Mr. Chadwick began to mumble some appropriate remark, the sound of his voice put her into action. She closed her eyeglass with a snap, and swept on. Before she had gone many paces, she turned and surveyed them again. Their eyes followed her in round apprehension.

'How *did* those people get here?' she asked, with no modification of her usual voice, so that every one in the immediate neighbourhood, including 'those people' themselves, heard distinctly. 'How do trades-people get the tickets? I impressed on all ticket-sellers that they must be most careful, but in spite of all I can do, the tone—the TONE is lowered year by year.'

Some people were amused, some displeased, but Noel Yarde blushed with discomfort and wished Mrs. Greenwood violently in hell.

'Was that the girl out of the shop, Sylvia?' went on Mrs. Greenwood.

'It was—and did you see that funny little feather in her hair, Noel? I never saw such a funny little thing in my life.' She turned round to look at it again.

'I'm afraid not,' said Noel coldly. 'I was wonder-ing where I had seen her before. I think I rescued her hat once in a wind.'

'Did you?' Sylvia was surprised at that.

'Did you really?' she asked again.

'Yes. Will you excuse me? Vining is coming for you, I think.'

He left the party with relief.

Mrs. Greenwood was considerably upset by the sight

of the Chadwicks and Jane. As Queen Victoria, in
her time, had been determined not to countenance the
advance of democracy in England, so Mrs. Greenwood
was determined not to countenance the advance of the
working-classes in Tidsley. Mr. Fenwick, the furrier,
might buy a house near hers on Hill Rise, he might
go about Tidsley in a Daimler equal to her own, his
daughters might attend the same dancing classes as
Sylvia, she still refused to acknowledge the existence of
Mr. Fenwick or his wife or anything that was his.
She was nevertheless aware that she could not stop
Mr. Fenwick's advance on territory hitherto sacred to
her and her like. Mr. Chadwick, however, was of
softer stuff ; she would squash him. She cast a wither-
ing glance again in his direction. He saw it and
winced.

'Oh, Bertha,' he groaned, 'we ought never to have
come.'

They sat miserably together. Jane, under the shade
of the minute feather, knew it to be ridiculous, since
Sylvia Greenwood had laughed at it. She sat with
downcast eyes, and did not see Noel Yarde watching
her.

'She must have heard the old fool's remarks,'
he thought uneasily. 'And she must be having a
rotten time here. Damn it all, I'll ask her for a
dance.'

When Jane slipped away to the cloak-room to
remove, with violence, the little feather, he intercepted
her on the staircase on her return.

'Excuse me,' he began. 'I once rescued your hat.
That ought to constitute an introduction, I think.
Don't you ? '

Jane was completely taken aback by the encounter.

She blushed and the eyes she raised to his were startled.

'Does it?' she said in a husky voice. Then coughed, and pressed her fingers nervously to her lips.

'I think so.' Her embarrassment communicated itself to him. He wished he hadn't let himself in for this business.

'Have you a dance to spare?'

Jane bowed her head over the pink programme whereon Mr. Chadwick's hieroglyphics danced fantastically.

'Oh dear . . . oh dear . . . oh dear . . .' she clamoured in secret panic. She was terrified and charmed by the young man.

'Yes, I have,' she said at last.

Ought she to have said Thank you? Did you thank men when they danced with you? Or was it grovelling? What did you do? If only she knew what people did! Never had she been so conscious of her lack of social knowledge.

'Let's see what we can arrange, shall we?' He took the blank and shameful programme and compared it with his own.

A little later, Mr. and Mrs. Chadwick were amazed to see their young charge dance by in the arms of a cavalier.

'Well . . .' gasped Mr. Chadwick, half rising. 'She's got a partner. Oh, God bless my soul! It's Miss Sylvia's young man! It's Mr. Yarde! Now the fat *is* in the fire! There'll be trouble now all right. Mrs. Greenwood will be more offended than ever. And she'll have every reason. Whatever possessed the girl to go dancing with Miss Sylvia's young man? She ought to have more sense. She ought to know

her place better than that. I do wish we'd never come,
Bertha. I do wish we'd never come.'

Bertha tried to console him with reminders of Fenwick. But they only upset him the more, and made
Fenwick's power of carrying things off the more mysterious and indisputable. He rubbed the knees of his
dress trousers restlessly.

Trouble was brewing, he could see. Sylvia Greenwood turned her head continuously to keep Noel Yarde
and his partner in view. In passing her mother, she
made a sign to her, and Mrs. Greenwood raised her
glass and glared through it with unspeakable indignation. All of which Mr. Chadwick miserably observed.

The cause, meanwhile, of this agitation was far from
happy. She knew she was dancing badly, and she
knew she was being dull. She could think of nothing
to say. Nothing. She was acutely conscious of Noel
Yarde's hand on her back, of his breath on her cheek,
of his hand on hers. Dancing had a new and strange
significance ; it overwhelmed her. It was extraordinary that she should be in this intimate contact
with this young man. She could not get away from
that idea.

She was relieved, yet disappointed, when the dance
ended. He led her to a chair, and they sat side by
side in mutual embarrassment. He, too, was deficient
in small talk.

' Good band, isn't it ? ' he remarked at last.

' Oh, very,' agreed Jane.

Silence fell between them like something heavy that
one of them must soon pick up. Jane was determined
it should be her. But she felt again like one in a
nightmare ; a nightmare in which you labour to speak
and cannot. With a physical effort, she opened her

mouth. She did not know what she was going to say, but it would have been something at least—had not the band at that moment struck up and left her gaping.

Noel Yarde rose with relief, and was on the point of withdrawing when Dick Elliott caught him by the arm.

'Who've you picked up?' he whispered. 'Looks refreshing. Introduce me.'

'Nothing in your line, I'm sure. You'll not get any fun there.'

'How d'you know? You're no judge! Introduce me.'

There was nothing for it but to introduce him, and Jane, to her amazement, found herself with a second partner, and simultaneously in possession of her full senses.

Noel Yarde, looking over the fair fluff of his partner's hair, was surprised and a little chagrined at the change in her.

'She gets on better with Dick than she did with me,' he thought.

Elliott himself was delighted with his find. She danced well, she was lively, and a good many people were looking at them. He was glad about that. He liked to be noticeable. He liked to be taken for a dog ; to pick up a girl at a dance, and annoy the dowagers and the girls of his own set. And so he danced delightedly with Jane, backwards and forwards under Mrs. Greenwood's nose.

He had purposely left this dance unbooked, because, after it, the band retired for an interval. There was, therefore, more time to have some sport with a suitable girl.

During this interval the entire company walked out
into an adjoining room, where the elders walked about
or stood in groups, and the young people sat behind
screens and palms, when they could get to them in
time. Elliott made a dash for a screen with the
unsuspicious Jane in tow.

She sat on a cane couch, with a desiccated palm
overhead and crumpled red felt underfoot, and smiled
to think how interested Maggie would be when she
told her all this. She chattered to Elliott, and he con-
tributed a ' Quaite ' at intervals. It was the day of
' Quaite.'

She did not notice that his pale eyes were amorous,
and that he was edging nearer on the tremulous cane
couch.

' I say,' he broke out at last, ' what jolly eyelashes
you've got ! '

Jane, unversed in the reception of compliments, made
a little, but charming, snort down her nose. It was
done to deprecate, to stave off—but it had precisely
the opposite effect. Dick Elliott completed the distance between them in one bound, and Jane was horri-
fied to find his lips on hers.

' Ugh ! ' she called out, bending her face backwards
from his.

' Don't ! Get away. . . . Let me go ! Let me
go ! '

He held her tighter, laughing. He liked them to
put up a bit of a fight. He was too excited to notice
what a noise she was making.

But Jane did not fight like a lady ; she fought like
something wild.

She pushed him with her hands, she twisted round
in his arms, and, in doing that, flung out both feet.

With a hollow flap, the screen collapsed outwards. They were revealed to the entire hall.

For a fraction of time all motion was suspended. The hall presented the appearance of a wax-work show ; Elliott's arms round Jane, Jane with a tail of hair on her neck, the rest of the company, faces turned with one accord, staring with mouths agape and eyes wide.

The fraction of time passed, and they all came to life.

'Good God!' cried Elliott, righting his tie.

Jane sprang to her feet. She looked round wildly. They were all there : the Greenwoods, Noel Yarde, Mr. and Mrs. Chadwick—all the familiar Tidsley faces. They had all seen. She lowered her head and went through them to the cloak-room.

Once in that refuge, she covered her face with her hands and whispered over and over again :

'Oh dear . . . oh dear . . . oh dear . . .'

She heard footsteps and removed her hands to stare in apprehension. It was Mrs. Chadwick.

'Will you get ready, Miss Carter?' she said in a queer, squeezed voice. 'We are going.'

'It wasn't my fault,' faltered Jane, longing to speak of the thing.

'Wasn't it?' said Mrs. Chadwick, as if she didn't believe her. 'It was very . . .' her voice stuck in her throat and then burst out into ' disgraceful! '

There was evidently no sympathy to be had from Mrs. Chadwick.

Jane put on her coat, and when the dancing had begun again upstairs, she followed Mrs. Chadwick from the disastrous scene in silence. Mr. Chadwick did not look at Jane ; he addressed no word to her.

He behaved as if she was not there, and walked on in front with his wife, the blue and white pom-poms of whose fascinator bobbled bleakly under the moon. Poor Jane came on behind, carrying her slipper bag, in the bottom of which lay the broken ostrich feather.

CHAPTER NINE

I

THE next day was Saturday and wet. A grey
steam of rain hung over the town. The market, viewed from Chadwick's, was a depressing sight
with the rain running from the canvases on to the
hunched, protesting shoulders of the stall-holders, and
dun streams coming from all quarters underfoot to
unite and gurgle in the gutters.

In Chadwick's there was a bloom of damp on the
counters and a smell of flannel. Jane was pale and
chilly and felt a gnawing grievance against the inadequacy of the oil-stove. She had hardly slept at all,
and life seemed indeed weary, stale, flat and unprofit-
able. Even Maggie was unsympathetic and had
received the account of Jane's excursion into the polite
world with an annoying reiteration of ' Didn't I tell
you ? '

Mr. Chadwick sat at his desk. His eyes were puffy
and his mouth peevish. He had not addressed a word
to Jane since their exit from the Hospital Ball.

The morning dragged on. A wet Saturday was bad
for trade. Jane longed for a customer to come in and
break the depressing inactivity. About quarter-past
eleven a malign fairy granted her wish. The door
opened and Mrs. Greenwood came in, followed by her
daughter and a gust of rain.

Without a glance to right or left, that lady advanced on Mr. Chadwick, who slipped from his stool and stood bowing.

'What can I do for you, Mrs. Greenwood, Madam?' he asked falteringly.

'You can do nothing, Mr. Chadwick,' she began in an ominous voice, 'except give me a few moments of your attention.'

Mr. Chadwick gulped nervously. Sylvia sat down to look on with interest.

'I am, as you know,' resumed Mrs. Greenwood, 'the chairman of the Hospital Ball Committee, and I have come to complain, officially, of the disgraceful behaviour last night'—she turned suddenly and glared at Jane—'of this young woman.'

Jane blanched and looked wildly away. Mrs. Greenwood turned again to Mr. Chadwick.

'I was amazed,'—Mrs. Greenwood's voice was thick and soft with emotion,—'amazed by the scene in the hall. This girl with her frock half off her back and her hair coming down—and poor Mr. Elliott put into such a dreadful situation! I have no words for it, Mr. Chadwick. I was standing with Lord and Lady Pelmer at the time, they having come from Farne specially at my request, and I may tell you I was never so ashamed in my life. What must they think of us— of the committee—of the town? I ask you, Mr. Chadwick?'

But Mr. Chadwick could not answer. He had shrunk into his morning-coat and his hair was damp on his brow.

Jane, twisting string from the string-box in her fingers, began to speak in a rapid, husky voice.

'I am sorry—I'm very sorry, but it wasn't my fault.

Mr. Elliott had no right to think he could behave like that just because I am a shop-girl. . . .'

' Miss Carter,' Mrs. Greenwood raised one hand and closed her eyes, ' I do not wish to discuss the matter with *you*. You quite understand, I hope, Mr. Chadwick, that such a thing cannot be allowed to pass. The Hospital Ball is our most important charity function, and its dignity must be kept intact, and I may tell you, Mr. Chadwick,' said Mrs. Greenwood with meaning, ' I intend that it shall be kept free of the people who are likely to cause such disgraceful incidents.'

' Certainly, Mrs. Greenwood, Madam,' murmured Mr. Chadwick unhappily. She was getting at him ; he knew it.

' The mistake, Mr. Chadwick, was in taking the girl to the ball at all. It is not fair to the girl herself ; her behaviour cannot, naturally, stand such a test. Why, she danced with Mr. Yarde without an introduction of any possible kind ! '

' Mr. Yarde asked me to dance,' Jane burst out. ' He picked up my hat once. I knew him.'

' Miss Carter,' said Mrs. Greenwood sternly, ' I have already said that I do not wish to discuss the matter with you.'

' But it's not fair to expect me to stand here and not say a word for myself,' cried Jane indignantly. ' I'll explain if you'll let me. Mr. Elliott tried to kiss me and I wouldn't let him and I knocked the screen down by accident. I was just as ashamed as you or Mr. Chadwick or anybody. . . .'

' Mr. Chadwick ! ' Mrs. Greenwood gobbled like an infuriated turkey. ' This is too much. Things are coming to a pretty pass when I cannot enter a shop without being addressed against my will by the shop-girls. And in such a manner ! I am not used to being spoken to like this, and I may tell you that I shall not risk it again. I shall not come into a shop where such a thing is possible.'

'Oh, Mrs. Greenwood,' cried Mr. Chadwick beseechingly, 'it shall never happen again. I promise you that. Such a thing has never happened before in all the twenty years of this establishment. You are quite safe, Mrs. Greenwood, Madam dear. She disgraced me last night and she disgraces me again this morning before my most valued lady-customer. It is too much. She must go.'

'Ah,' said Mrs. Greenwood triumphantly, looking round at Jane, 'in that case there will be no need to withdraw my custom. And I confess I should have been sorry, Mr. Chadwick,'—she raised a hand and her voice almost coyly,—'very sorry, Mr. Chadwick. You have always served me very well and I like to encourage such an old-established and respectable shop as yours.'

Mr. Chadwick, a little restored, bowed.

'You are very kind, Madam,' he murmured.

The little comedy was roughly interrupted by Jane.

'It's most unjust,' she said in a shaking voice, ravelling the string and staring at them with a painful intensity.

At that Mr. Chadwick broke into activity. He ran round the counter, and made for her like a small and ineffectual bull.

'Go into the back !' he cried, pushing at her with his hands. 'Into the back, I say. . . . Go away ! Speaking like that ! Madam, don't listen ! Don't . . .'

Jane hurried before his hands into the kitchen. She was glad to get there. She felt such a tide of anger rising in her that in another moment she would have been carried away on it. She was filled with wild words. Mrs. Greenwood . . . puffed up with snobbery and money. . . . Nothing but a loud voice and an ugly old body . . . cruel, spiteful . . . and Mr. Chadwick . . . mean, petty, a coward and a snob . . . and a toady . . . ready to throw her as a sop to Mrs. Greenwood . . . turn her off as if it meant nothing ! She hated them . . . hated them. . . .

She trembled so violently with anger that she had to sit down on the wooden chair near the door.

Mrs. Greenwood's loud voice ceased. She must have left the shop. There was silence.

Jane became a little cooler.

' I've done for myself now,' she thought.

She drew up her heels to the rung of the chair, and, leaning her chin on her fists, considered the position.

She could not get another job as good in Tidsley ; if she would get one at all in the town. A row with a customer could not be satisfactorily explained ; the customer was always right. That was the shopkeeper's slogan. ' The customer is always right.'

What could she do ? Where could she go ? Where did you go when you had nowhere to go ? The dreary prospect clouded her eyes with tears. She flicked them away with her forefinger. No time to cry.

The kitchen clock ticked on. Lily stumped about overhead.

Jane got up from the chair at last. Her mind was made up on one point ; Mrs. Greenwood was not going to get the better of her so easily. She would not

let her living be taken from her without a fight.   She
walked into the shop to begin it.

When Mr. Chadwick beheld her resolute approach,
he began to scrabble among his pens in a frenzy.   He
felt he could not put up with any more ; not any more
of anything.   The morning had been terrible.   And
Bertha was out ; he hadn't been able to get the relief
he so badly needed by telling her about it.

' Mr. Chadwick,' Jane began.

' I'm busy,' he cried fretfully.   ' I'm very busy.   I
can't be interrupted any more.   And nothing you can
say will alter my decision.   Besides, you brought it
on yourself.   Don't blame me for what you did
yourself ! '

' Please listen to me for a few minutes,' begged Jane
earnestly.

' No, I can't.   I'm too busy.   I don't want to,
either.'   He bit his best pen in his flurry.

' Please don't be so unjust to me,' said Jane.   ' Remember it was you who wanted to go.'

' It may have been,' cried Mr. Chadwick, taking an
unnecessary look under the lid of his desk.   ' It may
have been.   But how did I know you were going to
behave like that ?   Wild horses wouldn't have dragged
me to the ball if I'd known.'

' But how did I know, either, that Mr. Elliott was
going to behave like that ? ' interrupted Jane eagerly.
' You couldn't expect me to stand it, could you ? '

' I don't know anything about that,' said Mr. Chadwick testily.   ' It's no affair of mine.   Besides, the ball
was bad enough, but this morning was worse.   I shall
never get over it.   Never.'

' But, Mr. Chadwick, how could you expect me to
stand by without speaking up for myself ?   In common

justice, how could you? Would you be talked over the head of as if you were some creature without sense or a tongue—someone not quite clean or something— someone too inferior to be noticed? Would you? No, you wouldn't. And if you did, you'd be a worm. No, I don't mean that! Yes, I do—but not like you think,' said Jane, in agitation. 'But do listen, Mr. Chadwick—do listen! What happened at the ball was no fault of mine, and what happened to-day was hardly any fault of mine, placed as I was. Mrs. Greenwood has no right to speak like that; she oughtn't to be in a position to speak like that. . . .'

'Now, Miss Carter,' said Mr. Chadwick, wriggling. 'No socialistic notions here, please. Will you please keep a civil tongue in your head about Mrs. Greenwood?'

'All right,' said Jane, 'I'll not say what I think of her. What's the good, after all? But I just want to ask you, Mr. Chadwick . . . will you seriously consider . . .' She looked at him with such earnest eyes that she held his gaze in spite of him. 'Am I more use to you than Mrs. Greenwood?'

'What?' gaped Mr. Chadwick.

She said it again.

'Aren't I more use to you than Mrs. Greenwood?'

'Whatever do you mean?'

'She spends about thirty pounds a year with you; a very small amount, compared with what the Boyds and Wilkinsons and Smiths and Porters and many other people spend.'

Mr. Chadwick gaped wider. How did the girl know all this? He had never let her see the books.

'I only keep my eyes open,' said Jane in answer to this unspoken question.

' I do think,' she went on, ' that I am worth more
to you than Mrs. Greenwood.'

Mr. Chadwick was, as he put it later to Bertha,
' flummoxed.' Such a thing had never presented
itself to his consideration.

' I have increased your sales, haven't I ? And I
have developed the trimmings and dress materials,
haven't I ? '

He wouldn't answer.

' A lot of customers ask my advice now,' pursued
Jane, ' because, you see, you can't advise them on
dresses. Of course a man can't. Can a man ? Not
advise on dresses altogether ? '

She paused inquiringly, bending her head to look
into his face. But he wouldn't answer.

A little dashed, Jane was silent for a moment, running her finger along the edge of the desk. She began
again :

' And what about the ready-made department ? If
you decide to start that, you would need me, wouldn't
you ? You couldn't go fitting on ladies' dresses,
could you ? Besides, I'm rather good at that sort of
thing,' said Jane, blowing a little blast on her own
trumpet. ' Aren't I now ? Choosing frocks and
knowing what people want. And if you don't hurry
up and get some of that trade, Fenwick's will. They're
showing tweed costumes now, and they'll be on to coat-
frocks in no time. It'll cut frightfully into your trade,
you know. People won't be buying materials for
Miss Bowen to make up ; they'll be buying the frocks
ready made up by Venner's and Metton's and all those
firms. Do you really think it would pay you to get
rid of me ? ' she ended breathlessly.

Mr. Chadwick still gaped at her. She was amazing.

To talk to him like this ! And the queer thing about
it was that she had worked it out all right. She *was*
useful to him. She had made a difference to his
business, and would go on making a difference. He
knew he had never had a girl like her, and would
probably never get one like her.

' How can I keep you on ? What about Mrs. Greenwood ? She'll take her custom away,' he wailed.

' Where to ? ' asked Jane practically.

Mr. Chadwick's face lost its piteous creases. Where
to, indeed ? His mind ran over the dearth of drapers
in Tidsley.

' But what can I say to her ? ' he asked her.

' You can say that I apologized to you and asked
you to apologize to her and that you've decided to
overlook it this time. Say I'm indispensable to the
new department, or something like that.'

Mr. Chadwick considered, nervously.

' Very well, Miss Carter,' he said, ' I'll overlook it
this time.'

She had won.

II

Christmas was drawing near. Battersby's, the poulterer's, burst into unparalleled display of pendent
turkeys' necks ; fringe upon fringe of turkeys' necks ;
with curtains of rabbits over the door, and rows and
rows of plucked ducks and geese laid out with yellow
fat over them for decoration.

Mr. Chadwick thought it very fine. His own ideas
for Christmas lay along the same lines. He liked to
hang up specially sumptuous eiderdowns and cram his
windows with embroidered covers of every conceivable
kind ; covers for beds, cushions, tables, chairs, side-

boards, brushes-and-combs, night-gowns. Everything
was covered in 1913 ; it was a discreet age. Jane
besought him to depart from his usual procedure.

He gave in to her, but not without irritation. He
felt he could not cope with her ideas. Youth and
enthusiasm can be fatiguing to those who have lost
both. Mr. Chadwick, however, had enough shrewd-
ness to know that, though her ideas made him tired,
they were nevertheless good ideas. So he left her
to it.

In one window she arranged folded and snowy
linens, tied with green ribbons, and bearing little cards
inscribed ' Gifts.' Mr. Chadwick did these himself,
writing elegantly with a paint-brush dipped in green
paint. They restored his temper.

The second window was given over entirely to bait-
ing Mrs. Greenwood. Since she had discovered, three
weeks ago, that Jane was to be kept on, Mrs. Greenwood had not entered the shop. Jane was very
anxious to lure her back, to pacify Mr. Chadwick, who
was peevish about the loss of such a customer.

So in the second window Jane laid a blue frock, the
advance-guard of the ready-made department. It was
just the sort of frock that Sylvia Greenwood liked.
Jane hoped she would insist on having it.

She did.

In the afternoon, when the shop was at its busiest,
Mrs. Greenwood came in. Jane demurely lowered
her eyes, so as to make the lady's entry as little em-
barrassing as possible. She had never thought she
would be so glad to hear Mrs. Greenwood's bellow
again.

' What is the price of that gown, Mr. Chadwick ? '
Mrs. Greenwood's eyebrows were up and her voice

haughty. Her manner implied : ' You are a trades-man, and I shall use you because it suits me to do so. But my displeasure is unabated.'

' Six and a half guineas, Madam.' Mr. Chadwick judged it wiser not to interpolate ' Mrs. Greenwood ' as he had been wont to do. ' Would Miss Sylvia care to try it on ? We have now a fitting-room upstairs.'

' Miss Greenwood will try it on at home. Send it on approval.'

Wonderfully avoiding a glance either to right or left, Mrs. Greenwood steered herself straight out of the shop.

' There ! ' cried Jane, running to Mr. Chadwick, her eyes shining. ' I thought we'd get her with that frock. I thought she'd come in for her daughter if she wouldn't for herself.'

Mr. Chadwick pinched in his lips and was silent. This girl had got everybody sized up. She was getting a bit too clever.

She had swept him off his feet about that ready-made department. Before he had half realized it, she had made him interview travellers, and order dozens of dresses. She had helped Lily to clean out the box-room, and herself had stained the floor. She had unearthed a square of carpet, and made him have a long piece of looking-glass framed to fasten on the wall. She had wanted a pier-glass, but he hadn't given in to her. He wasn't risking more than he could help. He wasn't at all sure how it would turn out. He felt nervous and irritable. Things were getting out of his control.

Still, it had been gratifying to say to Mrs. Green-wood : ' We have now a fitting-room upstairs.'

III

Jane woke reluctantly to the sound of church bells. She remembered it was Christmas Day, and tried to go to sleep again. This was Christmas ; you worked up, at ever-increasing pressure, to Christmas Eve, and then you went flat like a burst balloon. She had almost collapsed from fatigue when the shop finally closed at something after eleven the night before. She hoped Mr. Chadwick was pleased with his Christmas rush ; he jolly well ought to be.

As for her, she was worn out ; drained of life. And too hungry to sleep. She had been too tired to eat her supper. It would be in the scullery still. Cold tripe. How like Mrs. Chadwick to provide cold tripe at midnight !

She rolled to the edge of her bed, and looked with heavy eyes round the room. She looked at the bulk of Maggie's body under the thin, red cotton eiderdown, at Maggie's head in curlers, her clothes tumbled on a chair, on the brush fuzzed with Maggie's hair on the dressing-table. Distaste filled her.

Christmas Day ! This was the day on which you needed, more than any other, a family and a home. It wasn't pleasant, she reflected, to have to disregard Mrs. Chadwick's hint that she would prefer the girls to go elsewhere on Christmas Day. But she had to disregard it, because she had nowhere else to go. Even her stepmother had left Elton.

If her father had lived, how she would have cherished him ! She tried to remember her mother, but could only conjure up the picture of someone who stood her on a chair to button up her frock, and the faint echo of a pretty voice—a Scotch voice, she supposed. But it was all vague and long ago. Strange that they should both be gone, and she, a part of them, should go on.

It was awful to have no one belonging to you, and to belong to no one.

'Oh, well,' sighed Jane, rising from the protesting bed, 'it makes no odds.'

This queer phrase, picked up from somewhere, was her favourite answer to Fate. She flung it out, as needed, in defiance, or resignation, or bitterness.

When she reflected that Noel Yarde, after the incident at the Hospital Ball, would think she was a cheap sort of girl and that Elliott would encourage him to think so, she told herself that it made no odds.

She dressed. She looked through the blind at Christmas morning. Nothing met her eyes but the great market-place littered all over with rubbish from last night's market : straw, paper, bits of holly, bad oranges, vegetables, derelict boxes. At the far end, two old scavengers were beginning fitfully to clear it up. She dropped the blind and went downstairs.

While she was waiting for the kettle to boil, steps came up the yard.

'Here's Lily,' she thought, and got ready to call out 'Happy Christmas.'

But the steps ceased at the door and a knock followed. Jane found a young man there in broken boots, smiling sheepishly.

'Lily can't come,' he began. 'She's been took bad. The district nurse come in last night, and says she's to keep to 'er bed. She says Mrs. Chadwick 'll say she's done it a purpose, but she 'asn't, Miss. She'll try to be 'ere to-morrow, and she said I 'ad to give you this 'ere.'

Jane took a thumbed envelope. Inside were two celluloid cards, one bearing a livid rose, and the other two violets and a cross. One was inscribed : ' To Miss Pie with love from Lily ' ; and the other : ' To Miss Cater with love and respek from Lily.' Three crosses followed : ' X X X '

Jane was a little embarrassed by this differentiation between herself and Maggie.

' Are you Miss Carter like ? ' asked Bob, with diffidence. ' I thought you must be. She talks a lot about you, does Lily.'

' Does she ? '

Jane looked at Bob. He was not at all what she thought a drinking husband would be. He was a well-set-up young man, with an honest face.

' Well, I'll be getting back,' he said.

' Wait a minute ! I've got a present for Lily.' Jane turned to fetch it. ' But no,' she said, coming back to the door, ' I'll bring it round this afternoon, shall I ? Then I can see how she is. D'you think she'd like me to ? '

Bob hesitated. He was alarmed at the prospect of this young lady finding out what a poor way he'd brought them to. He blushed.

' Well . . . I don't know,' he stammered.

But Jane wanted to do something for Lily. She was touched by the naïve expression of affection on the celluloid card.

' She won't mind my coming. You tell her I'll just come for a few minutes this afternoon to see how she is.'

' All right,' said Bob, putting on his cap with a desperate air, and diving down the yard.

IV

The town was deserted ; the entire population was indoors digesting Christmas dinners. Only Wilfrid moved restlessly in Chadwick's alley, waiting for the girls.

In his pocket he had a bottle of scent for Maggie, and in his hands a parcel at which he gazed continuously.

Would she like it ? Would she notice that mark on the leather in one corner ? How he had worked at that mark with a silk handkerchief at nights in his bedroom ! It was mean of Eddleston's to sell him a book with a mark in the leather. He hurriedly undid the parcel to look again. Where was it ? It had miraculously gone. Thank Heaven ! But no, there it was ! Its faint shadow was on the blue leather, and on his spirit.

Atalanta in Calydon. Would she like it ? Perhaps he ought not to have written in it : ' J. C. from W. T.' ? But she couldn't object to that really. It was distant and decorous enough for anybody. He did the book up again in its paper.

Chadwick's back door opened and closed. He knotted the string hurriedly. Steps came down the yard and the door opened. She stood there. He gulped and stared.

' Hello, Wilfrid ! You are early,' cried Jane. ' Merry Christmas ! Maggie won't be long. We've had all the washing-up to do ; Lily's ill. I'm just going to see her.'

She was so busy arranging a fluffy scarf—a present from Mrs. Briggs—that she did not see Wilfrid's face.

' Aren't you coming ? ' he managed to say at last.

'No, not this afternoon,' said Jane with cruel uncon-
cern. 'Are you cold out here? I wish we dare ask
you in, but we daren't.'

'Do come,' he begged hoarsely.

'I can't,' said Jane, half regretfully. 'I said I'd
go. No one asked me to; but now I'll have to.'

She looked at him, and he made an attempt to
smile. He was badly hit. She had done it again.
Always saying she would come and then going off
somewhere else. Lily might be ill—but what about
him? He felt he was dying at times like this. He
swallowed with difficulty, his eyes on her face. He
held out the book.

'Will you have this?' he said. 'Please.'

Jane went red with pleasure.

'Oh, Wilfrid, what is it? A book? Oh, you are
good! What a lovely book! What a lovely name it
has!' She took his hand warmly in hers.

'You are good. I do wish I had a present for you.
But I didn't know . . .' She meant she didn't know
whether you gave presents to other people's young
men. She trailed off into embarrassment.

Wilfrid smiled more easily. Her pleasure in the
book warmed him a little.

'Can't you come this afternoon?' he tried again.

Jane shook her head.

'I can't, Wilfrid. I must go to see Lily. Perhaps
nobody's looking after her. And I must take her
present. I made her a little apron, because one of
the things Bob drank away was a fancy apron with
roses on. She's always talking about it. It meant
something special to her for some reason or other.
I've made her another. I must see how she likes it.'

She talked fast, smiling into his strained face. He

made her very uncomfortable to-day. She must leave him.

'Good-bye, Wilfrid. Maggie won't be long. Thank you so much for the lovely book. Thank you so much.'

She got herself round the alley corner very quickly. She did wish he wouldn't look at her like that. She wished he wasn't so pale about everything.

'Oh, dear me!' she said half-irritably, adjusting the fluffy scarf again.

The feel of it distracted her thoughts from Wilfrid. It was a lovely scarf, so warm. Good little Mrs. Briggs to give it to her! Good, darling Mrs. Briggs! She hoped she liked the collar she had made for her; a stock collar on a black ribbon. Just the thing for Mrs. Briggs.

She walked along Baker Street, up Meadow Alley, Burn Street and came into York Street. She counted up until she came to No. 11 and knocked on the door.

She was confronted by a dozen faces at different levels : men, women and children all looking out at her. A hot, stale smell rushed out before them as if glad to escape.

'Does Mrs. Blackledge live here?' she said.

They let her in and one of them showed her the way upstairs. They opened a door without ceremony and Jane went in to find Bob with a cloth in his hand, looking round the floor he had just washed.

'Eh, well . . .' he greeted her. 'It's 'ardly dry yet —but I dare say it won't be long.'

Lily was lying in a thin, sagging bed with red ribbon bows on a dingy night-dress and a strange cap of print on her head. She smiled shyly at Jane.

'Fancy you coming to see me!' she murmured.

I

'Eh, I 'ave been bad, 'aven't I, Bob?' Her voice strengthened with pride. 'Something awful I was last night with pains in me side—but it's going off a bit now. Bob's been doing up the room a bit for you. 'E's been at it all morning.'

'Well, I'll be going now,' said Bob awkwardly.

'Don't go tert pub to-day, being Christmas Day, Bob,' begged Lily.

He turned on her.

'I'm not going,' he said fiercely. This was a nice return for all his labour. 'Who said I was going? I never said so, did I?' He looked sideways at Jane with anxiety. 'Well, I'm not. So don't shout before you're 'it.'

'I'm sorry, Bob love.' Lily gazed at him tearfully. 'But you know . . .'

'Now then,' he shouted. 'I've told you I'm not going, 'aven't I? Told you I'm not going? Well, shut up, then.'

He felt that by pouring out a torrent of words he could stop her mouth. Giving him away like that! Although he felt he shouldn't be making such a noise.

'Good afternoon,' he said suddenly to Jane, and cast a black look at Lily.

They were left together in the bedroom.

'You must excuse 'im.' Lily looked beseechingly at Jane. ''E's a good lad—but 'e's got in with such a wild lot. But 'e's been very good to-day . . . scrubbed everything.'

She looked round the room and Jane's eyes followed hers. No wonder the back bedroom at Chadwick's seemed a bower of ease to Lily! This room was so ugly as to make her want to shut her eyes; walls scaling as if with some hideous eczema, broken panes

in the window, a tortuous tubing attached to the gas
to light a cooking-ring, pans, broken pots, huddled
clothes, rags dangling from a line, and the smell—the
smell that was all over the house.

Lily did not like the look of it, either. She turned
her head under the print cap to Jane.

' I 'ad a 'ouse to meself once,' she said. ' Just two
up and two down . . . but it was lovely.'

Jane remembered the apron.

' Oh, Miss . . .' cried Lily, struggling to sit up in
the bed. ' Eh, of all the bonny things . . . bonnier
than t'other one ! It is ! It's bonnier than the apron
I 'ad once . . . it's nicelier made. Eh, well . . .
aren't I going to be a swell ? '

Lily held the rose-bestrewn apron at arm's-length
and glowed at it.

' Eh, y'are good,' she said fervently. ' To bring it
yerself an' all. I was right glad when I 'eard you was
coming. They lent me their pillows off of their beds,
and Sally gave me this 'ere red ribbon to tie on me
night-dress—and I 'ad this 'ere cap. Wasn't it lucky ? '

Lily swallowed excitedly and hurried on :

' You know when you made yourself that boodywar
cap—like that one you'd seen in Manchester ? Well,
I went and copied it—only I 'ad it in print so's it 'ud
come in fer dustin'. This is it. 'Ow do I suit it ? '

She cocked her head at Jane, and Jane said, ' Very
well.'

Lily chattered on.

' Eh, we 'ave 'ad a lot of bad luck this Christmas,'
she said. ' You know, 'is uncle promised us a duck
for wer Christmas dinner. Yes, fancy ! A duck.
'E keeps them in 'is back-yard. Well, we was looking
forward to this 'ere duck. I've never 'ad duck, 'ave

you ? But would you believe, when Bob went down
yesterday to fetch it, duck were ill ! Yes, it were ill,
and we couldn't 'ave it. And 'e never said nothing
about us 'aving it when it were better neither. And
Christmas comes but once a year. Isn't it disap-
pointin' ? '

'Terribly,' agreed Jane.   'But perhaps you wouldn't
have been able to eat it, now. Being in bed.'

'Not eat it ! ' Lily turned wide eyes on her. 'I'd
'ave eat it if I'd died after it. I'm that 'ungry,' she
went on. 'I keep thinking I'll pull that glycerine
jujube off the window—only I know th' glass 'ull fall
intert street if I do ! '

'Oh dear,' cried Jane. 'Have this, if you don't
think it'll make you ill.'

She hurriedly took a slab of chocolate from her bag.
It was part of Maggie's Christmas present to her.

'Eh, no . . .' demurred Lily.

'You must . . .' Jane broke it into pieces, and
laid it by Lily's hand on the bed.

Lily took a piece shyly. She giggled and pulled the
bed-covers higher.

'Well,' she said, 'I am 'aving a Christmas day.'

Downstairs, Bob sat in the din, trying not to go to
the pub.

CHAPTER TEN

I

SPRING came back to Tidsley and the scent of flowers from the market was wafted in at Chadwick's open door. The ready-made department flourished there like a green bay-tree, and was to Jane a source of pride and interest. It was also a source of irritation, because Mr. Chadwick hampered it terribly by his timidity and caution. Lively skirmishes took place nowadays in the room behind the shop when Jane and the travellers combined forces to get Mr. Chadwick to buy. Sometimes he gave ground, but more often he stood stubborn and immovable. Jane and the travellers sighed over him when he went back to his desk.

'Pity you can't run this business yourself,' said Mr. Bates of Venner's.

Colour rushed into Jane's cheeks at the very idea.

'Wouldn't I love to!' she cried. 'But there's not the slightest chance of that.'

'Well,' remarked Mr. Bates as he folded and packed, 'I've never seen a young woman with a better idea.'

Jane threw that little sop to her ambition, but it did not satisfy long. She was full of plans these days; full of mighty plans to grasp the whole globe in her two arms. But when she came to put these aspirations to the test of practicality, they narrowed themselves

133

down to such small, commonplace things as learning
French from a first French book lent by Wilfrid, going
to Liverpool on a half-day trip to see what Liverpool
was like, going to a different church every Sunday
night : Church of England, Roman Catholic, Wes-
leyan, Baptist, Unitarian, Spiritualist. She was avid
of experience, restless and dissatisfied. It was the
Spring, she told herself.

She was not the only one to feel the effect of Spring.

Mrs. Greenwood still walked up the Road with Mr.
Briggs, but Sylvia, one Saturday morning in early
June, departed from her usual procedure of going
home tamely in the Daimler. She let herself be put
into the car as usual, but later, she astonished Schofield
by stopping the car and getting out at Thirlby Road.

'You need not wait, Schofield,' she said.

She hurried down Thirlby Road . . . skirted the
wall of St. Stephen's School, climbed Barker Brow and,
with a final excited glance around her, turned into a
little blind alley that smelt of ash-bins. A black-
coated figure, pacing the alley, darted towards her.

'You have come !' he cried. 'I was so afraid I
was not going to see you to-day, and oh, what an
empty day it would have been !'

He took her hand in his damp, trembling hand, and
side by side they leaned against the dirty wall.

From gazing at Sylvia in church, waylaying her at
bazaars and other parochial gatherings, calling at
Stanfield, the Reverend Edward Shanks, curate at St.
James's, had got to this.

'You did look lovely at Communion yesterday
morning,' said the Reverend Shanks.

'Did I ?' asked Sylvia.

She thought it was a beautiful thing to say. It did

not occur to her, nor to him, that it would have been more fitting if his thoughts had been on the Service.

Nothing like that occurred to the Reverend Edward Shanks. He used the pulpit to further his wooing ; growing impassioned in his exposition of Love, while Sylvia listened enthralled. He stood behind the brass eagle and put special emphasis on the word ' beloved ' whenever it occurred in the Lessons, and Sylvia thrilled to think he meant her, and nobody knew.

' I have brought that photograph I promised you,' said the curate, releasing her hand to fumble in his clerical waistcoat.

He brought out a postcard photograph signed ' Yours in sincerity, Edward C. Shanks,' in one corner.

' It's a very good one,' said Sylvia.

' Yes,' said the Reverend Edward, also gazing at it with enthusiasm. ' It is not quite like the one they're selling of me in Parker's and other stationers. You'll notice I'm looking directly *at* you in this one.'

' D'you know,' he confided, taking her hand again, ' Parker's tell me they sell dozens more of my photographs than they do of the vicar's. Isn't that strange ? '

' It is,' agreed Sylvia. It was the wrong reply, but she did not notice it.

' But you know the vicar isn't *really* popular, I'm afraid,' went on the Reverend Edward. ' He doesn't know how to get on with people. He may appeal to their heads, but he makes no appeal to their hearts. I always make for the *heart*. By the way, my Mothers' Union was a great success last night. You know, it was doing badly before I came ; attendance poor and all that. I promised myself I would pull the thing together, and I went round the parish looking all the mothers up, and, as I tell you, we had a very successful meeting last night. I spoke to them quite simply, but from the heart, you know. Some of them actually wept. Yes, I made them shed tears.'

He was proud of it, but Sylvia was restive. She was not very interested in this kind of conversation. Happily he changed it.

'How beautiful you are!' he cried. 'And what a disastrous effect you have on me! I hardly know what I do these days. Someone will be taking me for a madman. I know I look quite wild at times. My landlady, dear soul, is quite concerned about my appetite. And it is all your fault!'

'No,' protested Sylvia, hoping it was.

'Indeed, indeed it is,' he said, lifting her hand deliberately to his lips.

'You know, you inspire me!' he burst out.

'Oh, do I?' breathed Sylvia.

'You inspire me! You make me feel I shall do great things. I think I shall be a bishop some day.'

'Oh, do you?' Sylvia was enthusiastic. That really would be a good thing, because then her mother would not object to the marriage.

She was quite willing to marry the Reverend Edward. She was sure he adored her; and when she was adored, she was happy. She expanded as far as she was able and bloomed afresh in beauty.

They were a simple pair, blushing and smiling in the alley. Neither was critical enough to notice any lack in the other.

They kissed and kissed again in mutual delight, but when the clock from the almshouses struck one, Sylvia hurriedly disengaged herself from his arms.

'One o'clock!' she cried. 'Oh, I do hope Mother hasn't arrived home before me. I must fly.'

The curate agreed. He was afraid of Mrs. Green-wood and did not feel himself prepared, as yet, to encounter her displeasure.

'Good-bye,' said Sylvia.

'That hateful word!' he said. 'But since there is no other : Good-bye!'

'Beloved!' he cried, running after her down the alley. 'I shall look at you just as I go up to read the Lesson to-morrow. Be ready for me.'

'I will! I will!' promised Sylvia.

She arrived home just in time to witness, from her bedroom windows, the stately, yet cordial, leave her mother took of Mr. Briggs at the gates.

II

One night in June, Maggie did not feel well.

'I'm bad,' she said, 'I must be. I can't tackle that brawn. Isn't it a waste? I'd better go to bed. You go and change your books by yourself to-night. Give my love to Wilfrid.'

She went upstairs with a Daisy headache powder and a cup of hot water, and Jane went out into the June dusk in which the lighted lamps bloomed softly like flowers. She ran across the empty market-place, feeling very light in her thin shoes. She sang to herself.

She sped up Exchange Street, gloomed over by the Municipal Offices, and tip-tapped across the tiled hall of the Public Library. Through openings and avenues in the books, she saw Wilfrid standing at a high desk, reading. It was like looking into a picture. The strong light in the high ceiling burnished Wilfrid's black hair and threw his eyes into caverns in his head.

He looked up intuitively and saw Jane standing at the counter. His hands fell to grasp the sides of the desk and he remained staring. She gave a little beckon with her head, smiling. A slow flush crept over Wilfrid's high cheekbones. He wrenched at his tie and came to her. His trousers and his sleeves reminded her of thin drain-pipes. At twenty-four he was still gawky and wistful.

'Have you got *Fraternity* for me?' she asked.

He had.

'I shall be out in five minutes,' he said, stamping the book with great care. 'Can I walk round with you?'

'Yes, if you want to,' said Jane, and told him about Maggie's headache.

She read her book under the porch lamp until he came out, bareheaded as usual.

'What a lovely night!' he said, breathing it up. A thin shaving of silver shone delicate and fine in the soft, deep sky.

'I've never seen such a wisp of moon before,' said Jane.

'Must you go in straight away? Couldn't we take a turn in the Park?' asked Wilfrid, his heart beating wildly at his temerity.

Jane received the suggestion with calm pleasure. Wilfrid breathed more naturally; it had been wonderfully easy.

They went through the little swing gate in the Crescent. Outside in the road, the lamps shone and people walked up and down in twos and threes, with sudden bursts of laughter and shouting, but in the Park there was only the diffused light of the stars and the moon, and no one to be seen, and silence. They

climbed the path up the hill and sat down on a wooden
bench set in a space among the trees. They talked
a little at first, but by and by drifted into silence.
Jane took off her hat, and moved her head from side
to side with delight to feel the soft air on her forehead.
She sat anyhow on the seat, relaxed, her hands fallen.
The trees stood around and there was the cool sound
of running water behind her. She lost herself, a lovely
sense of peace filled her. She felt as if she were floating in a pool—out—out. She was only aware of
Wilfrid inasmuch as he was no bar to this peace.

But he was aware only of her. How lovely she was
—still and dreaming like this ! It seemed to him that
her hair was radiant like the moon, and the curve of
tilted mouth and the curve of her throat made him
tremble.

He lifted her hand in his. She turned her head
slowly and smiled. There seemed to be no significance in what he did. Her hand lay loosely, unaware
of the fierce sweetness it set up in his.

He bent his head nearer. She did not move. Her
eyes were on the spaces of the sky.

Lost now himself, he laid his cheek against hers.

' Oh, Jane . . .' he murmured, and turned his lips
inwards to hers.

The spell of the night broke harshly. Jane jumped
to her feet. Her hat rolled away over the path. She
stood in a panic. Poor Wilfrid sat as she had left him,
one arm over the back of the seat where her head had
been ; his face white under the moon. She saw the
appeal of his eyes and mouth, and a nervous irritation
beset her.

' Let's go home. We're late,' she said. She went
after her hat, and turned her back to him while she

put it on. She did not want to look at him again.
She was all jangled now.

'Whatever made me do that?' she asked herself
over and over. 'Do come, Wilfrid,' she urged aloud,
fiddling with her hat.

He was too shaken to protest. He followed her as
she hurried down the hill and ran down the steps, her
heels tapping lightly and quickly—as fast as his heart.

'Oh, Jane!' he tried to say as they were leaving
the Park.

'I'm going to be late,' she chattered. 'I shall be
locked out. Don't come any further, Wilfrid. I
must run. No, don't come any further. Good-bye.'

She ran off down the road. He stood watching her
recur under the arc lamps, coming out into the light,
running on into the shadow, coming out into the
light, running on into the shadow—until she was
altogether gone.

III

Jane was breathless when she arrived at Chadwick's
alley. She leaned against the back door in the dark
and tried to recover herself.

'What did I do it for?' she asked herself. 'Why
did I? Why did I? . . .'

'What made me kiss him? Why did I rush off?
I should have had it out straight away.'

Her behaviour was ridiculous and mean.

'I've been mean to Maggie. . . . The first time
I'm alone with him, I go and kiss him. . . .

'I didn't want to kiss him. I didn't like it,' she
said. But she couldn't accept the excuse for herself.

She wanted to rush upstairs and tell Maggie what
she had done; confess the thing and get rid of it.

But it wouldn't do. Maggie wouldn't understand. Nobody would understand, of course. She must keep quiet and trust Wilfrid to know how she felt about it. He would never kiss her again ; that would be easy, because she would see that he was not alone with her again.

Poor Wilfrid ! He was a friend, a good companion, but she never wanted to kiss him. She remembered suddenly and inconsequently that his coat smelled of hot-pot or something like that.

If she kept out of Wilfrid's way and said nothing to Maggie, everything would be as before. Wilfrid and Maggie must not be disturbed ; they must go on in their own ways. Because she felt that she herself had really nothing to do with them ; that they would pass out of her life and she, in some unforeseen way, would go on.

She went into the kitchen at length, and finally upstairs, hoping Maggie was asleep. She began to undress in the dark, but Maggie moved.

' Is that you ? ' she asked. ' You can put the light on. I'm not asleep.'

Jane came to lean over her, feeling despicable.

' How are you now ? '

' My head's a bit better—but it's not gone yet. What a time you've been ! '

' We went into the Park.' Jane was surprised that neither her voice nor her face gave her away in the least.

' Did you ? ' Maggie was quite undisturbed. ' Was it nice ? '

' Mmmm,' said Jane, oppressed.

She went to her drawer and, seizing a handkerchief, she damped it in the jug and poured on the entire

contents of her minute and precious bottle of eau-de-
Cologne. She put the bandage on Maggie's head.

'Ooooh . . .' breathed Maggie, with closed eyes.
'How lovely! But your odyclone! You shouldn't
have done that, Janey.'

Jane pressed the handkerchief closer and said
nothing.

CHAPTER ELEVEN

I

IT had been a dull day ; very hot and hardly a
customer to break the monotonous and minute
business of ticketing stock. Jane looked out now and
then at the languid straw in the market-place and
sighed to think of the little stream they had visited
at Bowley on Sunday. It would be running under
the alders still, singing to itself. There had been
a dripping moss in the wood ; the loveliest thing ;
green threaded with crystal. How cool to the hand
it would be now !

She must go there again ; but alone. Wilfrid had
ruined her enjoyment on Sunday by gazing at her
with such unhappy eyes. She had not wanted to
go with them ever again ; but Maggie, who found the
walks dull without her, had insisted. It was all very
uncomfortable.

She drew in her breath to sigh again, but never
sighed. With Mr. Chadwick and Maggie, she stared
in amazement. Mr. Fenwick had come into the
shop ! He had walked right in, bareheaded, a paper
in his hand. Such a thing had never happened before.

' It's war all right, Chadwick,' he said.

' War ? '

Jane and Maggie gaped. They had never heard
the word used with any significance before.

' War ? '

Mr. Chadwick got down from his desk and came to read the paper over the elbow of the man whom, above all others, he admired and envied.

' Does it really mean that . . .? ' he said, and after a slight pause added ' Fenwick ? '

' It does,' said Fenwick gravely. ' A terrible business . . . terrible ! '

He began to talk about it—more to himself than Mr. Chadwick. Mr. Chadwick listened. He wished he had read the papers more carefully of late. He was, unfortunately, more interested in the local than the international.

Even now, he could not help noticing with lively interest as he looked at the *Tidsley Post* over Fenwick's elbow that Mr. Greenwood, in his capacity of magistrate, had been very severe with a man who had stolen five pounds. Made quite a speech about the beauty of honesty, evidently. He and Bertha must read about that. He jerked his attention back to this war that Fenwick was so serious about.

' Ah, well,' sighed Fenwick, ' it'll be a long, bad business for us all.'

He walked out of the shop as abruptly as he had come. Mr. Chadwick gazed after him for a moment, and then hurried upstairs to tell Bertha about the amazing and flattering visit, and the war.

' I say,' cried Jane excitedly, ' I must get a paper and see what it's about. I'll just fly after that boy.'

' You'll cop it,' warned Maggie, but Jane was out of the door and across the market-place. She came back breathless and triumphant.

' Did he come in ? ' she asked.

Maggie shook her head.

' Let's see what this 'ere war is,' she said.

They bent over the paper, spread out on the counter. A figure darkened the doorway and they thrust the paper aside. But it was only Mrs. Briggs. She came in and sat down in a chair, wiping her face.

' Eh, isn't it 'ot ? I was just passing, love, and I saw you was alone, so I thought I'd just ask you what's this about a war ? Can you explain to me ? I can't quite make it out. I've just seen young Mr. Yarde and 'e's that excited. Says all the Terry Toryals 'ull go—and 'e's a Captain in them, you know. Eh, these lads ! What will their poor mothers do ? Well, Willy can't go, anyway, because '—she leant forward confidentially—' 'e's ruptured. Yes. And I always looked upon it as a trouble and now it's going to turn out to be a blessing.'

Mrs. Briggs looked gravely from under her eyebrows at the inscrutable workings of Providence.

' What does it say in t' paper ? ' she asked.

Jane began to read. As she was reading Mr. Chadwick came downstairs again. She looked up guiltily, but Mr. Chadwick, merely nodding to Mrs. Briggs, went, bareheaded, out of the shop door and across the corner to Fenwick's.

' Good gracious ! ' cried Maggie. ' Wonders 'ull never cease ! Fancy him going out without a hat ! '

' And to Fenwick's too ! ' said Jane. ' This war is fairly turning things upside-down.'

It was all tremendously exciting.

In the evening she stood with Maggie and Mr. Chadwick at the shop door looking at the unusual activity in the market-place.

K

A figure in uniform approached. Jane raised admiring eyes and met those of Noel Yarde. As she gazed at him, he lifted a hand and smartly saluted her. Her heart jumped ; that gesture brought home to her the fact that there was war and that he was now a soldier. She stood looking at him with a strange, sharpened consciousness. She called mutely, ' Stop ! Speak to me ! Speak to me ! '

But Noel Yarde, rather glad to be saluting anybody on this tremendous day, walked on unaware.

II

It was Mrs. Farnworth who inadvertently opened Mrs. Greenwood's eyes to what was going on between Sylvia and the curate of St. James's. Mrs. Farnworth took an innocent interest in everything and everybody ; the front curtains of her little house had a permanent bend in them from being held aside to peep out. As a bee goes from flower to flower gathering honey, so Mrs. Farnworth went, in her compact little coat and skirt of grey, with, summer and winter, a round straw hat on her head, from house to house gathering gossip.

She went, whenever she could, to Stanfield. Being far from wealthy herself, it was a delightful novelty to sit in the grand drawing-room and see Collins bring in the massive silver tea-service and hand round hot scones and delicate sandwiches and several kinds of cake.

Mrs. Farnworth took small bites out of her hot scone, partly because it was genteel so to do, and partly to make it last longer. Collins did not hand the scones quite as often as Mrs. Farnworth

could have wished ; she got on to the egg-and-
cress sandwiches too quickly, in Mrs. Farnworth's
opinion.

Mrs. Farnworth found herself the only visitor on
this particular day ; so she talked as much as she
could to entertain Mrs. Greenwood and repay her
for the delicious tea and the comfortable pink arm-
chair.

Mrs. Farnworth's principal subject of conversation
was the church, the vicar, the curate, the sewing class,
the bazaar and other parochial activities. But as the
church was also Mrs. Greenwood's church, Mrs.
Greenwood was interested, and the afternoon was
passing very pleasantly when Mrs. Farnworth made
her unfortunate remark.

' Yes,' she said, ' I think we are very lucky in our
curate. He is such a dear young man, isn't he ?
Such feeling about him. And isn't he popular in the
parish ? From what I can hear there are several
broken hearts about. But of course we all know,'
said Mrs. Farnworth, coyly biting at her scone, ' where
his own heart is bestowed.'

' Ah ! ' said Mrs. Greenwood, unconscious of the
blow about to fall. She sat upright, holding her cup
and saucer elegantly under her chin. ' And where
may that be ? '

Mrs. Farnworth, who was after all not very intelligent, leaned forward to take another scone, laughed
and said :

' Well, well . . . who should know better than you,
Mrs. Greenwood ? '

Mrs. Greenwood's eyes flew open.

' Better than I ? ' she said. ' What exactly do you
mean, Mrs. Farnworth ? '

Mrs. Farnworth put down her plate hurriedly on the small table at her side. She seized the embroidered napkin, which she always tried not to crease unduly, and pressed it to her lips. Over it she looked in alarm at her hostess.

'More scones, Collins,' said Mrs. Greenwood peremptorily, and Collins rushed into the kitchen to tell the chauffeur who was having his tea that it was all coming out.

'It's all coming out about Sylvia and the parson-chap,' she whooped excitedly. ' 'Ere, cook, give me some more of them scones quick. I don't want to miss anything.'

But she was disappointed. Mrs. Greenwood dismissed her with a wave of the hand, and when the door was closed, turned again to Mrs. Farnworth.

'Come, Mrs. Farnworth,' she urged, tapping her hand on the arm of her chair in her impatience at being trifled with, 'I shall be obliged if you will tell me all you know.'

'But I don't know anything,' protested Mrs. Farnworth. 'Do you mind if I move out of the sun? I feel rather warm.'

'Come over here,' said Mrs. Greenwood, 'and let us get to the bottom of this matter, please.'

'I should never have mentioned it if I had thought you didn't know about it,' said Mrs. Farnworth unhappily.

'That, Mrs. Farnworth, would not have been the action of a friend.'

Mrs. Farnworth was silent. It was better not to say anything. She had said too much already.

'Tell me what you have heard,' continued Mrs.

Greenwood, ' about Sylvia and this—this *presumptuous* young man.'

Mrs. Farnworth received another shock. She was a simple soul, and it had not occurred to her that there was presumption in the Rev. Shanks falling in love with Sylvia Greenwood. She thought being in the Church made him the social equal of what she vaguely termed ' anybody.'

' I don't know anything really, Mrs. Greenwood,' she protested feebly, ' except that he admires your daughter.'

' What opportunity has he for admiring my daughter ? ' pursued Mrs. Greenwood inexorably.

' I don't know . . . but . . . well . . . I mean . . .'

There was no escape. Mrs. Greenwood got it all out of her.

Mrs. Farnworth went away with trembling legs. Mrs. Greenwood should have been a barrister, she thought, cross-examining her like that. It had been a most unfortunate visit in every way. She had made the remark at the scone stage, and in consequence never got on to the sandwiches at all.

Collins, having removed the tea-things, reported in the kitchen that the old woman was all of a twitch.

' Thumbs an' all, scrattin' at the arms of the chair. Eh, she does look mad ! Somebody's going to cop it all right.'

But it was not Sylvia.

Mrs. Greenwood was beside herself with rage at the presumption of the curate. She was galled, and deeply surprised at the gossip that was evidently going on in the parish. She had always felt above gossip ; had always been sure that whomever they gossiped about, they would never gossip about *her*. But they had gossiped about her, it appeared. However, she would deal with it ; she would cause the gossip to disappear as mist before the sun. She would deal with the curate. But how was she going to deal with Sylvia ?

She had made a mistake with Sylvia, she reflected. She was no longer a child. She was, in fact, a very beautiful young woman. Unless she was provided with men of her own set, she would naturally find others—eminently unsuitable.

No, Sylvia was not very much to blame. Except that she should never have demeaned herself to wander about back streets.

That was what Mrs. Greenwood pointed out to a startled and tearful Sylvia, when she came in from a long and satisfactory meeting—her last as it proved—with the Rev. Edward.

The Rev. Edward fared differently. At an early hour the next morning Mrs. Greenwood, driven by the interested Schofield, visited him at his lodgings in Bennington Street. As a result, the Rev. Edward Shanks appeared shortly afterwards in the uniform of a chaplain to His Majesty's Forces. It was his grand riposte to Mrs. Greenwood. He preached a farewell sermon on ' Man's Inhumanity to Man,' hoping it would be rightly interpreted as ' Mrs. Greenwood's Inhumanity to Me.'

He then went to the Front, and Sylvia had to forget him as best she could.

Mrs. Greenwood, however, never forgot him. She was determined to prevent such as him from happening again. Sylvia must be amused. Mrs. Greenwood supplied a choice of suitable men, all now officers.

She invited them to recuperate at her house. She gave dances and dinners to them. Sylvia remained lovely and unattached. Mrs. Greenwood was puzzled, but undaunted. She kept on.

CHAPTER TWELVE

I

IT was not long before the War ceased to be exciting in Tidsley.

For Jane and Maggie it gradually resolved itself into a struggle to get enough food from Mrs. Chadwick. The War called Mrs. Chadwick's full powers into play ; she lived vividly. She could now scheme and stint to her heart's content. She enjoyed the difficulties in the way of procuring food ; she enjoyed setting off early in the morning with a hard little basket for a shop 'up Benham' a mile away where there were, she heard, some currants to be had. She spent exciting moments stealing down to her own scullery, when the girls were out of the way, to take parings from their margarine allowances with a razor blade. She would pop the stolen pieces into the pot where her husband's supper was cooking, and watch it melt and add to the general goodness, with a greater satisfaction than she had known when she could put ounces of best butter in and never miss them.

She kept herself and Mr. Chadwick plump and comfortable all through the War. She did her bit.

Mr. Chadwick, too, was full of activity. The War and Jane had brought him prosperity.

Jane, hearing from Mrs. Briggs that Northgate, a great house on the fringe of the town, was to be turned into a V.A.D. hospital, suggested to Mr. Chadwick that he must tender for the supply of bed-linen, table-linen, towels and so on. Jane went to Manchester and returned with a specimen V.A.D. uniform, dressed a wax model in it, and announced that such uniforms were supplied within. Jane got to know about the Y.M.C.A. hut to be opened near Northgate, and Jane again procured the blue overalls and veils for the voluntary helpers. Mr. Chadwick was busier than he had ever been in his life before ; money rolled in. Yet he paid Jane one pound a week, and Maggie thirteen and sixpence, and looked with complacency on his wife's schemes to deprive them of their food rations.

In spite of the increase of business, Mr. Chadwick refused rigidly to extend his premises. When a small shop two doors away fell vacant, Jane begged him to take it for the dress department. But although he was thrown into a nervous irritation by the dazzling prospects she held before him, he would not budge from his hold-tight policy.

' This war's going to last a long time,' he would say. And then in direct contradiction : ' They'll soon not be needing any more uniforms, and then what shall I do with those premises on my hands ? '

' He'll never do anything,' said Jane with scorn. ' He'll never get anywhere. He can't see beyond his nose. He daren't risk so much as a pin.'

Life did not go well for Jane at this time. She was underfed, overworked and oppressed by the War.

Mr. Chadwick often remarked that he was ' doing well out of mourning.' It was hideous, Jane thought. He would have done even better, if she had not prevented him. She saw to it that the black trappings he provided for the heedless mothers, wives, sisters, were no more expensive and unnecessary than need be.

It fell to her to go to the afflicted homes, and fit the mourning clothes on the indifferent bodies. The saddest visit she made was to Dick Elliott's home, where his mother cried incessantly for her son so that Jane, in the hall, heard her. The maid, weeping, shook her head dumbly at Jane when she came down the stairs, and Jane put the box down and went away with that cry in her ears.

It was all so terrible. . . .

The only way, it seemed to her, to stop this killing was for more men, for every man to go out and kill. Every man ought to go. Wilfrid ought to go.

It irritated her intensely that Wilfrid should hang about gazing at her while other men fought.

'Why don't you join up?' she asked him at last.

Wilfrid flushed painfully.

'I don't think war is right,' he said. 'It's mad.'

'It doesn't matter what you think,' said Jane coldly. 'We're in it. We've got to get out of it. We never shall if every man gives way to his personal feelings. While you're here arguing about right and wrong, other men are dying in hundreds.'

It was easy to talk like that, and burn with righteous indignation like that in those days. Afterwards she wondered how she had dared to speak. She was terribly ashamed afterwards. But at the time she did not spare Wilfrid.

Maggie added her pin-pricks too.

'Eh, I do wish he'd join something,' she said. 'If it's only the Salvation Army. He would get into a

uniform then, at any rate. I never thought the day
'ud come when I'd be shamed by a navy-blue suit,
but it 'as. Conchy or no Conchy, 'e 'should think of
me.'

One morning, as Wilfrid stood motionless at his
high desk, his hands thrust deep in his hair, his eyes
on a catalogue, Birtwistle squeaking over the tiles in
his rubber soles, a decision formed in him. He was
afraid of it. He had a sinking sensation in his stomach,
and his heart beat in a sickening flutter.

Was Jane right? Was it contemptible to stand out
safe with your principles while other men died?
But if you never stood out for your principles . . .
Oh, God! All over again. All over again. He was
tired to death of his own arguments. Jane despised
him. She hated him. That kiss had meant nothing.
It had meant too much. It had shown her that she
did not love him. Once, she had liked him, but that
was all changed now. She despised him . . . because
he wouldn't join up . . . and perhaps she was
right. . . .

With a sudden dash, he crossed the room and
knocked on the librarian's door.

The librarian, a comfortable soul, looked up.

' Well, Thompson? '

' I want to join up, sir,' said Wilfrid, looking wild.

The librarian rose at once from his chair.

' Well now, that's fine,' he said, reaching for Wilfrid's hand, reluctantly submitted. ' That's splendid.
I'm proud of you, Thompson.'

He was also relieved. He had been asked about
Thompson by the Attestation Officer, and hadn't
known how to broach the subject to the boy. These
things were so awkward. It had worried him, and

now the problem had solved itself. Queer, he reflected, how often problems do solve themselves, if you just wait. It was his favourite philosophy.

He beamed on Wilfrid.

'This is a red-letter day for you, Thompson, and for me. Wait a minute ! I'll come down to the place with you myself. I'm proud to escort you ! I'm too old to join up myself, unfortunately, but I'm proud to have a clerk of mine answer the Call.'

Wilfrid smiled in a wry fashion, and the hearty librarian felt a little less hearty. It occurred to him that he would not be sorry to see the back of the gloomy chap for a bit. He would take care to get someone brighter in his place ; a nice girl, perhaps.

II

Jane and Wilfrid and Maggie walked on the high road above Enderby once more. Jane went first, her hat in one hand, a bunch of wild roses in the other. Maggie flounced along in a frock printed all over with large flowers ; she looked like something upholstered, and ate caramels without pause.

Wilfrid came last in a creased uniform the colour of stale mustard, with a little cockled basque at the waist. Gone was the old lift of the head, the old deep inhalation of the air and the peace. He knew it and blamed Jane. She—she had destroyed his secret fount of happiness ; she had pushed out his dreams and visions and given him nothing to replace them but an ache.

He raised his hot eyes and looked at her. How could she be so cool and remote—walking like that, when he was so wretched that he could have sunk down in the road and clutched at her skirts and wept ?

For one second he very nearly did it ; but he pulled himself together and kicked savagely at a stone.

' Clumsy ! ' remarked Maggie with ready and maddening cheerfulness.

Maggie ! The inevitability of Maggie infuriated him. She was always there. Why couldn't she get out and leave him alone with Jane ? If he once got Jane alone—he'd tell her what he thought of her ! She'd pushed him into this damned way of life ; this sleeping and eating and walking and sitting with innumerable men. He was maddened by it. He looked at her with smouldering resentment. She just walked on. A sense of futility overwhelmed him. What could he do ? If she wouldn't love him, she would not. That's all. He stumbled against a stone.

' Those Army boots,' remarked Maggie, plucking a caramel from its paper with her teeth, ' don't seem to fit. Eh, raspberry, this is—me favourite ! 'Ere— 'ave a sweet, old man. Buck you up ! '

She advanced on him, caramel extended. She tried to put it into his mouth.

' Get off ! ' cried Wilfrid, raising his hands.

Maggie mistook him. She loved a little horseplay.

' Now come on with you ! ' she cried delightedly, rubbing the sticky sweet over his lips. ' Better open your mouth—or else you'll be stuck up soon. . . .'

Wilfrid caught her wrists and threw her roughly aside.

' Did I say leave me alone or didn't I ? '

' Here ! ' cried the astonished Maggie. ' What's up ? Who're you knocking about ? You've hurt me.'

She went as red as her wrists and stood staring at

him from under her crooked hat. Jane stopped and
stared too. Wilfrid stood at the side of the road,
breathing quickly, staring back at Jane.

'What's up?' said Maggie again, looking from one
to the other.

'Oh, go away!' cried Wilfrid impatiently. 'I want
to speak to Jane.'

Jane went extremely pale.

'No, Wilfrid,' she murmured imploringly. 'There's
nothing to say. I've nothing to say. Don't.'

'Here—what's this?' insisted Maggie. 'What is
it? What does he want to speak to you for? What's
the matter with you, Jane Carter? What've you
been doing with him? What's been going on between
you behind my back?'

'Oh, don't, Maggie . . .' begged Jane. She could
see that Wilfrid was at the end of his tether. She
dropped the wild roses and began, without knowing
what she was doing, to put on her hat.

'Don't, indeed!' cried Maggie, planting her hands
firmly on her hips. 'But I'm going to, let me tell
you, Miss Carter! Come on, tell me—one of you!
There's been some nasty deceitful work going on
behind my back.'

'Be quiet, Maggie,' said Wilfrid hoarsely—'and go
away. I want to speak to Jane. I'm going to-night,
and I might never see her again.'

'No—and you might never see me again, neither,'
interrupted Maggie furiously. 'But I suppose that
doesn't matter now. She came butting in and took
you from me, didn't she? She's been meeting you
on the sly and sweethearting with you all this time—
and pretending to be my friend. . . .'

Maggie bit her lip and tears flooded her eyes.

'Oh, Maggie . . . I haven't.' Jane jumped to her side and took her hand, but Maggie shook her off.

'Don't touch me . . . sneak!' she burst out again. 'What've you been doing with him, then? There's something behind all this.'

Wilfrid had been startled out of his own nerve-storm by Maggie's sudden outburst.

'It's nothing, Maggie,' he said flatly. 'I wish there was. It's nothing Jane's done.'

Jane stood trembling on the grass. She didn't know what to say.

'If it's nothing she's done, what are you behaving like this for, then?' persisted Maggie. 'Go on—you'd better tell me. Let's have the truth for once.'

'I love her.'

Maggie's bosom rose on an audible heave.

'Oh, you do, do you? And what about me? What about me?' Her face was crimson and convulsed. Jane made another movement towards her, but Maggie turned on her like a fury.

'Don't you come near me! Haven't I told you? You've wormed yourself in and taken him from me, you nasty, sneaking thing! And I suppose you've been having me on all this time—the two of you—sneaking off together and kissing behind my back. Ah! Now I've caught you. . . .'

She advanced on Jane and stared into her face with accusing eyes.

'He says you've done nothing! But you've kissed him. I can see by your face. Own up, now. You've kissed him, haven't you?'

'Once,' said Jane gravely. 'And I was sorry straight away.'

Wilfrid laughed shortly.

' Once,' scoffed Maggie. ' D'you think I believe you ? I'll never believe another word you say, Jane Carter—because you act lies. And I thought you was a friend. You make me sick. It's all right, Wilfrid, I don't blame you—not much, anyway. You was all right before she came butting in. She's a great deal cleverer than me ; more in your line, I dare say. But she won't stick to you, you'll see. You're not good enough for her. She's on the climb, she is.'

Maggie sneered. Jane flushed red and her eyes, hitherto troubled, became fixed on Maggie in an angry stare.

' She's going to get on, she is,' went on Maggie. ' I've heard that till I'm sick. You're not good enough for *her*, Wilfrid ; so don't you waste no time thinking you are. She'll never have *you*.'

' Oh, be quiet, Maggie ! ' Wilfrid made a weary movement of his head. ' You don't know what you're talking about.'

' Oh, don't I ? ' Maggie's voice rose to a scream that sounded noisy, intrusive, ugly on the quiet moors. ' I tell you I do ! It's you that doesn't know what you're talking about, Wilfrid Thompson. You've behaved downright shabby to me, both of you, and y' ought to be shamed of yourselves . . . you ought . . . and me . . .' The words fell out of her mouth without meaning and lost themselves in incoherence. She covered her face with her hands and stood sobbing before them.

Jane was touched to the heart.

' Maggie, don't ! ' she said miserably. ' It's all been a frightful mistake. Wilfrid knows I didn't mean anything. Maggie ! '

'Oh, I've 'ad enough of you.' Maggie displayed a wet, distorted face to their view. 'And 'im too. You can keep 'im.'

She turned abruptly and fled over the rough road, the stones rolling under her feet, her ankles twisting.

They called after her.

'Maggie! Maggie!'

But she rushed on, hardly slackening speed along the whole stretch of road, and at last disappeared, a desperate, dishevelled figure, leaving the horizon as wide and empty as before.

Jane looked at Wilfrid then and found his eyes fixed on her with an expression she could not meet. She looked away quickly and twisted her fingers. She was torn between pity and nervous irritation. Why did he love her like this? She didn't want him to love her.

'Jane.'

She turned to him again.

'Don't worry. You can't help it.'

She thought he was referring to Maggie, but Maggie had disappeared from his mind as completely as she had from view.

'You can't help not loving me, and I shouldn't blame you for it. I don't, Jane.'

Jane looked at him with gratitude, but his eyes were unbearable. She evaded them again. It was terrible that such a love should rouse nothing at all in her.

'Jane,' he said again, after a pause that seemed endless, 'perhaps I shan't see you again, so will you let me kiss you?'

Jane swept round, startled.

'Oh,' Wilfrid smiled strangely, 'you don't need to kiss me this time. Just let me kiss you once—to remember.'

L

Trembling, Jane held up a pale face. He kissed her cheek.

' Good-bye,' he murmured against it.

She caught his hands.

' Oh, Wilfrid,' she burst out, ' I'm so sorry. I can't help it. Why do you love me ? I'm so sorry.'

' It's all right.' He held her hands very tightly, pressing them down. ' You must forget that I do.'

Jane struggled not to cry.

' But I feel . . . mean . . . to you.'

' No. It isn't mean at all. You can't help it.' Wilfrid had had as much as he could stand. If she wept or softened, it would be all up with him. He would drown her in his unwanted love, and she would loathe him. Far better leave her thinking kindly of him. He pushed her hands still further from him and said :

' Can you find your way to the car ? I'd rather walk on a bit if you don't mind.'

She nodded.

' Let me know how you go on,' she said hoarsely, without looking up, ' and . . . keep safe.'

Wilfrid gave a last hard pressure to her hands and let them go. His lips were stiff and would not speak. He turned and went down the road, and Jane, not trusting herself to look after him, went the way Maggie had gone, weeping too.

And so these three who had set off together returned each alone.

III

Jane, back at Chadwick's, filled with misgiving and anxiety, went straight upstairs to Maggie. She was lying, in her crumpled frock, on the bed with her broad back to Jane. For a moment, Jane thought she was asleep ; then she saw a movement of the hand still clutching a sodden handkerchief. She hesitated nervously at the dressing-table. Surely it would be all right, surely Maggie would understand that she had never meant to hurt her. She *must* see. Jane made a rush to Maggie's bed, bumping against the bed-post in her haste ; she threw herself down on the floor beside it.

'Maggie . . . listen to me . . .' she began imploringly.

She had spoken too soon ; this was not the moment.

Maggie, with a heave of her body, confronted her. Her face was pitifully swollen and tear-stained, but her voice was controlled and determined.

'Look here, Jane Carter,' she said, speaking slowly, 'for the last time—I've finished with you.'

'Maggie . . . don't be so silly . . .' begged Jane. 'Why can't you be just ? I don't want Wilfrid, I tell you. I never wanted him. . . .'

'What difference does that make ? You acted as if you wanted him. You kissed him.'

'Once . . .' pleaded Jane, 'and I didn't think what I was doing . . . it was just as if I might have kissed you, Maggie . . . because I was happy. . . .'

'Bah !' Maggie spat it out. 'Tell that to the Marines. I've told you I'll never believe another word you say, and what's more, I'll not work with you no more. Either you get out of here, or I do. I leave it to you. If you don't go, I shall.'

'Maggie !'

'That's my last word,' she said with deadly determination from the pillow.

Jane got up slowly from the bedside and walked

back to the dressing-table. The whole thing had
become extremely serious. She couldn't manage the
situation any longer. She aimlessly fingered the
things on the table ; she picked up the pot of cold
cream, unscrewed the lid, smelled it, screwed it up
again, replaced it and looked round for something else
to do. There was nothing. She looked again at
Maggie on the bed. She could do nothing with
Maggie ; neither comfort nor persuade her. She
went out of the bedroom and closed the door softly.
She went down to the kitchen ; it was strange to be
there at half-past three on a Sunday afternoon. The
fire, having cooked the dinner, was out ; a pile of
soft rusty ash disfigured the grate. The window was
open and the air from the back-yard moved the
dirty lace curtain to and fro. Jane sat down and
leaned her elbows on the red cotton tablecloth.
Things had moved so suddenly to this astonishing
climax.

'Either you get out of here, or I do.'

Maggie had said that—and she meant it. It was
stupid ; it was incredible. But she meant it.

Jane was completely floored.

CHAPTER THIRTEEN

I

JANE thought Maggie would not be able to keep it up. But she was wrong. She had to admit that she had been wrong about so much ; quite wrong in her estimate of Maggie, and wrong in her estimate of Maggie's feeling for Wilfrid. Maggie loved Wilfrid with the tenacity of a slow nature. It had never occurred to her to doubt that he loved her. He went about with her ; she took the rest for granted with her usual easiness.

Jane was amazed and bewildered by the implacable resentment Maggie showed. They ate and slept together as before, but Maggie's tight lips spoke no unnecessary word, and the expression of hatred never left her eyes under the untidy mop of hair she did not trouble now to curl at night.

Jane was wretched. She spent her nights devising ways to bring Maggie round ; but none of them had any success in the mornings.

And all for a kiss that meant nothing ! Nothing at all. As poor Wilfrid, gone to the Front, knew now.

' I should have told her that night,' Jane said to herself again, changing from one tired foot to the other at the counter.

' Yes, Madam, that lace washes well,' she said aloud, and sighed almost audibly.

And she would have to leave Chadwick's. It was unbelievable!

'To go round the top of the camisole?' She cast an experienced glance at the customer's bust and said, 'A yard and three-eighths.'

When the shop was empty again, she tried again.

'Maggie, I want to know definitely if you mean me to leave here.'

'I've told you,' said Maggie. 'Either you go, or I do.'

'Very well,' said Jane, 'but I must say I think you are taking a very big revenge.'

'I've told you,' said Maggie again, and moved off.

After this, in case Maggie should think she was trying to save her own skin, Jane tried no more. They went on together in silence.

When Mrs. Briggs came into the shop, Jane's pale face brightened. In her distress, she had almost forgotten that the world still held a friend.

'A packet of pins!' said Mrs. Briggs hastily. 'I only popped in to ask you to come to tea on Thursday. Th' Mester 'll be away for the day, so we'll be able to have a nice long chat. And I've just 'ad a present of a pound of butter. Lucky, isn't it? I'll see as you get plenty on your bread. Will you come, love?'

'Oh, of course.' Jane was fervent.

'Now I come to look at you, you do look washed out. What 'ave you been doing to yourself? You look fit to drop. What's the matter?'

'I'm all right,' whispered Jane. 'I'm not ill, I mean. I'll tell you on Thursday.'

'All right.' Mrs. Briggs smiled and nodded and went away.

Jane went about her business a little more briskly
after that ; but Maggie looked sour. She wanted Jane
to be friendless and alone.

On Thursday afternoon, in the garden, Jane told
Mrs. Briggs all about it. Mrs. Briggs sat bolt upright
in her camp-chair during the account, following every
word with the closest interest, throwing in an indignant
' Eh ' every now and then. Her feet were set sturdily
apart, and her stockings, like Hamlet's, were down-
gyved, because she could not bring herself to put her
trust in anything but the garters she knitted herself
out of white worsted, making them long enough to
wind round and round.

When Jane finished, Mrs. Briggs leaned back in her
chair to consider.

' Well, it beats me,' she said at last, looking at Jane
over the spectacles she wasn't wearing. ' Why you've
to leave a good place because you kissed a young man,
I can't see. If that girl's so set on not working with
you, let 'er leave 'erself, good gracious me ! Nay,
come, love, you're not showing much sense, are you ?
It's not like you. I've never known you to be insen-
sible before.'

Jane smiled wanly.

' You know you're wore out,' said Mrs. Briggs, lay-
ing a hand on Jane's knee. ' You're run down. Why,
your eyes look as if you could hardly raise them up.
You worry me to look at you. What you need is a
little rest. You'd look at things different then.'

Jane shook her head.

' Can't you take a little 'oliday ? ' inquired Mrs.
Briggs, her head on one side.

' I haven't been able to afford a holiday since I've
been at Chadwick's,' said Jane. ' This year Maggie

and I were going to her aunt's in the country for holiday week. But of course that's impossible now.'

Mrs. Briggs suddenly hitched forward her camp-
chair.

'Wait a minute,' she began hurriedly. 'I've got an
idea.'

Her face grew rosy with excitement. She pushed
back the mushroom hat Jane had chosen the better
to see Jane. 'Th' Mester's going to London this
week-end on business. You know 'e's all the going
away to do now. Mr. Greenwood won't leave that
office a minute. You've no idea. 'E's getting quite
queer about it. 'Owever, that's neither 'ere nor there.
Th' Mester's going to London this week-end. Now,
what d'you say to you and me going to Blackpool from
Saturday till Monday morning?

'Nay . . . wait a minute!' Mrs. Briggs put up a
hand to stop Jane from speaking. 'You've no idea
what pleasure it 'ud give me to take you to Blackpool
for the week-end. See, love . . .' pleaded Mrs.
Briggs, 'I'd like to go meself and I've no one to go
with me. Th' Mester never goes to Blackpool now
and Willy's busy with his wife and children. Besides,
I wouldn't enjoy meself with them if they went, and
that's the truth.' Mrs. Briggs wrinkled her nose in
self-depreciation. 'It's me own fault, mind you. I
'aven't been able to keep up with them, and their
ways seems strange to me now. They get on better
without me. I forget me 'h's in hotels and I keep
eating with me spoon instead of me fork, if you understand me, and that sort of thing. It upsets 'em. Eh,
I 'aven't 'ad a 'oliday since goodness knows when!'
cried Mrs. Briggs, her face lighting up like a child's.
'Let's go to Blackpool for the week-end, do!'

'Oh, Mrs. Briggs!' breathed Jane, 'if only we could! But how could I?'

'You can go to Mr. Chadwick,' said Mrs. Briggs, speaking deliberately and punctuating each phrase by a tap on Jane's knee, 'and you can say, Mr. Chadwick, you can say, I'm not very well, you can say, and I've worked years for you, you can say, without a *h*oliday.' Mrs. Briggs brought that aitch out very carefully because she felt that Jane would not miss it in this speech to Mr. Chadwick. 'Well, now I want Saturday afternoon off, you can say, and you don't need to pay me, because I'm going to Blackpool with Mrs. Briggs, and if you don't say yes not another stitch does Mrs. Albert Briggs buy in your shop and you can tell him that from me.' She backed away from Jane to see what she thought of it.

'Now then?' she inquired.

Jane's eyes shone.

'Oh, I wonder if I could get off! Oh, Mrs. Briggs, wouldn't it be lovely? I've only been once for the half-day, and the sea was splendid.'

'Yes,' said Mrs. Briggs complacently. 'They can say what they like about Blackpool, and call it common, and go to St. Anne's when they've made their money if they like, but Blackpool bucks you up when no other place will, let me tell. And speaking for meself, I can't abide St. Anne's. Nasty, flat, mild place,' said Mrs. Briggs scornfully.

'But there I am again, you see,' her face changed wistfully. 'That's another of their ways I 'aven't been able to keep up with. Genteel folks always likes St. Anne's. They never mentions Blackpool.'

'Whatever does it matter?' cried Jane. 'Why should they know any better than you what to like?'

'I don't know. But they reckon to. But what about our little 'oliday? It would do you all the good in the world. And you must promise not to give your notice to please that girl. You'll look at things very different when you've been to Blackpool.'

Jane shook her head.

'No. I'll have to leave Chadwick's. But I promise I'll not give my notice till we get back. That is, if we get there. Oh, Mrs. Briggs, d'you think we shall?'

II

She got there. She arrived with Mrs. Briggs and two small discarded bags of Albert Briggs's at Talbot Street Station at 1.30 on Saturday afternoon. They came out on to the Front and stood dazzled by the radiance of the sunlight and the glitter of the sea.

Jane drew in a long breath. Blackpool was all sea and sky—clear, wide and shining. Her sight, bound in Tidsley by the market-place, stretched like something long cramped and reached out with almost physical relief and delight to the far distances.

'Oh, Mrs. Briggs!' she murmured.

She would have liked to stay where she was and be filled with light and air.

But Mrs. Briggs was practical.

'Come along, love. Let's get the apartments first. Then we'll be free to do as we like.'

They turned to the south, and walked past the long line of boarding-houses whose windows showed tables set out ready with peaked napkins, but empty. Soon they would be full of visitors in white shoes, and the sea full of orange peel and paper bags; but the holiday weeks were not yet.

Mrs. Briggs scrutinized the face of every house with an expert eye.

'Blinds pulled up crooked there ; that won't do.'

'Bell out of order there.'

'Dirty curtains.'

'Something to hide there, covering up the windows with net like that.'

She came to a halt at last before a clean and discreet little house, pinched narrow by tall neighbours.

'We'll try here,' she said.

The landlady, narrow, with compressed elbows like her house, looked them over every bit as carefully as Mrs. Briggs looked her over. Reassured, but not amiable, she said she had a little sitting-room over the front door and two bedrooms at liberty. They went up, and Jane found herself and Albert Briggs's little bag in a small back bedroom which seemed a veritable bower of delight. It had furniture of the same yellow kind as that in the bedroom at Chadwick's, and almost the same wall-paper, but it was clean and filled with pure air. Jane sniffed it up and washed her hands and unpacked the little bag in happy excitement. She went back to the sitting-room over the front door ; it was filled with the same crisp air and brightness. Mrs. Briggs was already there, looking into the cupboard, where there was a bread-board, a glass dish for cake, a cruet and a sugar-basin.

'Clean and respectable,' she pronounced. 'But she's a grudging woman, isn't she? Never mind, we're not going to be 'ere long enough to bother about that. Now, love, shall we go and buy in? She suggested 'am and tongue for tea, but I said no. I could see,' whispered Mrs. Briggs, nodding her head, 'that she didn't want to bestir 'erself to cook anything, so

I said we'd probably 'ave fish.'   She puckered her face
at Jane like a child getting the better of an elder.

Even shopping was an adventure.   Even the bread
was different at Blackpool.   Jane kept feeling at the
shape of the cottage loaf through the paper ;   comfortable and homely it felt.   They bought a pot of honey,
because Jane had never had honey ;   and a plaice just
out of the sea.   For Sunday's tea they bought two pots
of shrimps, very special, and covered with butter, from
Miss Jenkin's.

'Expensive, I must say,' remarked Mrs. Briggs.
'But there's none like them and there's fourpence on
the pots.   We'll take them back on our way to the
station on Monday.'

They bought potatoes, mint and peas, and tarts and
cakes and buns, and butter and tea and eggs, until
their arms were full.

'What a lot of food !' said Jane happily.

'I brought a bit of lamb in me bag,' confided Mrs.
Briggs.   'I thought it 'ud be awkward with meat cards
here.   I 'ope that woman cooks it proper and doesn't
dry it to tinder.'

Jane smiled in secret.   Mrs. Briggs was adding
interest to her holiday by a little wholesome antagonism
to the landlady.

They filled the cupboard with good things, and Mrs.
Briggs having firmly requested the landlady to cook
the fish, they emerged again upon the promenade.

'Shall we go on to the pier ?   There's a band,' said
Mrs. Briggs.

On the pier, young men and girls walked round and
round making a hollow ringing with their heels on the
wooden boards.   They laughed backwards at each
other and made swift war-time acquaintance.

Jane peered down the spaces between the boards and saw the sea far below, deepening silently.

Mrs. Briggs suggested they should have stamp photographs taken, and then she suggested they should have vanilla ices. Jane sat in a little glass perch over the sea and scooped very small hollows out of her ice with a bone spoon.

' Ooooh, I am enjoying myself ! ' she burst out suddenly. Her cheeks and the end of her nose were already burned by the sun.

' That's right, love,' said Mrs. Briggs, beaming from under the mushroom hat.

At tea, a comfortable meal with Mrs. Briggs behind the teapot, Jane looked at the sea as she ate ; she could not bear to lose sight of it for a minute.

Next morning, after sound sleep—Chadwick's, Maggie and all forgotten—she got up very early and went out on the shore. In the radiance and the silence, she ran on the vast expanse of hard, smooth sand, beside herself with joy. Ah, when you only have a holiday once in a while, what a happiness it is ! Each golden minute had to be held and perfected before it was let go.

It was in the afternoon, just after dinner, when Mrs. Briggs had settled down for a nap in the horse-hair arm-chair, that the Great Idea formulated itself for the first time.

Mrs. Briggs had crossed her hands over her waist and arranged her face for sleep. Her thoughts were evidently still active, because her eyelids twitched incessantly, and her lips puckered over unspoken words. Jane smiled as she sat in the window. She found Mrs. Briggs endearing in all her ways. She turned to the window again and gazed at the sea. The breeze fluttered the curtains and a dog barked far away at the edge of the sea. She started at the sound of Mrs. Briggs's voice.

' 'Ave you ever thought, love,' said Mrs. Briggs, opening her eyes, ' of setting up for yourself ? '

Jane turned round, and looked at her in mild surprise.

' Why, yes,' she admitted, ' many a time. I hope I shall be able to some day.'

' I don't mean some day,' persisted Mrs. Briggs. ' I mean soon.'

' Oh no,' cried Jane. ' It's impossible. How could I ? I've been nearly six years at Chadwick's and I've only saved seven pounds. My mother left me fifty-two. I can't do much on fifty-nine pounds, can I ? Although it's a beginning. It'll grow in time, if only I can get a decent job.'

' How much do you need to set up shop ? ' inquired Mrs. Briggs.

' I worked it all out once,' said Jane, ' and I reckoned I'd just manage on a hundred and fifty pounds. You see, I could get extended credit from several houses. I should only have dresses and hats. No haberdashery for me ! It's a lot of trouble and there's no money in it. Besides, I don't like it. My taste lies in dresses and hats . . . ' she babbled on, not noticing Mrs. Briggs's anxiety to get a word in.

Mrs. Briggs broke in at last and to some purpose.

' How'd it be,' she said, ' if I lent you the £150 ? '

The animation died out of Jane's face ; she became very still, staring at Mrs. Briggs. She put up a hand, and with a long-forgotten gesture, took hold of a strand of hair and put it behind her ear, the better to see Mrs. Briggs.

'If you lent me a hundred and fifty pounds . . .'

'Yes, if I lent you a hundred and fifty pounds,' repeated Mrs. Briggs. 'How'd it be?'

'How'd it be?' echoed Jane.

The hair escaped with elasticity from behind her ear. She snatched it and put it back.

'Mrs. Briggs . . . do you mean it?'

She left the window and came to stand and stare at Mrs. Briggs at closer quarters.

''Course I mean it,' said Mrs. Briggs. 'It's just come over me.

'I've got more than that put by. You see, it's this way. Th' Mester gives me more money for the housekeeping than it takes. I make do very well on about 'alf what 'e gives me. But I don't give it 'im back. No . . .' said Mrs. Briggs with a wise shake of the head. 'He throws 'is money about something awful. We might be short some day. You never know. So I put it by. And 'e doesn't know anything about it. It's quite a nice bit now. And I could lend you a hundred and fifty pounds very comfortable because I know you'll get on and pay me back. You're right smart and you've got such ideas. I know you'll do well in a little shop of your own. And to tell the truth, I can't bear the idea of you leaving Tidsley to get another place,' she finished.

'Oh, Mrs. Briggs, you've taken my breath away,' said Jane shakily. 'It's unbelievable—this. Would you really lend me a hundred and fifty pounds? No . . . you're too good! It's unheard of . . . I can't grasp it.'

'Well, do . . .' said Mrs. Briggs delightedly. 'It'll not sting you! I tell you, I'll lend you a hundred and fifty pounds and welcome.'

' Good gracious ! ' Jane flung herself down at the table and cooled her scarlet cheeks in her hands.

' One thing bothers me,' resumed Mrs. Briggs. ' You're very young. Do you feel too young to tackle a shop ? '

' Too young ! ' cried Jane. ' Not I ! I feel I could tackle a shop all right. I should think I do ! But I feel I daren't take your hundred and fifty pounds.'

' Go on with you ! ' protested Mrs. Briggs. ' If I'm willing to take the risk, why shouldn't you be ? Besides, I feel sure and certain as you'd make a success of a shop.'

' I could ! I think I could ! I've thought about it so often. But I never thought of this. I thought it would be years before I could start. Oh, I say . . . Mrs. Briggs ! How queer all this is ! ' Her voice sank to something approaching awe. ' Because that little shop two doors from Chadwick's is still to let ; that man that's got it filled up with tinware only has it on a weekly lease, that I do know. It's the very place ! Just the front shop and a little room behind and a scullery ; the Joneses still want to keep the upstairs premises. Why, I could sleep behind the shop and be as safe as houses with the Joneses above. The rent's eighty pounds a year. I know all about it because I tried to persuade Mr. Chadwick to take it. It's the very place for a little dress shop. Oh, Mrs. Briggs ! '

She precipitated herself on the floor and clasped Mrs. Briggs's foulard waist in her arms.

' You're too good. I can't thank you. You've been so good to me all along . . . and now this . . .'

Tears were bright in her eyes. Mrs. Briggs blinked too.

'Well, love, I took a fancy to you from the beginning,' she said, 'and now you feel like one of me own. I don't know what to do with that bit of money I've saved, so why shouldn't I help you with it? There's nothing much in that as far as I can see.'

'Nothing much in it! You don't know what it means to me, then! Yes, you do! You're only pretending not to know how good you are! Oh, goodness . . .' said Jane, getting up restlessly. 'I can't believe it! To be on my own!'

She leaned her elbows on the mantelpiece and contemplated, with unseeing eyes, the black funereal clock.

'I've thought about it so often . . . what I'd have . . .' She walked to the window and gazed out. 'Small fittings of course, glass-fronted drawers all on one wall—behind the counter, with the blouses in . . . and one-colour window displays, you know. . . . Venner's are very good people. They know me now, and that traveller from Elwin's—he told me a lot. . . .'

She came back to stand in front of Mrs. Briggs, but she hardly saw Mrs. Briggs either. Her mind was leaping from this plan to that like a grasshopper.

'Bless me,' said Mrs. Briggs, peering forward at the clock, 'it's a quarter to four. Hadn't we better get a blow before we'se teas?'

They went out; but Jane hardly saw Blackpool now. She unfolded plan after plan to her friend, and before long Mrs. Briggs was almost as interested as Jane herself.

'We'll go to Yarde and Ramsworth, the solicitors, and have everything done proper for you,' said Mrs. Briggs. 'Mr. Ramsworth's a very nice old gentleman. I know 'e'll not tell Albert.'

'You know, it'll be half your business, Mrs. Briggs.

M

Yes, it *shall* be half your business. We'll arrange that
with Mr. Ramsworth. I'll make it pay for you, you'll
see ! It'll be hard work at first. But I'm not afraid
of work, am I ? I've worked hard enough for other
people, so I shan't mind working hard for us two,
shall I ? . . .

‘ Goodness, there'll be an awful lot to see to. You'll
help me, won't you ? You know you've got experience, and you're so sound, Mrs. Briggs darling. You
can help me an awful lot. . . .’

A warm feeling of importance came over Mrs.
Briggs. It was new to her. She had not felt important since Willy was a little boy and they lived in
Sarah Ellen Street. She expanded almost visibly, and
put her feet, in the flat slippers with bows on, with
conscious firmness on the promenade. This shop, she
dimly felt, was going to mean almost as much to her
as to Jane.

They made strange progress along the promenade
that Sunday afternoon. Jane, with pink cheeks and
eyes dark with excitement, talked rapidly and kept
bending down to look under Mrs. Briggs's hat. They
often came to a complete standstill to look at each
other. That was when some knotty point cropped up.
Sometimes they found themselves leaning over the
railings by the sea ; at other times they dangerously
crossed the tram-lines and got among the oyster-bars
and the stalls of Blackpool rock.

There was no sleep that night for Jane. With the
sound of the sea in her ears, she tossed and turned
and talked to herself in the alien bed. She longed
to get back to Tidsley to look at that little shop two
doors from Chadwick's. She was feverish with anxiety
in case anyone should have taken it during her absence

—because it was the very place ; just the very place !
It served Mr. Chadwick right ! It was just the very
place. . . .

They were still so vitally interested next morning
that they packed their little bags without regret. Jane
had projected herself into the future and almost
carried Mrs. Briggs with her. Almost ; but not quite.
Mrs. Briggs was still able to remember, after having
paid the bill and got as far as the end of the garden,
that they hadn't got the shrimp-pots to take back to
Miss Jenkin's.

She handed her bag to Jane and returned to the
front door. The sour-faced landlady met her on the
threshold.

'I've forgotten my shrimp-pots,' called Mrs. Briggs.
'There's fourpence on those pots.'

'Shrimp-pots !' ejaculated the landlady so loudly
that Jane heard her at the gate.

'Yes, shrimp-pots,' repeated Mrs. Briggs mildly.
'Whyever not? They're mine, aren't they?'

'Allow me to say, Madam,' said the landlady, hug-
ging her elbows and flashing glances from the middle
distance to Mrs. Briggs and back again, 'that I never
heard of anyone coming back for shrimp-pots before.'

'Well, you live and learn. I'll have my shrimp-
pots, if you please.'

Jane, wondering at the delay, came back up the
path.

'I refuse to give you your shrimp-pots on principle,
Madam,' said the landlady. 'I have never been asked
for such things before. All empties are the property
of the house. And may I say that I have had a colonel
and a captain staying with me, and families bringing
their nurses and their own car. I am used to the best

people, Mrs. Briggs, not such as you who come back to ask for two shrimp-pots. You're no lady, Mrs. Briggs.'

'Did I say I was?' inquired Mrs. Briggs angrily. 'And who are you to talk, I'd like to know. You're not even an honest woman. Give me my shrimp-pots.'

'I shall not give you your shrimp-pots, Mrs. Briggs,' said the landlady, 'for the precise reason that they have already been returned to Miss Jenkin's, and I defy you, Mrs. Briggs, to get the fourpence out of my skirt-pocket.'

Mrs. Briggs stood on the doorstep, completely routed.

'Well . . .' she said to Jane.

The landlady banged the door, and Mrs. Briggs allowed herself to be led away by Jane.

'Have you ever?' she said. 'Well . . .'

All the way to Tidsley the conversation was divided between the shop and the shrimp-pots.

CHAPTER FOURTEEN

I

MAGGIE bit her nails and gazed at Jane from a dark corner of the shop.

What was she up to? That question nagged at Maggie like a sore place. What was she up to? What had changed her? She had gone away pale and peaked enough to satisfy even Maggie. Maggie had been fiercely glad to see her brought so low.

'Yes, my lady,' she exulted, 'I've brought you down. You made me and Wilfrid suffer—and I've paid you out! A lot of dirty tricks you played me; pushing into the shop and taking first place. I let you do that; and then you went and took Wilfrid. . . .'

She took Wilfrid and kissed him and then didn't want him. Why couldn't Wilfrid see what she was? Oh, men! Men! You made yourself a door-mat under their feet, and then they treated you rotten and went with your friend. Friend? Bah, thought Maggie bitterly.

What did Wilfrid see in her? Nothing about her; thin and pale and all eyes. There was only that book-reading that Maggie could think of. When people got book-reading together it was, it seemed, dangerous. Well, Jane might be clever, but she'd brought her down!

That was over now. Maggie was filled with an

infuriated helplessness and a burning desire to know
what Jane was up to. Why did she keep going out
at dinner-times? And where did she go at nights?
A new job couldn't keep her running backwards and
forwards like this. A new job meant hunting round
with an anxious face. Besides, Maggie felt sure there
were no new jobs in Tidsley that could make Jane so
excited and keep her making notes on odd scraps of
paper.

Had she got a job with Venner's? Maggie had
found out that she'd had tea with the traveller on
Thursday at the Victoria Café. She would fancy herself going out with travellers!

'Wonder if she kissed *him*,' said Maggie sneeringly.

Jane's mysterious behaviour continued. Maggie was
tortured with curiosity and a dreadful premonition that
Jane was going to get the better of her, after all.

Jane was always out with Mrs. Briggs. She seemed
to have got friendly with the Joneses all of a sudden.
Whatever had she up her sleeve? Maggie felt her
head would burst if she didn't know.

Then one day she knew. She heard Jane give her
notice to Mr. Chadwick. She felt quite dizzy with
excitement.

'Now then!' she cried mutely. 'I've made you do
it! I've downed you! Made you leave, haven't I?'

She edged her way along the counter, drawing out
the length of towelling with her. She must hear what
Jane said.

'I'm going to set up for myself,' Jane said.

The towelling slid to the floor. Maggie leaned
heavily forward on the counter. What had she
said?

'I'm going to set up for myself.'

Mr. Chadwick dropped his pen and stared at Jane like a man suddenly bereft of his senses.

' Going to set up for yourself . . .' he repeated in a soft voice. ' Going to set up for yourself ? '

The meaning of the words reached him at last.

' Going to set up for yourself ? ' he repeated clearly. ' That's a nice trick, Miss Carter.'

Jane stood by the desk, nervous, embarrassed and wishing the interview over.

' A nice trick ! ' cried Mr. Chadwick, clasping his trembling hands. He had not many words at his disposal ; he used them over and over again.

' It's not meant to be a trick,' said Jane.

' It's a trick ! ' shouted Mr. Chadwick, banging the desk with sudden rage. ' A nasty, low-down trick ! '

' Same as she served me,' said Maggie aloud, but only Jane heard her.

' You come here and learn my business and poke round until you find everything out and then you go and set up for yourself.' Mr. Chadwick spat profusely in his rage. ' And then you say it's not a trick. I say it *is* a trick.'

' Has no one ever to set up for themselves ? ' attempted Jane. ' I can't stay on here for ever at twenty-five shillings a week.'

' What's the matter with twenty-five shillings a week ? It's as good a wage as you'll get anywhere in the town.'

' I know. That's why I must set up for myself.'

Mr. Chadwick dug at the desk with his best nib in pitiable agitation.

' And where are you going to set up for yourself, may I ask ? '

This was the question Jane was afraid of. She blushed.

'The only shop empty—and suitable,' she stammered, 'is Joneses'.'

There was a silence ; broken only by a gasp from Maggie.

'Do you mean to tell me,' said Mr. Chadwick, livid and deliberate, 'that you have actually taken Joneses' shop—two doors away from here ? '

'Yes.' This was awful.

'But you can't do it ! I'll stop it ! ' announced Mr. Chadwick. 'I'll stop it by law, let me tell you. I'll stop it by law.'

'No,' said Jane, 'you can't do that. I've seen to all that.'

'You've seen to all that ? ' Mr. Chadwick began to feel rather mazed in the head. She had seen to all that ! Oh, she was deep. . . .

'I'm not setting up the same sort of shop,' said Jane. 'Only ready-made dresses and blouses. I shan't touch your real business, Mr. Chadwick. Your materials and household stuff. You'll never make a success of your ready-made department. You won't expand. Remember I tried to get you to take this very shop. You can't really blame me.'

'Can't blame you ? ' said Mr. Chadwick with a snort. 'Can't I ? I tell you the whole town'll blame you. Setting up two doors away ! You'll not get any business. Dirty tricks never pay. Never ! ' hissed Mr. Chadwick into Jane's face.

He got down from his stool. His legs felt queer. He must go and tell Bertha. He felt an urgent need to go and tell Bertha about this viper that had turned in his bosom.

Jane saw with relief that the interview was at an end.

'So I give a week's notice,' she said, 'or a fortnight, if you would find it more convenient . . .'

'A week!' snapped Mr. Chadwick. 'I don't want a sneak in my shop any longer than need be, thank you.'

He hurried to the stairs, and Jane was left alone with Maggie.

It was all very uncomfortable, she reflected. But it would be worth it. She bolstered herself up by visions of the little shop. The walls were being distempered in French grey to-day. She was dying to see how it would look.

Had those glass drawers arrived yet? Mrs. Briggs was going to wait there to receive them. Mrs. Briggs was being a wonderful help.

Jane stole a glance at Maggie. Maggie closed her eyes at her and turned away.

Mr. Chadwick came back into the shop.

'Miss Carter,' he began in a conciliatory voice, 'I'm afraid I was a little hasty with you just now.'

'Oh no,' Jane protested. He was going to make it hard if he took this line.

'I know it must look awful to you, Mr. Chadwick,' she burst out. 'I hadn't thought of leaving for years, but the opportunity came, and I must snatch it. You would in my place, wouldn't you?'

'I hardly think so, Miss Carter,' said Mr. Chadwick politely. 'I think you are making a great mistake. You are very young. You are too young to carry a business. To tell you the truth, Miss Carter, that is why I have kept you back about the ready-made department here. Business is full of pitfalls, Miss Carter, which you are too young to see. You haven't the experience.'

Jane regarded the buttons in her hand and was silent. It was no good saying anything.

Mr. Chadwick, encouraged by the downcast eyes, continued :

' Now I'll tell you what I'll do, Miss Carter.'

Jane looked up. There was a catch in it somewhere, it appeared.

' I'll take that shop,' resumed Mr. Chadwick, ' and we'll transfer the ready-made department to it, and put you in charge. With me behind you, you'll be all right—and you shall have thirty shillings a week. Now then.'

Jane shook her head.

' Thank you, Mr. Chadwick. It's a very generous offer—but I can't. . . .'

' Wait a minute, Miss Carter—don't be in such a hurry.' He raised a hand and looked at her persuasively, except for his eyes, which gave him away. ' Remember this, Miss Carter. . . . I can't carry on this business for ever. I have no one to carry it on after me. If you stay here and work with me, who knows but what I might hand it on to you ? ' He knew perfectly well that he would sell it to the highest bidder and retire on the money to St. Anne's, but he and Bertha had decided it was a good bait. Jane, however, didn't even look at it.

' Mr. Chadwick, you are very kind indeed—but I must go now. Everything is arranged. I must be on my own—and really I shan't damage you in any way. I'll see to that. I'll keep strictly to my own line.'

' You're making a mistake, Miss Carter,' said Mr. Chadwick, pinching in his lips.

' That may be. . . . But I'm going on with it.'

' How can *you* set up for yourself ? ' Mr. Chadwick
was getting worked up again. ' You've no capital.
Where did you get this money from ? '

' That's my affair,' Jane reminded him.

' If you've got yourself into the hands of money-
lenders I pity you,' said Mr. Chadwick with emotion.
' I pity you, Miss Carter. Surely you have never been
so foolish. . . .'

' No, I haven't.'

' I am relieved about that.'

Mr. Chadwick cast about in his mind. How *had*
she got the money ? He wondered about his own till.
But it had been all right. Nothing had been missing.
He leaned nearer Jane.

' I hope, Miss Carter . . . there has been nothing . . .' Jane's clear gaze made him shuffle a little.
' I hope there is no man behind this ? '

It took Jane a little time to grasp this.

She shot up like a flame before him.

' How dare you suggest such a thing ! ' She had no
position to remember now. She could let him have
it. ' I'm leaving. I'm setting up for myself. That's
all you need to know. I've worked my hardest for
you for six years. I know I'm leaving your business
in a better state than I found it. I've doubled it for
you. I've treated you far and away better than you've
treated me. I've had to screw my wages from you ;
you've stolen—yes, stolen '—she emphasized to his
livid face—' my commission dozens of times. I was
helpless. But I'm not helpless now and I'm going a
week from to-day.'

' Very well,' said Mr. Chadwick with venom. ' Very
well. Go. But don't come whining here to be taken
back when you've lost every penny of this mysterious

money somebody's been silly enough to lend you.
Don't come round here asking for help when the sale
bills are up in your shop windows, and you're in the
Bankruptcy Court, Miss Carter. Because that's where
you'll end up. You mark my words ! That's where
you'll end up . . . and before the year's out, too.
The Bankruptcy Court—and serve you right ! '

He turned and rushed back to Bertha.

II

Jane lingered over her supper. She was in a fever
to run to the little shop and see how it looked. But
there was something she wanted to say to Maggie,
and she had to be so careful in her approach. Jane
looked at her many times as she sat by the window
looking with sullen eyes through the curtain at the
back-yard.

At last she spoke.

' Maggie.'

A blink of the eyelids alone showed that Maggie
heard.

' Maggie, you heard what I said to Mr. Chadwick
about setting up for myself. Everything's nearly
ready. I think it's going to be all right. It will be
uphill work at first and I'll have to live—keep myself
and clothe myself and everything on fifteen shillings
a week, I've reckoned, or even less if I can. There
won't be anything for more than one for a bit, but
when there is—will you come in with me ? '

She waited, holding her breath for Maggie's answer.
Maggie turned a lowering face on her.

' Don't speak too quickly, Maggie,' urged Jane.
' Think a minute ! You can go equal shares with me
later. Will you, Maggie ? '

Maggie went a dull red to the roots of her hair.

' No.' She thrust her face forward. ' No, I won't. I hate you, Jane Carter. I'd rather starve than accept any favours from you. So now you know.'

Jane got up from her chair. Her fingers trembled as she put on her hat. She went out of the kitchen. Maggie sat on by the window. The fierce exultation had returned. She had got her own back, after all !

CHAPTER FIFTEEN

I

A S the market clock struck nine Jane, addressing an invisible public, declared her shop open.

'It's open,' she said, standing on the step in the quiet radiance of the morning.

She looked round the market-place with new eyes. This Square, in which a delicious mist still hung, would witness her failure or her success. For a moment, a nervous apprehension shook her. She went out on to the pavement and looked again at her shop, with anxiety.

The sight of it reassured her. It was a real shop; it was there; it was realized. It did more than reassure her, it filled her with the wildest excitement. She gazed with ecstasy at her name hanging in bronze letters in the window:

'JANE.'

She had always disliked that name for a plain, old-fashioned one, and now it inspired her with the sharpest delight. Not only was it adequate, and, by a turn of fashion, modish, but it was a symbol. Under this name the venture was launched, like a very small ship in an uncertain sea. This name must carry Mrs. Briggs and herself through to success. This brief name bore great responsibility.

It seemed to its owner to be making a good start at least. In the window beneath it, against the background of grey, was an elegant white embroidered frock with a yellow necklace laid on it. Three equally elegant white embroidered blouses were disposed on the other side of the window ; and just where it should be was a bowl of yellow globe flowers to point the colour of the necklace. Jane thought it discreet, fresh and delicious, and feeling it impossible to behave like a sober shopkeeper if she looked at it any longer, she went inside.

There was nothing much left to do. She had been up at six o'clock, and about half-past that hour, as she was vigorously dealing with the camp-bed, Lily arrived at the back-door, sheepishly requesting to wash the step and the shop floor.

Jane was embarrassed.

' Oh, Lily—I wish I could have you to clean for me,' she said at last. ' But you know I can't afford it. I shall have to do my own cleaning.'

Lily blushed and looked reproachful.

' Eh,' she began, breathing hard. ' Don't talk like that. Don't mention such a thing. I wasn't cadging for work. I don't want payin'. I just wanted to 'elp you a bit like before I begin there.' She nodded her head in the direction of Chadwick's. ' Only don't tell them, for mercy's sake, or they'll up at me with somethin' 'ard and tell me to 'op it. Eh, mud's your name there, you know. 'Anging's not good enough for you. But never you mind. Can I come in ? '

' I can't let you,' said Jane. ' You work so hard. Let me do it myself. I've plenty of time.'

' Eh, no,' said Lily gravely. ' That wouldn't do. You can't be down on your knees scrubbing step one

minute, and up be'ind the counter the next. It isn't
the thing. Besides, you'll spoil your 'ands. Silk
stuff 'ull catch on them when you're tryin' on, and the
ladies won't like that. Very particler, ladies, I've
always found.'

So Lily washed the step and the floor and had a cup
of tea and told Jane how well she was doing on her
separation allowance. She had a house of her own
again, and actually a blue toilet-set with roses on,
exactly like the one Bob drank away.

' I'se 'ave it all lovely by the time 'e comes back.
Eh, the war '*as* done 'im good,' she said gratefully.
' 'E's right enjoyin' 'imself—drivin' motor lorries.
You know 'e was always one for machines. When
anybody's mangle went wrong in our street, they
always sent for Bob, and 'e generally nearly always
could put it right—when 'e were sober. 'E writes
me such lovely letters,' said Lily tearfully. ' God bless
you till we meet again, 'e says, and such-like ; beautifully put together, they are.'

She went away, damp and happy, saying she would
come again the next day.

And Jane went on polishing fittings, cleaning
windows, dusting and arranging until all was done,
and she could squeeze herself behind the counter to
wait for the first customer.

' What a good thing I'm thin,' she thought.

It really was a box of a shop, but to Jane its horizon
was unlimited.

She looked at herself in the mirror on the opposite
wall ; considered herself from every angle. She had
never had enough time to look at herself before. She
wondered if she really was nice-looking or not. She
couldn't decide. Anyhow, she had the right figure

to show off dresses ; that was useful, she could be her own mannequin. She patted her shining hair, curving her fingers as she had seen the cinema heroines do ; and assumed sets of airs and graces one after the other. All at once she began to sing loudly, throwing up her head like a bird. She ceased as suddenly.

'No—that won't do,' she said aloud. 'What if a customer came in ? They'd think I was mad ! Nobody would want to buy blouses from a lunatic.'

She laughed to her reflection in the glass.

'Suppose I was a lunatic—and made the customer put her legs through the blouse sleeves . . .?

'You know the best of it is—being *alone. That's* why I'm so happy. I've never been alone—in the daytime—since I can remember. Oh, I am happy. I've never been so happy before—and perhaps I shan't ever be again. My shop, my shop, my adorable shop ! Bless Mrs. Briggs, bless Mrs. Briggs, bless Mrs. Briggs ! '

She began to open the glass-fronted drawers one after another and go through, with loving hands, her little stock of silk stockings and blouses and jumpers and camisoles and princess petticoats. It was quickly done and she soon found herself turned round to the counter again, waiting. Even waiting can be enjoyed sometimes.

She stood at her counter slackly, her eyes wandering. She smiled to see Mr. Chadwick go by, with his hat on, pretending he had been somewhere, casting surreptitious glances at her window. She saw venom and apprehension in his eyes. He was sure her downfall would be swift, and yet was afraid it wouldn't be swift enough.

N

She wished a customer would come in while he was passing, and suddenly a customer came in. It was Miss Barton from the 'Empire' Bar; a dressy lady, Jane knew. She admired the embroidered blouses, and if there was one in an outsize she would have one. Jane produced an outsize, and, disguising her excitement, helped Miss Barton to dispose the blouse on her ample person. As Miss Barton was considering the effect in the mirror, the shop door opened again and Mrs. Briggs came in. She motioned to Jane not to notice her, and walked creakily through to the back premises. Her face was hot and important. She stood behind the curtain and listened to the transaction. She beamed when she heard the till ring and the door close on the customer.

Jane came flying out.

'Well, I've sold the first blouse. Fifteen and eleven!' She hugged Mrs. Briggs and then straightened her friend's hat. 'And Miss Barton was very nice and admired everything and says she's sure I'll do well. Does everything look all right?'

'Lovely,' said Mrs. Briggs. 'I just popped in to see how you were going on.'

Mrs. Briggs kept on popping in to see how things were going on. She came down to get parcels off by the tram-boys; she came down to see that Jane had a cup of tea in the afternoons, bringing cakes of her own making, and little additions to Jane's supper.

Jane worked harder and harder as the shop got under way. All day long she was kept busy with customers, accounts, travellers, parcels, tidying up, telephoning.

She took thirty-four pounds in the first week and was beside herself with joy.

'Thirty-four pounds!' she said over and over again to Mrs. Briggs.

It was only at night, when the shop was shut, that she realized how tired she was. So tired that she could hardly drag her feet round the Square. She forced herself to do it, though ; remembering Wilfrid's insistence on a 'breath of air.' Poor Wilfrid ! She wondered where he was. She had written to him, but he had not answered.

II

Mrs. Greenwood was in her element as Commandant of the V.A.D. Hospital at Northgate. She went about in a stiffly starched uniform with a broad red cross on her bosom, giving orders and putting everything to rights. She knew everything that went on,—even to the number of onions peeled in the kitchen by the newest V.A.D.s, weeping copiously and involuntarily the while. She was dreadfully efficient. She could even speak French to the Belgians.

'Quel bel après-midi que cet après-midi !' she would bellow to them as she passed.

And when one of them tried to commit suicide in the bathroom, she dealt with him. She got him back to bed and talked to him for the good of his soul for half an hour. The poor fellow did not understand a word she said, but he did not attempt suicide again.

Sylvia, very pretty in blue and white, followed her mother about sometimes. At the beginning she tried to be useful. She went into the laundry. But when she boiled the flannels and the matron made such a fuss about the hard little things that had been the men's shirts, she withdrew in hauteur.

She was driven to spend a good deal of time writing

to Noel Yarde and other officers she knew. She
wrote in a large open hand, sloping backwards. She
put question marks instead of exclamation marks, and
anything she wanted to emphasize she put in inverted
commas.

'Noel dear,'—
　　(She had seen this inversion of the usual in a
novel and thought it very smart.)
　'Ever so many thanks for your letter. What is it
like at the Front? It is very cold here; not at all
like April. I am still wearing my fur coat? "Isn't
this war simply putrid." It will finish me off completely before long. Mother is always at the hospital
and Father is always at the mills and poor little me is
left all alone. Aren't you sorry for me. I go to the
hospital sometimes but I don't like it much. Mother
has started a Y.M.C.A. hut now and I help in that.
You should see me in my blue veil? Who do you
think was helping last Thursday. "That girl from
Chadwick's, the draper's." Mrs. Briggs brought her.
Mrs. Briggs is always being a trial to us. Mother was
not at all pleased about it. The helpers generally
have tea together but Mother told Mrs. Briggs she
couldn't have tea with the "shop-girl," so Mrs. Briggs
and the girl had to have tea afterwards. Why does
she keep pushing in with us. "Do you remember the
excruciating feather she wore at the Hospital Ball."
It did make me laugh? Didn't it you. I do wish the
war was over and you were back again. Can't you
wangle a leave and come and cheer me up. I feel
very lonely.

　　　　　　　　　　　　'Ever
　　　　　　　　　　　　　　'Sylvia.'

Noel Yarde came on leave. He was in high spirits, enjoying everything—his clean bed, his shaves, his bath, with unlimited hot water and soft towels. He even listened enraptured to a bird singing in the garden.

' By Jove—how lovely ! What a long time since I heard a bird sing ! '

It was exquisite. And how dear his mother was to him ! And Mary, his sister, how quaint and delightful ! He had never really appreciated them before. He even loved the maids for looking so trim and cheerful.

And Sylvia was a miracle of beauty. How she had come on while he had been away ! What an enchanting pout she had ! How could he ever have thought she was spoiled ? How lovely she was to look at after those women they came across in France ! How could fellows go mad about such women ? Want to marry them ? That was madness, if you like. So superfluous—and yet they did it. How could they ? Old Abbott, for instance, dragging a dirty snapshot of that Laure out of his pocket-book every five minutes. Just wait until he showed them that last portrait of Sylvia. He turned his head to look at it again. She was too lovely for words.

Mrs. Greenwood was being quite a good sport. Giving him a very jolly time.

When Mrs. Greenwood suggested that he should take Sylvia over to the Adelphi in Liverpool to dance, he jumped at the idea. And when she said they were going to London for a few days' gaiety to cheer Sylvia after her hard work at the Hospital, and would be very pleased to see him there, he jumped again.

He jumped at everything, and when she hinted that

he was getting Sylvia talked about by his intimacy with her, he cheerfully jumped into the net she had spread for him and asked Sylvia to marry him. And so well had Mrs. Greenwood done her work that he imagined he had had a hard fight for Sylvia, and was a lucky man to win her in the end. He returned to the Front, extremely infatuated, and exhibited with possessive pride many exquisite portraits of Sylvia to his fellow-officers.

CHAPTER SIXTEEN

I

JANE was on her way, for the first time, to London. She was going in person to Venner's, Elwin's, Sutherland's, Brock's and Metton's, in search of dresses for the Greenwood-Yarde wedding. She was going on what Tidsley called a 'trip'; travelling by night, spending the day in London, and returning by night. In that way, because Thursday was early-closing day, she would miss only Thursday morning in the shop. Surely Susie would be able to manage in the morning; saying, in answer to inquiries, that Miss Carter was buying in London, but would be back to-morrow. Jane had been obliged to take Susie Howarth to help with the packing of parcels and errands. She was a sensible little girl of fourteen and worked hard for her five shillings a week, which was all Jane could afford to pay.

Jane fingered her 'Buying Notes' in the dark.

> 'Dress for Mrs. Briggs'—to be left entirely to Jane's discretion.
> 'Dress for Mrs. Briggs Junior'—who fancied, unfortunately, royal blue satin.
> 'Dress for Mrs. Parks'—long lines, grey, trimmed fur.
> 'Mrs. Bentley, green, large.'

And so on. She must keep all the details in her mind.

Such a lot to do and to think about. Life was so full and so unexpected in places. Customers were often strange creatures ; so incredibly confidential. Miss Parsons, for instance, disclosing her life's sorrow— the hairs on her legs. She had refused an offer of marriage because of these hispid limbs. All her life she was condemned to virginity because of them. Rather grim, thought Jane. She wondered if Guy de Maupassant would have made a tale out of it. A woman resisting temptation with inexplicable virtue ; the reason to be revealed in the last line with dramatic effect : ' Ses jambes étaient couvertes de poils.'

Jane knew enough French for that now.

Unexpected again had been the proposal of Mr. Goodwin from Brock's. She burned again in the dark to remember it.

' D'you ever go away for the week-end ? ' he had said.

' No,' she said airily. ' I can't afford to.'

' Would you like to ? '

' Yes, if I could afford,' she said again, with surprising naïveté.

' Well, what about it ? ' said Mr. Goodwin. ' A little week-end at Southport ? At the Crescent, say ? Tip-top place ; band ; good grub ; all the best people. You see life at the Crescent all right.'

Jane overcame a qualm of sickness by an effort.

' D'you mean—with you ? ' she asked to make sure.

' Mmm. Not a bad chap, am I ? '

A look inherited surely from her hardy young mother came into Jane's eyes.

' Mr. Goodwin,' she said at last, having thought how

to put it. 'You are here on business. Will you keep
to it ? Or shall I ask your firm to send another
traveller ? '

'All right. All right.' Mr. Goodwin was in no
way perturbed. In fact, it seemed to her, though
hardly credible, that he was relieved. 'No offence
meant. I see you're not that sort. Beg pardon. I
won't mention it again. Week-ending is looked upon
as quite the thing ; some expect it.'

Jane did not forget the incident. She woke sometimes in the night, and found herself filled with loath-
ing and fear. Alone in the room behind the shop in
the middle of the night, life took on strange and
terrible aspects. But when the day came with its
brimming measure of work, she was confident and
happy again.

Life was mixed, she decided, trying her elbow again
on the inadequate window-ledge of the compart-
ment ; mixed, but interesting.

She fell into an uncomfortable doze, not losing consciousness of the fact that she must keep a tight hold
on her bag and her ' buying notes.' . . .

In the early morning she arrived at Euston. Going
chilly and heavy-eyed to have what Lily called a ' wash
and tidy,' she found the tempting offer of ' Baths ' in
the cloak-room.

' May I have a bath ? ' she found herself saying like
an experienced traveller to the attendant. She was
astonished at her own behaviour, and kept saying to
herself as she lay in the comforting water :

' Fancy me having a bath in London ! '

The attendant was talking outside to someone about
a new hat.

' I think I'll 'ave a bough orn, wouldn't chew ? '

Jane said it after her with bewilderment. When the meaning reached her, she giggled. How funnily they spoke in London !

She dressed carefully in her dark blue coat and skirt. She hoped fervently that she would not appear too provincial in the eyes of Venner's and the others. She must not let it be seen that she was in London for the first time, either. That would never do.

She went out into the Euston Road, flooded now with October sunshine. What a place, what a rush, what a noise ! Not beautiful, certainly, but how exciting ! What cars, vans, buses, bicycles, horses —and what was that running with a roar under a grating ?

Five minutes to nine by the clock of a church standing gravely in the hurly-burly. She must get on ! She seized her moment and ran to the policeman. He was benevolent and, without ceasing to direct the traffic, told her how to get to Great Portland Street.

She boarded a bus with a sense of achievement and was swept away. The conductor promised to tell her where to get off, and as he seemed a man to have confidence in, she gave herself up to the excitement of looking out of one side of the bus and then out of the other.

' London ! London ! ' she kept saying to herself. ' I'm in London.'

Her heart gave ecstatic leaps now and then, so she clasped her buying notes over it.

Really Life . . . when you think of it . . .

' I've got here ! ' she wanted to shout to the great buildings.

She found Venner's with ease, and searched in its dingy exterior for the right door. She went inside at

last and stood in a vast and empty expanse of carpet
and windows. After some time, an exotic-looking
girl with stiffened eyelashes and a scarlet mouth in a
dead-white face walked across the expanse with an
undulating movement of the hips. Her shoes were so
extremely down at the heels as to be dangerous, but
she was indifferent to them, as to Jane, whose gaze
she crossed without returning.

'Well,' thought Jane uncomfortably, 'isn't anybody
coming to me?'

Two young girls appeared in a far corner of the
room. They stood together, laughing and talking, not
even troubling to glance at Jane on her door-mat. A
young man with a waist, who looked as if he would be
a good dancer and not much else, walked again across
the expanse.

'Queer manners they have in this part of the world,'
said Jane. 'Do they know I have a business? Do
they know I am here to buy?'

She walked resolutely to the chattering girls.

'Took me out and gave me a jolly good meal. You
know, a real pal, that's what he is. Of course, he's very
keen on me . . .' The girl paused in her conversation and turned an incurious gaze on Jane.

'I am buying gowns,' said that business woman. 'I
was told to ask for Miss Bootle.'

'Not here yet,' said the girl.

She looked with more interest at this phenomenon
who came to buy at quarter-past nine in the morning.

'What time will she be here?'

''Bout ten.'

Jane went out of Venner's, and stood again in Great
Portland Street. They did not hurry themselves in
London, she thought.

She went to Sutherland's higher up. Mr. Sutherland himself was there and they did business quietly and swiftly together, and Jane with more assurance went back to Venner's. Miss Bootle, embarrassingly amiable and as full of small-talk as a balloon of gas, arranged Jane in a satin chair and directed a thin girl with hair bleached to palest flaxen to walk up and down in the gowns Jane chose. Jane could hardly look at the gowns ; she was so interested in the people round her. In Lancashire you didn't see young men with waists talking to mannequins in petticoats.

She stopped gazing in their direction with difficulty and asked to see matrons' gowns in black, V front, long lines.

' A very nice number, don't you think, Miss Carter? I am very fond of this number—the godets are so smart. All the thing. . . .'

' Too fussy,' said Jane.

She went next to Metton's. While she was doing business pleasantly with a nice quiet girl, in came the proprietor himself ; a man with a face like a tortoise, and spots in his skin like a toad. He eyed Jane's legs and put his hand under her arm to lead her to the other department. Jane recoiled ; her body curled away from him with repugnance.

' Come into the office and have a drink,' he said amiably.

Jane refused. She hated him at sight ; leathery skin, dull eyes, thick lips and all.

He couldn't leave her alone. He followed her round the rooms and hovered over her while she chose. He repeated his invitation to come into the office, and Jane again refused. He asked her to lunch. She refused, but in no way put out, he accompanied her to the door and watched her walk away, ready to wave his hand if she turned round.

'Fancy having to deal with such people,' Jane fumed. 'The toad. . . .'

'Trade' presented you with unpleasant problems. Metton's sold good stuff, and it would now be repugnant to deal with them.

'Pity I ever saw him,' she reflected.

She forgot him among the shops of Regent Street and Bond Street; lost herself in wonder at the delicacy, the colour, the workmanship, the display. She went from one side of the streets to the other, crossing and re-crossing perilously, afraid of missing anything. Her feet ached intolerably before the afternoon, but she made them carry her on.

She found her way to Westminster Abbey and sat in the Poets' Corner for Wilfrid's sake. She wandered into the cloisters and was enchanted by the sudden glimpses of beauty—a flight of worn steps under a plane tree in one place; in another a square of garden shut away with its small sleeping fountain; all so quiet and holy.

She copied the inscription on the wall-tablet about the man who died of small-pox but presented an unspotted soul to God. She liked it so; Wilfrid would like it, too.

She left the muted, war-time London night and travelled back to Tidsley, feeling that she had taken a plunge into a most exciting and adventurous sea, and come up with a wonderful haul of new ideas, new views. She slept soundly from sheer fatigue, rolling about with unconscious abandon from the unbuttoned private on her left to a substantial old woman on her right.

II

Jane lay in the camp-bed in the middle of the room behind the shop and wondered why she had awakened with a feeling of depression.

It was still dark, but she could make out the bulk of the cardboard boxes piled in one corner and the dim white sheets of paper at the desk where she had been doing accounts until late the previous night. Perhaps the bills depressed her? That Mrs. Rhodes, who would not pay up, and had to be dunned into paying bits on account! If only people would pay for what they had! But it wasn't that weighing on her spirits. Waking fully, she remembered. This was the wedding-day of Sylvia Greenwood and Noel Yarde. She was to go to Stanfield to-day to arrange the bride's veil. Although her daughter's entire trousseau had been bought in London, Mrs. Greenwood had not hesitated to ask Jane to dress the bride. Jane disliked the idea, but knew it would not do to refuse.

'I'm sorry he's marrying her,' thought Jane heavily in the November dawn. 'I don't think she's anything in her. Very beautiful, of course, but empty.'

Strange how she went through her life, hardly thinking of Noel Yarde, and yet whenever she came into contact with him, she was aware of a curious sympathy; of a feeling that, in some inner consciousness, she knew him intimately. Well, it meant nothing; it was entirely unreciprocated, and here to-day was an end of it!

She got up and, with sudden recklessness, lit the gas-fire. It was usually lighted only for 'trying-on' customers.

Soon all the little skulls were glowing, and she was dressed and drinking tea.

The morning got on to half-past twelve, and Jane set out for Stanfield. The gates were wide open and the flight of steps carpeted in red felt. Jane was admitted and shown upstairs. The rich, dark house was all astir, doors opening and shutting, maids passing up and down, Mrs. Greenwood's muffled bellow sounding at intervals. As Jane reached the top of the stairs Mr. Greenwood came out of a room and stood there a moment. He looked nervous and— what? Jane wondered what it was that he looked. Furtive. That was it. A strange expression to wear on his daughter's wedding-day.

The bride was in her pink-and-white bedroom, sitting by the fire, looking cross.

' Miss Carter,' she cried, ' I thought you were never coming! There's a stitch gone in my frock. Some pearls are loose. I am nearly demented. Bennett pulled it when she took it from the wardrobe. Yes, you must have done, Bennett—so don't deny it. How could it have happened any other way ? '

Bennett wiped her red eyes again.

' I can soon put it right,' said Jane. ' Nothing to worry about.'

' It's so stupid of her,' Sylvia said. ' The clumsy creature! One would think she would be careful with a wedding-gown.'

The telephone rang in her mother's room.

' Mr. Yarde,' said Bennett, returning.

Sylvia ran out, leaving the door open. Jane, stitching at the satin, heard her speak.

' Yes, Miss Carter's here now. I shall soon be ready. No, I'm not at all nervous. Soon be over ?

Oh, I don't want it to be. Great fun . . . everything's lovely . . . my veil's a dream. Wait till you see me! Miss Carter's going to dress me now. I must go. Yes . . . do you? Mmmm. Good-bye.'

She ran back, flushed, excited, and stood like a child for Jane to dress her. She was lovely. Jane, kneeling in her black frock, looked at the contrast she herself made to the radiant vision in the mirror.

' I hope you will be very happy,' said Jane, when all was done.

' Oh, I shall,' said Sylvia. She had no doubt about it at all. She had always been petted and adored, and Noel would continue to pet and adore her.

She sat down very carefully, with her veil and train disposed around her, to wait for her wedding-hour.

Jane went further on up Hill Rise to see that Mrs. Briggs was all in order for the wedding. She found her nervous in black silk with Albert pacing backwards and forwards, a white carnation in his buttonhole, instructing her in behaviour. Mrs. Briggs cast rapid and beseeching glances at Jane, and her fingers twitched in her tight gloves. Jane could do nothing for her but smile reassuringly and leave her to Albert.

She went back to the shop and relieved Susie at the counter. No one came in. She stood gazing out of the window, bemused. By and by the cars began to stream past the window carrying the guests to St. James's. There came a pause and the bride's car went by. People in the street gaped at the satin and pearls and tulle and lilies within. A hush seemed to fall on the town ; the streets seemed empty. Jane stood at the counter, feeling empty too, bereft of her own self.

All round the market-place the shopkeepers were gathered at their doors to watch the cars come back.

'She'll be too grand, will Jane Carter,' said Maggie Pye to the new assistant in Chadwick's, 'to come out on the doorstep like the rest of us, but I bet she's peering through somewhere.'

She was. And the maroon car came slowly round the Square again. Noel and Sylvia were together now; together for always. She saw his happy face as he passed.

It was over now. She went to get a drink of water from the scullery tap and came back to the shop with resolution. Venner's traveller was coming in, and she must go through her stock of jumpers and blouses.

CHAPTER SEVENTEEN

I

THE February night was cold ; a thin wind fluttered the blue veils of the Y.M.C.A. workers as
they came out of the hut to meet the trains with
buckets of tea. When the trains went out again, the
station was left in dismal emptiness of parallel lines
and perspective, with a gleam of rain under the lamps
at each remote end of the platforms. There was a
smell of smoke imprisoned under the glass roof ; the
book-stalls were shuttered ; only the posters, lettered,
it seemed, in blood, were left to point the grey night
with a terror nobody seemed to notice : 'Heavy
Enemy Losses ! ' 'Further Allied Advance ! ' 'Local
Casualties ! '

Inside the hut, Mrs. Briggs and a St. John's Ambulance man tended the steaming urns, and Jane came
when she could to stand near them and get a little
warmth. She still helped at the station, though it was
now a considerable effort for her to do it. The strain
of months of hard work and careful living were telling
on her, but she felt she must do something directly
connected with the War, which dragged on and on, all
the exhilarating hatred and fine fury gone out of it ;
nothing now but a grim struggle between worn men.

Jane was tired and took no part in the conversation
in the hut. When the whistle of an approaching train

was heard, she took the handle of a bucket of tea
or a tray of mugs and went with the others to the
indicated platform.

'The 10.45 is due,' said the St. John's Ambulance
man, looking at the time-table hung over the urns.
'A lot of wounded coming in.'

'There's the whistle.'

Tea splashed into the buckets and, with a clatter
of mugs, they went out.

Nurses and ambulance men from the Northgate
Hospital were already on the platform. The train
came in, filling the station with clouds of white smoke
of strange, tumultuous beauty. The doors opened,
letting out a helter-skelter of khaki-clad figures, who
hailed the tea with joy. They were, for the most part,
very cheerful.

'Men are splendid,' thought Jane.

She felt a deep admiration for men as men, looking
round for someone else to give tea to. She saw a
tall, thin figure silhouetted against the green gloom
of the lamps, a bulky outline, bulged by haversack and
bundles. He was walking away alone ; she dipped a
mug in the tea and ran carefully after him.

'Do have some tea.'

He turned under the lamp and the light fell full on
his face. It was Wilfrid.

The mug in Jane's hand shook so that the tea
spilled on the platform.

'Wilfrid !'

One sleeve of his tunic was empty.

'Wilfrid !'

He answered, but she did not hear what he said.
She stood staring at his sleeve. She put out a hand
to touch it.

' Wilfrid—what's happened ? Your arm . . .'

He took her hand in his.

' Don't worry, Jane . . . I'm used to it now.'

' Oh . . .' A sudden rush of tears choked her voice.

He pressed her hand.

' Don't, Jane . . . it's all right.'

Jane stood, shaken to the heart, holding to his hand as if she would never let go.

She tried to speak.

' Take that tea to somebody,' said Wilfrid. ' I must go.'

' Wait—wait a minute . . .' Jane brought out desperately. ' Where are you going ? '

' To the Northgate Hospital for a bit.'

' Shall I be able to see you ? '

' If you like.'

' Wilfrid ! Wait . . . don't go . . . Wilfrid ! '

She caught his tunic to keep him. He mustn't go. He must tell her. His arm . . .

' I must go, Jane. Don't worry about this. I don't.'

' Wait . . . a minute ! '

' I can't.' He loosed her fingers. Then something of what she felt, standing there shocked and afraid, made him speak more gently.

' Good-bye, Jane. When I'm a bit better, I'll be glad to see you. Good-bye.'

He waited for her to answer, but she did not. She watched him go away under the lamps, then she herself turned slowly back to the hut with the mug of cold tea. She was seized by a sudden longing to get away, to tell Mrs. Briggs she felt ill, as indeed she did. But she remembered that the men couldn't say they felt ill when the War was too much for them. She must not either. She stayed on, standing in the dark corners of the station to go over it again. Wilfrid—with an arm gone ! And so tired—too tired to be bothered with her. Simply too tired.

II

She waited with nervous apprehension for Thursday afternoon, so that she could go to Northgate and see Wilfrid. If it was true that he wanted to be left alone, if it was really true that he didn't want her to go, she told herself, she wouldn't go again. But this first time she must go.

But how must she be when she got there, she asked herself? How do anything but weep, and spread her useless pity before his indifferent gaze. It was terrible . . . terrible . . . and she didn't know how to behave in the face of it, so as not to hurt him, so as to comfort him somehow. It wasn't only his arm ; that, strangely, seemed to be the least of his hurt.

She went slowly up the gravelled drive of Northgate and rang the bell at the visitors' door. As she was admitted to the hall she found Mrs. Greenwood, starched and authoritative, talking to some V.A.D.s. Mrs. Greenwood turned her head stiffly in her collar at her approach.

' Ah ! Miss Carter, I see. What is it ? ' she called. She was as strict in her dictum of ' no followers ' in the hospital at Northgate as she was in her kitchen at Stanfield.

' I have come to see Mr. Thompson,' said Jane.

' Thompson ? Do you mean Private W. F. Thompson, 3rd East Lancashires, who came in last Monday ? Lost an arm ? ' Mrs. Greenwood was proud to show this girl who had once got the better of her that she knew every detail of her hospital.

'Yes,' said Jane.

'Do you know Thompson?'

'Yes,' said Jane briefly.

Something in Jane's level gaze reminded Mrs. Greenwood that it would be better to modify her tone a little. The committee had intimated to her that access to patients by their friends must be more freely allowed. The men had rebelled against 'Ma Hindenburg's' iron rule.

'Ah, you know him! Very well. You may spend half an hour with him. I don't think he has had any visitors to-day, has he, Nurse?'

'No. His mother and sister came yesterday,' said a young V.A.D., blushing at being referred to.

'See if you can rouse him, Miss Carter,' said Mrs. Greenwood, with sudden loud graciousness, as she turned away. 'He has lost an arm, which is very sad. But hundreds of brave fellows are lying dead at this moment. Surely that should comfort him. Stubborn, I fancy—and morose. *Good* afternoon.'

She crossed the hall with dignity. Jane, trembling a little, followed the childish V.A.D. down the corridor to the room with three great windows and an armorial fireplace where Wilfrid lay in bed. The other occupants of the ward were out on the terrace in the February sunshine. Jane was glad they were to be alone.

She sat on a papier-mâché chair by his bed. His hair was thick and dark against the pillow; a tiny muscle worked incessantly in his thin cheek. After the greeting, he lay staring out of the window.

Jane sat dumbly. There seemed nothing fit to say.

But the silence grew oppressive. She tried to talk.
She told him about Mrs. Greenwood in the hall.

A mechanical smile flitted across Wilfrid's face ; his
eyes smouldered on above it.

' Will you be able to come out for walks later ? '
Jane ventured again. ' This isn't a prison, is it ? '

She tried to lure him out of the dark place he was
in by talking of the spring and the country, reminding
him that something was untouched and lovely still.
There was no answering light in his face.

A numbing sense of helplessness beset Jane. This
War . . . what terrible things it did to men. How
strangely it had worked in the only two men she knew,
and how differently ! Noel Yarde had rushed from it
to warm himself at the first fire of life he came across ;
and Wilfrid had withdrawn into some cold secret wood
of his own where he brooded with God knew what for
company.

He must come out. He must let her help him. He
must let her reach him.

' Wilfrid . . .'

The door was flung open by an energetic hand, and
V.A.D.s trooped in with trays.

' Tea-time ! ' one called gaily to Wilfrid.

Wilfrid looked at her with hatred.

' God—for a little peace ! ' he muttered, raising
himself awkwardly in bed.

' Shall I go ? ' asked Jane.

' No, stay,' he said. ' You'll keep the men off.'

The men came in from the terrace ; cheerful,
facetious, ordinary. The room was filled with colour
and noise.

' You're his visitor,' said a V.A.D. to Jane. ' Would
you like to spread his jam ? '

' Oh yes,' said Jane, tearing off her gloves with eager haste.

Standing at the table, isolated by the shadow of her hat, conscious of the men laughing and eating round her, and the clatter of spoons and pots, she went through a strange, vivid moment. A passionate desire to protect Wilfrid, to care for him, to do things like this for him always, surged in her heart. She bent her head lower. It was not only pity, but something deep, yet indefinable. She stood a long time, handling the cheap knife, cutting the bread into meticulous fingers. She carried it at last to Wilfrid's bedside. That which Wilfrid had wanted so passionately was here now in her eyes. But he did not look up to see it. He merely took the plate of bread and jam with indifferent thanks.

Jane, chilled, turned away to put on her gloves again. She realized definitely that the old Wilfrid was gone. This Wilfrid, aloof, hardened, was his own man ; but he was a stranger.

CHAPTER EIGHTEEN

I

JANE sat doubled up at the desk in the little back-room, with her head on her blotting-pad and her heels on the rung of the chair. It looked like an attitude of pain, but was in reality one of relief and joy.

Mr. Robinson, the accountant, had just gone.

She had known, for some time, that she was making good, but now it was certain. Mr. Robinson had just confirmed it.

Her turn-over for the year was more than £3,000. Three thousand pounds. She trembled at it. Think of it ! And how many times had she paused, terrified by having started the business, terrified of going on with it ! She admitted that many a time she had felt Mr. Chadwick was right ; that she had no experience, that she must fail. But she'd gone on, dealing with things as they came, and here she was through her first year with more success than she had ever dreamed of.

It was a grand little business, thought Jane proudly. It seemed to have a sturdy, independent life of its own. It went on growing almost of itself.

And it had brought her in two hundred and fifty pounds. That, when rent, rates, taxes, telephone, gas and electricity had been deducted, and her own salary and Susie's wages, was the clear profit she had made.

And the same for Mrs. Briggs. Two hundred and fifty
pounds ! What wealth ! She felt rich beyond her
wildest dreams.

But what a grinding year it had been ! How she
had worked, early and late, doing everything, cleaning windows, polishing fittings, dusting, sweeping,
buying and cooking her own food, interviewing travellers, selling in the shop, stock-taking, having sales,
sending out bills, sending them out again and again,
insisting on payment, dealing hardily with troublesome customers, going to Manchester and again to
London to keep up with the times—Phew ! What a
year ! The struggle had matured her ; she felt more
capable, more confident, but older. She didn't think
that anyone, looking at her now, would say she was
too young to manage a shop.

She undoubled herself from the desk and put on her
hat. Tired though she was, she must go and tell Mrs.
Briggs all Mr. Robinson had said. Telephoning was
no good. Mrs. Briggs had never got used to the
telephone. She answered at random in a flat voice
and would never admit that she couldn't quite hear.
Besides, Jane wanted a sight of Mrs. Briggs's face when
she heard the news ; she wanted to get near her friend
and tell her again that she owed it all to her.

Mrs. Briggs was knitting operating socks in her
room.

' Eh, love ! ' she cried, whipping off her glasses at
Jane. ' Fancy you coming up at this time of the
night. There's nothing wrong, is there ? '

' No. It's all very right,' burst out Jane. ' Mr.
Robinson's been and we've taken over three thousand
pounds this year and we've got two hundred and fifty
each out of it. Two hundred and fifty each ! '

' You don't mean to say ! ' Mrs. Briggs was solemn with pride. ' Eh, well ! Fancy that ! '

' I can pay you your hundred and fifty back now.'

' Nay, leave it where it is,' said Mrs. Briggs. ' Leave it in the business. It's safe. I knew you'd got your 'ead screwed on right. Eh, 'asn't it done champion ? Now, 'asn't it ? '

They gazed rapturously at each other.

' Oh, Mrs. Briggs darling ! ' Jane burst out again, throwing her arms round her friend, operating socks and all. ' You have been good to me. You've given me the best year of my life. You've no idea what you've done for me, I don't suppose.'

' Nay, now.' Mrs. Briggs shook her head. ' If I reckon it all up, I couldn't 'ave spent a hundred and fifty pounds to better advantage. Let's be fair. I've 'ad one of the best years of my life too. I feel different, you know. Oh yes, I do,' she said emphatically. ' I feel I don't mind so much what people think of me not being a lady and that. I feel I can stand up to Albert and Willy and Lizzie and the servants. I don't know why, but that's how I feel. I'm a lot happier since I knew you, love. You've done me good, and the shop's done me good. Given me something to think about. It's a grand thing, is something to think about.'

' We'll have more than ever to think about now,' said Jane. ' I think when the Joneses move we'd better take over the whole premises. I need a fitting-room. I'll have to expand soon. I was thinking I'd better go and see the Manager at Lloyds.'

' Eh, d'you know, Mr. Ramsworth's dead. Isn't it sad ? We'se 'ave to see young Mr. Yarde when we go about the business now. 'E's the only one left in the firm. I do 'ope 'e won't tell Albert. Did you know his wife's going to have a baby? About Christmas, I 'ear.'

'Really,' said Jane, and hurried on to a mass of detail. She didn't want to think about anything uncomfortable or extraneous to-night. Only about her precious business.

II

The War was over. Tidsley burst into prosperity. The great mills shook with the ceaseless rattle of looms ; tacklers bought pianos. The streets were suddenly full of expensive cars, and women began to spend a great deal on dress. The Hospital Ball, once solitary in grandeur, was lost in a buzz of dances so wild that Elton and other little neighbours held up their hands in horror and looked upon Tidsley as Sodom and Gomorrah both. At these dances hitherto respectable matrons sat behind screens with young men, and an episode such as Jane's with Dick Elliott would have been considered a very mild joke indeed.

The gaiety was reflected in the shops. Wilfrid Thompson was dazzled by their blaze as he came out of Library Street on the fine winter night. There was only one smudge in the glittering row opposite. He looked to see what it was, and found it to be Chadwick's, the draper's, whose lights were, as of old, obscured by stalactites of eiderdowns.

'One way of advertisement, perhaps,' thought Wilfrid. 'Have your shop darker than anyone else's, and it will attract attention.'

He remembered how familiar he had once been, through Jane and Maggie, with the life of Chadwick's. Maggie was still there. It had been an awkward

moment the other evening when she came into the
Library, with Mrs. Chadwick's books. He happened
to be at the counter and nearest to her.

'Another of Ethel M. Dell's,' she said, pushing the
books at him with defiant cheerfulness.

'How are you, Maggie?' he said.

'Fine, thanks. How's yourself?' retorted Maggie.

She hummed a tune under her breath while he
remained at the counter, and was humming when he
came back. He did not know how she had stared
after him when he went to the book-shelves, or how
she rushed into Chadwick's alley to cry against the
back-door. He only wondered how on earth he had
ever gone out with her. The simplicity that had been
able to take any pleasure in the company of Maggie
Pye was gone out of Wilfrid for ever.

His eye was caught by Jane's little shop, as clear as
a crystal in the frosty night, with two green gowns in
the window and a plant of pure white cyclamen at one
side. The window was a poem in itself, and Wilfrid
gazed at it with pleasure.

He was tempted to go in and tell her his news. But
just then she looked over the curtain-rod into the
window, and at the sight of the foreshortened oval of
her face, the dark arcs of her lashes, he turned away.
It was safer not to go in ; he must keep safe and free
and unfeeling.

Besides, what was it to tell? Only that he had
to-day been appointed Assistant Librarian to the Tidsley Public Library. He had got the job because the
Chairman had seen a poem of his in the *Observer* and
been impressed. The Chairman was an earnest man
who made long speeches smelling strongly of the midnight oil, and believed in encouraging local talent.

Wilfrid hated to be local talent, but he accepted the
job with concealed gratitude.

He idled on, past Jane's shop, and in front of Harris's, the hairdresser's, he saw Noel Yarde examining
the window with anxiety.

' *He* got through without a scratch,' thought Wilfrid,
and walked out of the brilliant light of the town into
the semi-obscurity of the road.

Noel Yarde remained where he was, looking in
Harris's window, weighing the merits of a pink powder-
puff in a glass box against pots of something or other
tied up with yellow ribbon. That was the sort of
thing Sylvia liked ; and he must take something home
for her.

He had been doing a good deal of thinking that
afternoon, sitting in his comfortable office, staring
from the Turkey rug to the old map of the ' County
Palatine ' on the wall, and out of the top of the window
at the smoke-grey Tidsley sky. The fire burned softly
in the grate, and the muted tip-tap of a typewriter
came from the outer office. One or two clients came
in ; he interviewed them with the assistance of Varley,
his chief clerk, a little man with a domed head and
small dry hands, who knew everything. When the
clients had gone, he fell back into his brooding.

He thought of Sylvia. Like an ardent boy he had
rushed to pick a rose that tormented him with its
beauty, only to find that it wasn't real. Not real ;
made of some artificial stuff. No scent ; no secret ;
just beautiful. That was what he felt about his wife
already.

He thought of that, with a set face, staring at the
sky. Then he plunged forward in his swing chair and
took his long legs from under the desk.

'I'm not being fair to her,' he said. 'She can't help it. It's the way she's been brought up. It's her mother.'

All his life, he and the rest of Tidsley had accepted Mrs. Greenwood as she was. They were used to her loud voice in the streets and in the shops and at concerts and theatres. Her figure was as familiar to them as that of Queen Victoria in front of the Town Hall. But Noel Yarde found that though it had been easy to accept her from a distance, it was a very different matter to find her every night, as he did now, installed in his mother's chair in the drawing-room at Greystones, vociferously engaged in brightening Sylvia by all the devices she had employed for the twenty-odd years of her daughter's life. She treated Noel as if he were some privileged dog of Sylvia's to be tolerated in the room on condition that he behaved himself.

'I hate her,' muttered Noel Yarde, balancing his letter-scales. 'I really hate her. Why can't she stop in her own house and leave mine in peace?'

It had been so peaceful in his mother's time, but she and Mary had withdrawn to the Isle of Wight on his marriage. If only he could find them at home to-night, and have a good laugh with Mary once more!

'That's what's wrong,' he said, throwing himself back in the chair. 'I never laugh now.'

Sylvia, poor child, hadn't a grain of humour in her composition. Not what he called humour. She didn't like *Punch*. That was his test. She laughed at hats sometimes, but he couldn't remember that she ever laughed at anything else.

He pulled himself up again.

'Jolly hard to have a sense of humour when you're having a child.'

And she had started having the baby so soon.

' Jolly hard lines, poor little girl ! '

Hard indeed for such as Sylvia to be caught in Nature's grip like this, forced into this slow, discomfortable travelling with agony and perhaps death at the journey's end.

Noel Yarde jumped up from his desk. It was caddish of him. Mean. Selfish. It was of her that he must think now ; not of himself. Always of her. He must help her, please her, amuse her—always.

He seized his hat and left the office to Varley. After long consideration before Harris's window, he bought a whole box of Elizabeth Arden's beauty preparations, and arrived home in a frame of mind chastened enough to satisfy even Mrs. Greenwood. They spent a comfortable evening in the long drawing-room. Sylvia read the book on how to use the things in the box, Mrs. Greenwood made lengthy comments, and Noel read quite a lot of the latest Wells.

CHAPTER NINETEEN

I

NOEL'S wish that his house should be left in peace was realized ; but in a way he had not foreseen. Sylvia decided she did not like living at Greystones ; the maids kept leaving and everything was so tiresome. She must go ' home,' as she called Stanfield, at least until after the baby was born. So Greystones was left in peace, with drawn curtains, and Noel was removed to chafe under Mrs. Greenwood's eye at Stanfield.

And here his son was born. They telephoned the news of his arrival to the office. Noel rushed to Stanfield in hot haste, and was put to cool in the drawing-room for the evening, where Mr. Greenwood glanced uneasily over the top of the paper, and Mrs. Greenwood came in now and then to report with importance what was going on upstairs.

A week passed before Noel had what he considered a really good look at his son.

' It seems to me,' he said then, ' that he's mistaken his latitude. He looks definitely Japanese.'

' Japanese ? ' cried Sylvia indignantly from the bed where she lay looking more than ever lovely under a pink marabout bedspread. ' How can you say that, Noel ? Japanese ! '

' Yes. He's exactly like one of those little Jap dolls you used to get out of crackers.'

'Noel, how can you talk like that? You know it isn't true.'

'My dear,' said Noel, rather flatly, straightening himself up to look at her, 'I'm only joking.'

'Well, don't joke about my baby. I won't have him called Japanese. Nurse, give him to me. I won't have him criticized.'

'You behave,' teased Noel, 'as if I had nothing to do with him.'

Sylvia gave him a deep look as she moved the Elizabeth Arden beauty box to make room for her son. The look meant that she was shocked. In front of Nurse!

Noel grimaced and kissed her. Let him get out of that bedroom where he felt so futile and unnecessary.

He walked down to the office for exercise. He felt the need of it. At thirty-one his Rugby days were over. He played tennis with vigour in the summertime, but the golf-links were three miles out from Tidsley and Sylvia did not like to be left for golf. So he walked up and down twice a day to keep himself as fit as might be.

Varley followed him into his room.

'A young lady by the name of Carter 'phoned, sir,' —Noel winced privately; he loathed 'phoned!—'to ask if you could see her at three o'clock this afternoon. She is a client of ours; the late Mr. Ramsworth dealt with her affairs, Mr. Noel. This young lady and Mrs. Albert Briggs, of Greenwood & Briggs, sir,'—Varley always felt he must explain everything to the present head of the firm,—'entered into an agreement about a shop, Mr. Noel; a dress shop. But I have all the particulars here, sir. Perhaps you would look them over before the ladies arrive, and then you would be in the know, if you would permit me to say so.'

He untied the papers and laid them before Noel.

'Good Lord!' thought Noel. 'He's been doing his hair again. He stinks to heaven!'

Varley did a little home-dyeing. He went about thinking nobody knew. Noel Yarde was always on the verge of suggesting that he should use something a little less pungent, but he was afraid of hurting the chap's feelings. He looked at Varley now with a wrinkled brow, and Varley went out wondering what was the matter. He was sadly afraid his young chief did not like the trouble of interviewing Miss Carter and Mrs. Briggs.

Noel applied himself to the papers.

Mrs. Briggs mixed up with a dress shop! What an incongruous combination! He remembered seeing, at rare social functions, her small face crumpled with anxiety, her eyes darting this way and that, looking for a way out. Mrs. Briggs was his mother-in-law's standing grievance.

At three o'clock prompt, Varley ushered in Mrs. Briggs and Jane.

'How d'you do, Mrs. Briggs?' said Noel, taking her hand, then offering his own to Jane. He'd seen this girl before somewhere, he knew, but where? He looked at her again as she sat by his desk. When her eyes were downcast, her face was rather wistful; when she looked up, he saw the practical one, the worker, in her clear grey eyes.

Mrs. Briggs began.

'I do 'ope, Mr. Yarde,' said she, resting both fists on her knees, 'as you'll treat this as confidential.'

'Of course, Mrs. Briggs. Nothing you say here will go beyond these walls, you know.'

'Well, I'm relieved,' said Mrs. Briggs. 'I was a bit

bothered, you being married to my 'usband's partner's daughter. You understand me. Because this business between Miss Carter 'ere and me is a bit of a secret, you see, and I don't want Albert to know about it. Well, now that's off my mind, we'll get on. Jane love, you'd better do the talking.'

Mrs. Briggs folded her hands across her front and left the floor to Jane.

Jane was strictly business-like. She broached the subject of a limited company. Her shop was doing well ; so far it had been a partnership, but now that she was going to launch out further, she didn't want Mrs. Briggs to be responsible for her debts if she failed. And if it remained a partnership, she would be, wouldn't she ?

They discussed that. Noel sent for Varley, got information, sent him out again.

The next subject on Jane's list was the question of profits. Here they had a tussle with Mrs. Briggs.

' I don't want to make money,' said Mrs. Briggs. ' I've got as much as 'ull do me. More. It's never brought me any 'appiness. What do I want any more for ? Money takes all the usefulness out of you, as far as I can see.'

' Come, come, Mrs. Briggs,' said Noel. ' You've been able to help Miss Carter with yours, at any rate.'

' Oh, well . . .' Mrs. Briggs dismissed that, but she wrinkled up her face and sniffed delightedly.

' If you won't have half,' said Jane, ' will you have a third ? '

' I don't want it,' said Mrs. Briggs firmly.

' Make her have it, Mr. Yarde. Put it down at that. She can quarrel with me later.'

' Eh, dear me . . .' Mrs. Briggs began, but her voice was drowned by Jane's next question.

They had decided, she and Mrs. Briggs, to take over the whole premises. What about the lease? And would Jane have the right to convert the first floor into fitting-rooms and the top floor into a flat? And the money for that would come out of her two-hundred-and-fifty and the two-hundred-and-fifty Mrs. Briggs insisted in putting back into the business. Would Mr. Yarde put in about that? And it was to be paid back at Jane's convenience, Mrs. Briggs interpolated.

If Jane needed any more money, should she borrow from the bank?

' Or from us,' suggested Noel Yarde.

Jane was pleased. He evidently considered ' Jane, Ltd.,' a sound proposition.

She finished her questions, and stood up to go. Her eyes were shining and her cheeks carnation-pink ; she had blossomed into such sudden beauty that Noel Yarde stared. It was the discussion of her business that made her look like this—alert, happy, ready to fly ! Without thinking at all of the man looking on, she flew to Mrs. Briggs, and with sundry twitchings and whiskings got her fur into place and straightened her hat, while Mrs. Briggs stood like an obedient and elderly child. It was obvious that she loved being pulled and patted into place by this girl.

' Come on, Mrs. Briggs darling. I invite you to tea at the Victoria.'

' Eh, do you, love ? I could just do with a cup of tea, and they 'ave such nice buttered oven-bottom cakes at the Victoria. Good afternoon, Mr. Yarde, and thank you kindly, and not a word to Albert, will you ? Nor to Mrs. Greenwood neither ? 'Ow's your

wife and baby? That's right. Remember me to
them. But no, perhaps it's better not. Good afternoon.'

It was not until she had gone that Noel Yarde
remembered that Jane was the girl at the ball. The
girl Elliott had made such an exhibition of. The girl
he had danced with.

' Good heavens! How she's changed! Who'd
have thought she had all this in her?'

He was impressed with Jane's grasp of her business.
He didn't know girls could . . . Of course, she'd
grown up with it. Very young, though, to be man-
aging all that. Not more than twenty-six, he thought.
If that. Her hair was short, he had seen ; it grew in
a point in the back of her neck. And that little mark
under the corner of her left eye looked like the faintest
touch of an artist's brush. He didn't know why, but
it gave an air of fragility to her face.

II

In the old days Maggie and Jane used to gaze with
longing at the dummy tea in the window of the Victoria Café ; a brown teapot, cream jug, sugar basin
and a plump currant teacake set out on a round
japanned tray. But now Jane went inside to tea.
She determined to go to dinner the very next Thursday that ever was. She chose Thursday, because that
was her early closing day and she could linger over the
food. Food was quite important to Jane because she
had never had very much of it.

The Victoria Café was peculiar to Tidsley and its
kind. It consisted of one large room furnished in plush
suites. There was a long table in the middle, and
small tables round the sides of the room ; all the tables

were adorned with aspidistras with twists of crinkled
paper round their pots. Miss Clegg, the proprietress
of the Victoria, was very proud of her aspidistras and
bought penny packets of food for them in the market.

They made a speciality of funeral teas, with ham,
at the Victoria, and if the defunct was a respected
client, Miss Clegg would do the aspidistra pots in
mauve paper and put a black bow on them here and
there. The afternoons at the Victoria were given
over to funeral teas and that kind of thing, but at midday Miss Clegg had what she called a ' high-class '
connection of lawyers, accountants, architects, municipal officials from the offices round about. That was
because Miss Clegg provided excellent fare, cooked
and served out, very slowly, by herself alone and taken
to the tables by a solitary and exuberant waitress
called Maud.

When Jane ventured into the Victoria on the following Thursday at quarter-past one and took a seat with
diffidence at a side table, Miss Clegg looked out from
the kitchen door and sent for Maud.

' Tell 'er to sit at big table,' she commanded. ' She's
got Mr. Eccles's place.'

Jane, blushing, approached the big table. There
was not a comforting female form in sight ; nothing
but a succession of waistcoats. That was as high as
she dared look. She sat down, and seizing the bill of
fare from Maud, ordered the first thing that caught
her eye.

' Calf's head.'

' Calf's head ! ' yelled Maud, rushing towards the
kitchen.

Jane sent a wild glance after her. If only she dared
call her back ! Whatever had possessed her to order

that? Calf's head! She had never seen such a thing before. She had a dreadful vision of it appearing before her on a charger like the head of—no, come!

She lowered her eyes to conceal her panic; her eyelids felt damp with apprehension. She fiddled with her knife and fork. She opened her bag and took out her handkerchief to hide her scarlet cheeks. The swing doors into the dining-room clapped together suddenly, and Wilfrid came in. In his prosperity as assistant librarian, he too had taken to dining at the Victoria. Jane signalled to him. She thought he was going to ignore the invitation because he was such a long time hanging up his hat. He was wishing she had not seen him. Far better, he said to himself, not to begin again. But he came to the empty chair at her side.

'Oh, Wilfrid,' she began hurriedly, in a low voice, 'I'm so glad you've come. I ordered a calf's head, and I'm so afraid of what it will be like. It's Miss Clegg's fault. She flustered me; she wouldn't let me sit at a little table. D'you think they'll bring me a whole head, Wilfrid?'

Wilfrid's remote gravity gave way. He laughed openly and aloud, because he couldn't help it. The idea of a whole calf's head tickled him.

'Oh, don't,' begged Jane. 'If they do bring me a whole head, will you pretend it's for you, Wilfrid? Would you mind?'

Maud issued from the kitchen door with a tray. Jane turned apprehensive eyes towards it. But Maud held the tray so high that she couldn't see what was on it.

'Oh, Wilfrid, it's not a joke to me at all!'

Maud came to tower over her with the tray. Jane

sat under her, gone very small. Her eyes were glued to the table, on which appeared from above bread, water, a minute dish with potatoes on one side and carrots on the other, and lastly a plate with a portion of something discreetly covered with parsley sauce.

After a brief stare, Jane shot upright, and helped herself to vegetables with confidence.

'May I have the salt?' she said briskly, looking about her.

A hand across the table guided the ancient cruet, a thing on wheels with a handle, towards her. She looked up.

Mr. Yarde! Had he been there all the time?

She could give no further consideration to the question because Miss Clegg's cruet boggled suddenly and threw out a shower of salt and the spoon.

'Sorry,' said Noel Yarde. 'But why do they have a thing like this?'

'It goes with the establishment very nicely,' said Jane. 'It's like a hansom cab!'

Relief about the calf's head made her speak with unusual gaiety. Every one looked at her. She withdrew a little into Wilfrid's cover and devoted her attention to the calf's head.

'Now, Wilfrid, don't keep it up!' she besought him in a low voice. 'Maud's coming. What are you going to have?'

'I'll have calf's head too, if you'll be kind enough to cut it up for me,' he said, composing his face for Maud.

He usually chose shepherd's pie, or beefsteak pudding, or something that didn't need to be cut up. He was still self-conscious about his single arm.

Jane cut up the food with concealed and maternal

solicitude. Wilfrid was more amicably disposed to her than he had been since that day on Enderby Moor. The calf's head had done it. She was grateful to the gelatinous substance.

Noel Yarde, who no longer went to Stanfield at midday, looked at Jane and her companion with interest. Who was he? What were they talking about? *Westminster Gazette* . . . what? Did she say his poem this week? He wrote, did he?

Noel looked again. He looked as if he did something like that. Poor devil, he'd lost an arm. Poor, poor devil. No golf, no tennis, no cricket—there was nothing else for him *but* poetry.

Noel ordered coffee, and kept an ear on the conversation.

They were an interesting pair, these two.

Then his thoughts caught on his own particular and painful hook, and he sat on at the table with a wan face.

Wilfrid and Jane talked on, finding their old pleasure in each other. Maud bustled to and fro with smoking plates and hearty words.

' Hot-pot's champion. Coffee? Right y'are! Just another minute! She's just carvin' it. She's that partitler, you know. . . .'

The smells of food thickened ; appetizing enough to the hungry, but superfluous to one who has eaten. Noel Yarde got up and went back to his office.

CHAPTER TWENTY

JANE'S days were now like a succession of crammed cupboards that would not shut on their contents. Things fell out in miscellaneous confusion and had to be picked up and put into the next cupboard, from which they fell out again and so on until they positively had to be attended to.

The back premises of 'Jane, Ltd.,' were given over to banging and clanging, but business went on at the front as usual.

'The cuffs a little tighter, Mrs. Mallett, I think. Oh, the noise! I do apologize for it. . . .'

Carpenters came, with their aprons in triangles at their waists and filled the place with the maddening rasp of the saw; plumbers came with noises like Vulcan himself, electricians appeared and disappeared, twisting themselves and their wires into the unlikeliest places. At last there was silence and the smell of paint, and Lily going up with mugs of tea; painters were a thirsty lot, she said. She only wished Bob would be as contented with tea! Now that he couldn't find a job, he was falling back into his old ways. Lily had left Mrs. Chadwick to cleave wholly unto Jane. Jane protested; but Lily insisted. And as Mrs. Chadwick refused to pay an adequate wage, Jane could do no more.

It came to Lily's turn at 'Jane, Ltd.' She brought

a friend, and there was the sturdy sound of scrubbing
and the slop of mops and the squeak of wash-leathers,
from morning till night.   Then the rooms no longer
rang when you spoke ; curtains and carpets caught
your words to themselves and buried them quickly.

During all this time Jane had been flying up and
down the stairs a dozen times an hour, and Mrs. Briggs
had been coming to stand about and see that the work-
men got on as they should.

Jane had engaged Miss Sutton to do the books,
Mrs. Megg to do the alterations, had taken Susie into
the shop, and a little girl to do the errands and the
parcels.   She was looking round for a woman to 'live
in' and clean and cook for her.   The expense of
all these changes alternately alarmed and elated her.
She went several times to Noel Yarde's office to be
reassured.

Almost every day now Jane escaped from the bustle
and upheaval of her shop to go to the Victoria, where
Noel Yarde now openly joined her and Wilfrid.   In
time, the trio took itself so much for granted that it at
last braved Miss Clegg and moved to a side table the
better to talk.   This interval at the Victoria was a
relaxation and a pleasure to each in a different way.
Wilfrid admitted to himself that he liked to be with
Jane.   He 'liked to be with her.'   That was as far as
he would go.   Jane liked to be with him ; she also
liked to be with Noel Yarde.   Noel Yarde had still his
old charm for her ; but she did not indulge in high-
falutin dreams now.   He was married, and she was
too busy.   So busy that the hour at the Victoria seemed
like something left whole, untouched amid chaos—
like a round complete globe held up over a confusion
of bits.

Noel Yarde found himself strangely stimulated by his new friends. They roused him ; they had points of view that he had missed. They had a shared interest in queer twists of life, grotesqueries, odd tags of conversation. Noel Yarde began to look about him with their eyes, and life took on a further depth. Gradually he found pieces of his own to bring to the conversation. Old Godber's nose, for instance. Jane did not know old Godber, the cotton magnate.

' I don't know how you've missed him,' said Noel, pleased that she had. ' He had the most extraordinary nose in the country, I should think.'

' What like ? '

' A real affliction.'

' All bubukles and welks ? ' asked Jane again.

Noel didn't quite know what she meant, but he covered his lack with a smile.

' Like Cyrano's, perhaps ? ' suggested Wilfrid.

Noel didn't know again. But it was a frightful nose, he said. Swollen, enormous, blue. Once seen, never forgotten. And as familiar a landmark on 'Change as the clock itself. But what he wanted to tell them was that old Godber had put up with his nose until he was nearly seventy, always looking as if he were asking you to excuse it ; gentle and diffident and sensitive about it.

' He put up with it all these years,' said Noel, ' but when his daughter came home from China a few months ago with her little son, the baby cried and wouldn't go near his grandfather. The nose frightened him. So old Godber's had an operation on it. They didn't want to do it. Said it might be quite serious, and certainly very long and unpleasant. But he would have it, and now the thing's almost normal and the baby goes to him without a murmur.'

He could see Jane was very interested in that story and he looked round for more. When he couldn't find anything new to tell, he rummaged like an endearing dog until he dug up some old joke-bone that he could lay at her feet to see what she thought of it.

Jane was amused and rather touched when he did this.

'It's a good thing I'm so busy,' she thought sometimes.

Her new premises were now completed. She opened them by giving a mannequin parade ; something new for Tidsley. Everybody came and sat in a double circle in the new room, while the mannequins swayed about, looking contemptuously over the heads of the assembly and uttering a laconic 'seven and a half guineas,' 'ten and a half guineas,' at intervals.

Jane made calm appearances in the room interspersed by rushes to the back premises to superintend the dressing of the mannequins. These exotic creatures stood about in her room in various stages of nudity. When hooks caught in their fashionable hair they called them 'bloody.' Miss Sutton and the alteration hand sent each other glances of intense disapproval. But Jane, in one of her exalted moods, was not shocked ; only interested in their attenuated bodies and scrappy underclothes, the scent of them and their undulations, their painted faces and sophisticated eyes. And when she went back into the new room, she was interested in all the Tidsley women sitting about in the clothes she had sold them. She knew many of their inmost secrets ; she knew their camisoles and petticoats ; their legs and shoulder-blades. She knew their personal habits and found some of them surprising.

Sylvia Yarde was there in pearls and pale grey.

'You know,' said Jane to herself, 'she's gone rather out of date. They don't put that type of face on chocolate boxes now.'

Mrs. Greenwood made loud remarks on the deportment of the mannequins. It affronted her. The girls made ribald fun of her in the dressing-room and Jane wished Mrs. Greenwood could have heard them. It would have given her such a good shock.

That night, when Jane was still tidying up at ten o'clock, Lily arrived and stood among the tissue-paper and cardboard boxes with a ravaged face.

'D'you still want someone to live in?' she began.

'Yes.' Jane folded and packed without pause. She was dead tired, but all this stuff must be got out of the way before morning.

'Will I do?'

Jane looked up.

'Why, Lily, what's the matter? What about your husband?'

'I'm leaving 'im. 'E went off with me antimacassars last night and the plant pots; and last week the rocking chair went—but to-day 'e's taken the wash-stand set—that bonny blue one, *you* know. Well, I'm not standing it no longer.' Lily gulped; her face convulsed. 'It's no good. All me beautiful things gone again—drunk away again. No, I'm not standing it. I'm leaving 'im. I've told 'im.'

Jane got up from the floor. She was so tired that she felt inadequate to the occasion.

'You'll not leave him, Lily. You'll go back, you know.'

'Nay, I'll not. Will I hec as like! Will y'ave me?' she besought piteously.

Jane was in a quandary. She did not think that
Lily would leave Bob for long. But Lily insisted that
she would leave him for ever. The wash-stand set
had done it. She couldn't forgive that. They talked
it out, Jane folding doggedly, limp with fatigue. They
settled at last that Lily should come to ' live in ' on
Monday. Lily was a little brisker after that. She
set the room to rights and prepared Jane's supper
of milk and biscuits. She herself preferred a cup of
tea.

' I'll work me fingers to the bone for you,' she told
Jane. ' I know I'll settle 'ere wonderful. It's a grand
little home is that kitchen and bedroom downstairs.
I'll show Bob I can get along without 'im. Drunken
thing that 'e is ! Thinks I'm so soft I'll stick to 'im
whatever 'e does. Going off with me wash-stand set !
You know it knocks all the 'eart out of a girl. . . .'

She talked on, battering Jane's tired ears with
sounds. . . .

For the rest of the week, Lily was full of talk.

' I'll soon get to know yer ways. We'll be very cum-
fertable, you in your little 'ouse upstairs and me in
mine downstairs.

' I'll get everything shipshape on Monday.

' Well, I'll be 'ere Monday morning with me things.
. . .'

She went away, sturdily independent.

On Monday she arrived pale and with no parcel.

' Where are your things, Lily ? '

' I've got me comb in me pocket,' she murmured.

' But where's your night-dress ? '

' I can sleep in me shimmy.'

' That won't do,' said Jane firmly. ' I'll give you
one.'

'Will yer?' said Lily flatly, without inquiry.

Jane plunged into her own work and forgot Lily. But at six o'clock, when the shop was shut and Susie, Miss Sutton and Mrs. Megg were gone, she went into the kitchen to see how Lily was getting on.

Lily was standing by the fire, looking lost. She gave a flaccid smile as Jane entered.

'Are you ready for yer supper?' she inquired.

'I am,' said Jane emphatically. 'It's been a long day somehow.'

'Long it 'as,' Lily agreed.

'Ah!' thought Jane, looking at her.

'Eh,' said Lily, on the top of a long sigh. 'It's a mess, isn't it?'

'What?'

'This 'ere livin'-in.'

'There now,' cried Jane accusingly. 'I knew how it would be. You said you'd settle, but I knew you wouldn't. Lily, you are a nuisance.'

'I keep thinkin' of 'im with no 'ome to go to . . . wanderin' about.'

'He's brought it on himself,' said Jane. 'But he's right about you; you're soft.'

'I know,' said Lily in a low voice. 'But bad as 'e is, I love 'im.'

'Well, get off home to him.' Jane was exasperated. 'You're no good to me.'

A gleam came into Lily's eye; she looked as if she was going to escape from a prison. Then she sagged back at the fire.

'I don't like desertin' you.'

'Well, you will, whether you like it or not.'

Jane went into the scullery and rattled cups in annoyance.

Q

' I don't like it . . .' whimpered Lily. She sniffed on by the fire.

' Eh, it is a mess,' she said quiveringly.

Jane went back to the kitchen and said more kindly, ' Go home now. I'll get someone else.'

Lily gazed at her over the apron she had applied to her tears.

' I suppose . . . I suppose . . .' she seemed to wonder if she dare go on,—' you wouldn't let 'im come 'ere ? '

' Let him come here ! ' cried Jane.

' Could 'e come and live in too ? ' Lily clutched her apron to her thin breast and went red with hope and excitement.

' Eh, could you let 'im and me live in this little place, and me do all the work and you pay me just a few shillings and me keep ourselves ? Eh, if I could 'ave 'im 'ere and work fer you at same time, wouldn't I be glad ? Eh, I'd be that glad, I'd bust . . .' cried Lily on a sudden high note. ' You know Bob's frightened of you. Oh yes, 'e is, 'e thinks you're such a lady and that clever. 'E wouldn't dare to get drunk 'ere. It 'ud be the saving of 'im.'

' Stop, Lily. You know it can't be done,' said the alarmed Jane. ' I couldn't possibly have Bob here.'

' Eh, but it's a very good thing to 'ave a man about the 'ouse ! There's lots of ladies—single ones and widders—as 'angs an 'at up in the 'all to make out there's a man in the 'ouse. But an 'at in a single lady's 'ouse p'raps might make a misunderstanding— except with a burgular.' Lily was letting herself go now. ' But you won't need an 'at if y'ave Bob,' she finished breathlessly.

Jane burst out laughing.

'Oh, Lily, you're very funny! I wish I could do something for you, but it's no good. I couldn't possibly have Bob here. Do have a little sense.'

'Couldn't you try 'im?' begged Lily. 'With you be'ind me, I feel I'd be able to keep him straight. 'E's not really wild, isn't Bob. What he wants is a job. Look 'ow good 'e was in the war? Champion all the time. If 'e could only drive a lorry fer someone, 'e'd be a grand lad again.'

'But I've no lorry for him to drive,' protested Jane.

'No,' said Lily, going flat again.

'You seem to think I'm a wizard,' said Jane. 'You look to me to put Bob straight and conjure up a lorry . . . but I can't. How can I?'

'No,' said Lily, tears beginning to roll down her cheeks again.

They were silent in the kitchen. Jane gazed uncomfortably at Lily's forlorn little figure.

'But I can't leave 'im,' said Lily hoarsely. I'se 'ave to go back. I don't know what 'e'll come to if I leave 'im. . . .'

There was silence again, and in it they heard someone moving about in the yard.

'What's that?' asked Jane.

Lily went to the back-door and opened it.

'I thought it were you,' she called out sternly. 'What d'you want?'

'Who is it?' asked Jane.

'It's 'im, of course. What d'you want?' she called into the back-yard again.

'I were on'y just bringing you yer wash-stand set. I've put it by th' doorstep.'

'Wash-stand set!' shrilled Lily. ''Ere! Bob, don't go! Come 'ere! 'Ow did you get it out?'

' I got a bit of work this morning——'

' Eh, did yer? And did yer get yer dinner all right? What did yer get?'

' Well, no,' murmured Bob, ' I didn't get any dinner. I didn't want none, though.'

' Did yer get yer tea, then?'

' No—not yet. . . .'

' Come 'ere, you great gormless thing you.' Lily stretched out into the dark. ' What did you go getting that wash-stand set out for before you'd got a bite of dinner. Think that's the sort of thing I want you to do?'

' Well, I oughtern't to 'ave took your set.'

Their voices were muffled. They whispered together in the back-yard.

' Bring him in,' called Jane with resignation.

CHAPTER TWENTY-ONE

I

JANE'S flat was finished. Mrs. Briggs kept quiet about it. Three green chairs in a yellow room with an outlandish mirror in a green glass frame did not constitute Mrs. Briggs's idea of furnishing. She was glad when Wilfrid Thompson added a picture ; though that was not much to her taste either, being a winter wood of silver birches, spectral, lonely, bleached under the fall of night. Mrs. Briggs thought it would look more homely if a sewing-machine stood beneath it.

Jane, however, was enchanted with all. Many a time before she went to sleep she would switch on the light in her bedroom to look again at the ivory walls, the leaf-green paint and the curtains sprigged with magenta. And every time she did it, she was visited anew by amazement and delight that this bedroom, this sitting-room, this bathroom should be hers.

She slept in security and precious solitude above, and Lily and Bob kept guard below. The arrangement was working well, and Lily's faith in Jane's power appeared to be justified. Bob, sober and happy, was driving a lorry for Messrs. Elliott Bros., China Clay Merchants. Jane had reason to be glad that she had cut off the back premises so thoroughly, because Lily sang all day long, swooping up and down the notes of sentimental dirges such as : ' Speak not her name, I loved her well.'

At night, when the shop was closed, Jane often sat alone, gazing at the room and talking to herself. About all sorts of things. People who said ' bin ' for ' been.' Mrs. Sykes-Bayne said ' bin.' It was very attractive. Jane would have liked to speak like that. But she realized the impossibility of it. You'd have to be born to ' bin,' she felt. She tried it :

' I haven't bin to Blackpool.'

It sounded very well in the empty room. People in Lancashire didn't often say ' bin.' They didn't say ' auf ' for off, either.

' I haven't bin to Blackpool.'

So true. A person who said ' bin ' would not go to Blackpool.

She repeated the conversation of Mrs. Batty :

' Mr. Batty likes this frock immensely, but he said to me, he said : " Now there is just *one* thing wrong ; quite, quite wrong. The top button should be moved a little to left. Like this." That is what Mr. Batty says, and, you know, he *knows*. He is *so* particular about my clothes. He won't let me have *anything* that isn't just right.'

So absurd when you knew that Mr. Batty was having an affair with Mrs. Grange and was completely unconcerned with the buttons of his wife.

Mrs. Thomas called underclothes ' neathies.'

' Neathies ! ' said Jane. ' Lord ! '

Her conversation wandered pleasantly and absurdly, her hands hanging over the arms of the chair. She was happy. The business enthralled her. Not only the making of money enthralled her, but the actual life of the shop enthralled her. The people who came

into the shop. Those women, now, whose sole interest
in life was clothes, clothes, more and more clothes.
Jane had often an entirely unbusiness-like impulse to
beg them to stop buying.

There was pathos in this urge for clothes. Mrs.
Mallett, for instance, with some secret flame burning in
her slender body and dark eyes—what did *she* keep
dressing up for? All those clothes she bought—red,
silver, black, white—what for? To play bridge in the
afternoons with the same women in the same drawing-
rooms? To dine with these same women plus hus-
bands, talk a little on singularly unstartling topics, play
more bridge and so home to sleep and a husband to
whom her beauty was a commonplace? Was it for
that Mrs. Mallett clothed herself so radiantly? It
couldn't be. She, in her secret self, held some excitement, some desire or search. She waited—but for
what? She herself probably did not know. Ah,
illusion! Nothing would come. But Mrs. Mallett
would go on dressing up to be ready for it.

Wilfrid began to come sometimes to her sitting-room.
He read his poems and articles to her, and talked about
his friend Sycamore, whom he had met in hospital.
Sycamore was a writer and lived in London. He
periodically urged Wilfrid to join him.

' Why don't you, Wilfrid? ' asked Jane. ' It would
be a splendid thing for you.'

Wilfrid looked at her.

' I'm too poor,' he said.

His real reason was that he couldn't bear to leave her,
and he cursed himself for a fool.

Jane found a very special pleasure in entertaining
Mrs. Briggs. Lily brought up the supper. Mrs. Briggs
liked something savoury with onions in it, and she liked,

with apologies, a glass of stout. They sat by the fire afterwards and discussed everything. On Jane's side, the shop, Miss Sutton, Susie, the new girl, Miss Blakey, Lily and Bob and the customers. On Mrs. Briggs's side, all about Willy and Lizzie and the children, and how Peggy was getting quite fond of her grandma, and how Lizzie had begun to play tennis and getting in with the bridge-playing lot.

Mrs. Briggs was vaguely worried about Albert.

' 'E seems to 'ave got it into 'is 'ead that Mr. Green-wood and Barker, out of the office, are keeping something from 'im. 'E thinks it might be,—only don't you ever mention this, love, because I tell 'im it's an awful thing to think,—'e thinks Mr. Greenwood is trying to do 'im out of 'is proper share of the money. But as I said to 'im, I said, what d'you want any more for ? I said I think you've done very well to get what you 'ave, I said. 'E said it wasn't just that, but because 'e 'ad an uncomfortable feeling that something was up. But I can't think a gentleman like Mr. Greenwood would ever do anything like that. Funny, isn't it ? . . .

' You know, I were flabbergasted at Albert tellin' me about it. It's a long time since 'e told me anything, or asked my advice. But you know I 'ave a good laugh to meself at times, because I can fair see 'im wondering what's come over me.' Mrs. Briggs crinkled up her nose in her endearing fashion and hugged herself closer with her crossed arms. ' I'm a lot more independent nor I used to be. And I don't try to be a lady, either. I just please myself. What should I go fagging meself to be a lady for ? I never got no thanks for trying. In fact, just the opposite. . . .'

The little room was a pleasant place at night. Noel Yarde, who had heard about it from Jane and Wilfrid, looked up at its light as he went home from the Borough Club. He wished he could go up and look at it.

'Strange life that won't let me do even that,' he reflected.

The segregation of the sexes seemed to him ridiculous and petty. A married man was allowed to know one woman only ; his wife. If he found a friend in any other woman, people began at once to pry and to whisper.

Noel Yarde was one of those men, far more numerous than women can believe, who, if the flat truth must be told, enjoyed the War. He had at any rate lived more fully during the War than he had ever done before or since. The War was his greatest adventure, his greatest experience. He had been stimulated by the discomfort and the danger. He had liked his men, had cherished the responsibility of his Captaincy. He had liked, in a boyish kind of way, his uniform and the really excellent field boots that Bull's used to make for him. He thought of those boots, now stuffed with tissue-paper and un-used, with regret.

He had returned to civilian life with great zest.

'Now ! . . .' he kept saying unconsciously. 'Now ! '

As if he expected that life would now begin ; some splendid way of life that would satisfy him wholly and make him completely happy.

But nothing happened. Nothing at all. Every-thing was very soon precisely as before. Noel began to feel less eager about life. There was nothing, it appeared, to be eager about.

He fell into a dull routine. He went to the office, where Varley did all the work really, he ate his luncheon, he went back to the office, and idled away the afternoon, generally dropping into the Club for tea, to look at the papers and play a game of snooker with Bolton or somebody. He came home at night and had dinner. After dinner he read the paper from end to end, even reading silly bits of news about the birth of a second lot of triplets to Mrs. Brown of Tooting ; letting his eyes run over anything until as often as not he dozed, waking to find it was almost time to take the dog down the hill and back again before going to bed. And another day was gone.

He was beginning to get introspective and moody. There was no effort in his life. No need to use his brain to make any more money ; Sylvia had plenty. No opportunity to use his limbs and his muscles.

This ' home ' idea, he told himself, was all wrong. It might have been all right once, when a man had to fight for the bare necessities of life, had to kill and hunt or be killed and hunted himself, and when women had to do all the cooking, washing, nursing, weaving and so on. But there was no meaning in home life nowadays when you had enough money to pay other people to do everything for you. Sylvia had done more than he had, he admitted. She had at least performed the primitive task of bearing a child. But he felt useless in the house.

His life was stagnant. There was no spring of happiness to freshen it and keep it moving.

He was utterly at a loss with Sylvia. She was treating him to a long fit of the sulks, because he had insisted on moving back to Greystones. She took up her abode in a different quarter of the house and met her husband only on the common ground of the dining- and drawing-rooms. He didn't know what she did with herself. She didn't take much interest in her son, and said many

a time she wished he had been a girl, because a girl was
so nice to dress. She went to Cooper's for coffee in the
mornings with her mother, and in the afternoon she
looked at the fashion papers or walked across to Stanfield to say how much she hated living at Greystones.
On Fridays she and Noel went to the theatre, whether
the play was good or bad, because every one else did.
On Mondays they went to the second house at the
Hippodrome for the same reason, and in between times
they went to the Pictures. It was maddening. It was
deadly.

They went out to dinner and had people in to dinner
in the limited permutations and combinations that
Tidsley society offered ; and Noel found them all
equally dull.

It would have been different if he had loved Sylvia ;
but he did not.

It took him a long time to dare to whisper to himself
that she bored him. But once he had done it, he went
on :

' She bores me. And I probably bore her. And
there we are—for life ! '

II

Jane was in London. All day she had been rushing
about the purlieus of Great Portland Street with buying
notes. She had interviewed the hateful Mr. Metton.
He had whispered that she should wear a petticoat
because he could see her legs, and pretty though they
were, he thought he ought to mention it. He asked
her to go to some Mrs. Paton's where they could always
get a drink out of hours. He never learnt.

In Venner's now they received Jane with deference.
All the big hats in the business came, one by one, to

speak to her now ; they all asked her if she had been to Ascot or whatever was on.

She had finished at last with sleeves and bits of lace and ' nice numbers ' and the ' newest thing ' and ' copies of Lelong and Patou,' and she emerged into the top of Regent Street with a sense of escape. Clothes sometimes made her sick.

She looked at the little church with the candle-snuffer spire. She loved it ; specially at night, standing white against the back-cloth of the dark.

She crossed Oxford Street and continued down Regent Street, and there, in a grey suit with a felt hat, his eyes on the patch of sky over Oxford Circus, was Noel Yarde coming up. Jane went and pressed herself against Liberty's window. The silks from India and China swam before her eyes. She felt in the hollow of her back as she did when boys with snowballs were behind her.

' He won't see me. Perhaps he will. Forty-five-and-eleven a yard. Forty-five-and-eleven. Forty-five . . .'

' Good afternoon.'

He was there. She laughed upwards with sudden happiness.

' Fancy meeting you here ! ' he said.

' Oh, you can come across half Tidsley here any day of the week ! '

' Are you here on business ? '

' Am I ever anywhere on anything else ? '

' Pity,' he murmured. ' Have you finished yet ? '

' Just.'

' Could you have tea with me ? '

Jane paused ; she didn't know why. Then said, ' Yes, I could, thank you.'

They turned. She lost all volition. A moment ago
she had been heading along Regent Street, cutting her
own way through life—and now she gave it up and
drifted at his side. It was a queer feeling. The
continuous stream of people flowed past them, pressing
them close together. They hardly spoke, and when a
Fuller's door appeared before them they went in as if
they had thought of it.

They sat at a little table and had tea. Jane's eyes
kept coming back to the red bow on the sugar tongs.
When did you come? I came yesterday. So did I.
The bow on the sugar tongs. When are you going
back? On the six train. So am I. Really! The
bow on the sugar tongs. I left my car at Preston.
You can get home an hour sooner if you go by car
from Preston. May I give you a lift? How kind of
you! The bow on the sugar tongs.

Jane had a piece of chocolate cake that seemed six
feet high. He had nothing at all.

They went out into Regent Street and drifted about.

' D'you know,' said Jane, ' I find the greatest
pleasure in just walking about and not being known.'

He agreed heartily that it was one of the worst
features of provincial life. You were so known. If,
in absence of mind, you walked into a lamp-post, the
fishmonger knew. And sitting in the tram, you had
to keep such a guard on your face ; you daren't look
worried, or absorbed, or even over-cheerful. It was
relief, pure relief, to come to London and be merged.

' Look at the church,' said Jane suddenly, as she
came into view of it again.

' I always do,' he said, looking at her.

' Do you ? ' said Jane.

Suddenly her spirits soared. She felt so happy that

she would have liked to stand where she was in Regent Street and hold the moment and say ' I am happy.'

But she walked on with Noel Yarde and nobody had any idea of the wild joy that was in her.

They went to Euston. They had a carriage to themselves. Fate seemed to be conspiring with them. Or against them. They were together for four hours. And at Preston they got into the car and drove away from the town. The night clove before them and flowed in behind them like a soundless sea. The trees appeared in solemn procession, all, it seemed, reaching with their arms to the stars. Every blade of grass was distinct, as if newly painted in a blue-green ; there were stiles in the hedges, over which, it seemed, you might step into the pit of night.

Jane was aware of his hands on the wheel ; all she could see of him ; two hands. She turned in the seat so that she could see them all the time, even when looking at the trees.

CHAPTER TWENTY-TWO

I

JANE'S greatest asset had been her superb health, but now it temporarily failed her. She was suddenly filled with such a dreadful lassitude that she went to bed without a protest when so ordered by Mrs. Briggs's doctor. A rest, he said ; and she thought she would be glad of it.

Once in bed, however, all desire to rest left her. She was ridden by nerves for the first time in her life. Through the long hours of the day and the longer hours of the night, she tossed and turned in the bed she had once thought so comfortable. Her thoughts ran about in her head like mice, and she couldn't trap them.

Mrs. Watson's dress . . . would it come in time for that wedding ? Had Miss Bootle understood that that lace wouldn't *do* ? Had Venner's repeated that georgette number ? Would Mrs. Watson's dress come in time for that wedding ? Had Miss Bootle . . . oh, where in the name of Heaven would she find a house that stocked the *right clothes* ? Was Noel Yarde wondering why she didn't go to the Victoria ?

She had Miss Sutton up and harangued her from her bed, and lay down again with a temperature to wonder if Noel Yarde missed her at the Victoria.

She had Lily up and gave her instruction on a dozen things, and alone once more, she thought of Noel Yarde.

Under her scattered thoughts, the thought of him persisted like a tune in her head that she could not get rid of.

She remembered his hands on the wheel of his car. To Jane it still seemed a rather wonderful thing to drive a car. His hands in the night. . . .

She wrenched her mind from him. If only she had been able to be busy !

' Oh, God . . . what am I doing ? ' she asked, and in turning over again dragged the sheets tightly about her body like a mermaid's tail. ' Spending my life selling clothes to women. Clothes ! Of all the frittering, silly jobs . . .'

She had never thought like that before. But all her life seemed to have gone sour in a few days.

Her thoughts crept stealthily back to Noel Yarde. She tried to project herself into his life. What did he think of ? What did he look like going about the rooms of his house ? What did he talk about to his wife ? Did he love her ? Somehow Jane knew he did not. Noel Yarde was not yet moored anywhere.

That thought gave her a fierce pang of joy. It also startled her. She steadied herself.

' What am I doing ? Where am I going ? '

She must stop thinking about him. She must. She looked despairingly round the room. If only someone would come. . . .

Suddenly she remembered Marcus Aurelius. She ran in her night-gown to her little row of books and seized the shilling volume. She went back to bed and turned the pages with determination. Long ago she had come across Arnold Bennett's remark that everybody should read Marcus Aurelius.

What could she find to keep her from thinking of Noel Yarde?

'How easy it is to repel and to wipe away every impression which is troublesome or unsuitable.'

'Is it indeed?' thought Jane. She read on.

'Wipe out the imagination. Stop the pulling of strings.'

She didn't agree. Her imagination was one of her greatest pleasures. Though here it was leading her wrongly. . . .

'The soul is dyed by the thoughts.'

'My soul must not be dyed by Noel Yarde. . . .'

'The cucumber is bitter. Throw it away. There are briars in the road. Turn away from them.'

He made it sound easy enough.

She turned her pillow, and smoothed the sheets. She settled herself more comfortably, and read on.

'Art thou angry with him whose armpits stink?'

She threw back her head and laughed aloud. It had given her such a delicious shock!

Marcus Aurelius was all-embracing. Even armpits came in for his Olympian attention. She laughed and laughed. She poked for a handkerchief to wipe away her mirthful tears.

She must tell Wilfrid that. No—hand him the page! It must be read to get the full effect. She picked up the book again.

When Lily came up with a glass of egg and milk Jane was asleep, still smiling.

II

She kept her Aurelian serenity to such good effect that she was up in her sitting-room by Friday morning. As she was reading her *Manchester Guardian* the telephone bell rang. She picked up the receiver and in a tranquil voice said :

' Hello.'

' Hello.' At the answering voice, her heart began to beat thickly. ' Yarde speaking. Are you better ? I'm so sorry you've been ill. I wanted to ring up before, but I was afraid to disturb you. Are you sure you're fit to be up ? I'm so glad you're better. . . . What I wanted to say is . . . er . . . I have some papers here for you to sign. May I call round with them ? Are you sure you're fit to be worried ? This evening on my way from the office, would that do ? Thank you. I'm so glad you're better.'

Jane replaced the receiver with a trembling hand. She stood by the telephone as if he were still within reach. His voice speaking like that—suddenly to her ! His voice ! It had shattered her peace. It was all to begin again now. No, no, it wasn't ! Marcus Aurelius could not quell this strong tide of happiness that flowed all through her. He was coming—in the evening ! What a long time to wait ! Papers to sign ! What papers needed to be signed in such a hurry ? He was coming because he wanted to see her !

It is a long day when something is to happen at the end of it ; a day wasted, deliberately got through. Jane wandered from the fire to the window. She looked out at the market square, where people crossed and re-crossed and assembled and scattered, like ants with umbrellas.

Perhaps the umbrellas alone distinguish us from ants, she thought.

Lily at last brought up her lunch on a tray.

' How are you getting on downstairs, Lily ? ' asked Jane idly, from her chair.

'Champion,' said Lily heartily. 'I'm just going to clean up. I'se wash the curtains through this afternoon. Just freshen them up a bit. Yes, I'm getting on champion. Bob's taking a lorry to Rochdale to-day. I was up at six making him some sangwiges. You know, I'm fair put to it at times to know what to make them sangwiges of. Sardine, I make, and cheese, and cold beef . . . but 'e likes belly-pork sangwiges best.'

'What?' asked the puzzled Jane.

'Belly-pork.'

'What is it?'

'What is it? 'Ave you never 'ad it? It's pig's stomach, of course; y'ask for belly-pork in the shop, then they know what you mean. Very tasty. I'll get you a bit if you like.'

'Not yet,' said Jane. 'I don't think I'm strong enough.'

'No, well . . . p'raps it would lie a bit 'eavy,' agreed Lily.

She descended to her lower regions, and Jane wore away the afternoon.

At half-past five she sat tensely in her chair, listening for his coming.

The Cathedral lay on her knee, but her eyes were fixed on the yellow wall opposite. Suddenly the blood ran up into her pale cheeks; a door had opened and shut downstairs. Lily was coming up. He was here!

She made an effort and presented an indifferent exterior to Lily.

'Mr. Thompson wants to know if you can see 'im for a few minutes.'

The tension slackened in Jane's body. It was only Wilfrid. How awkward that he should call just now!

'Ask him to come up,' she said.

Wilfrid came up. In the fold of the papers he carried were violets for her.

'I got them from an old man by the Market House. I thought they would be nice ones; they looked dim and wet under the light there—but they don't smell much, I'm afraid. I said to him, "Do they smell?" and he said, "Well, you can tell wot they are." Anxious to be fair, you see. How are you?'

He looked at her carefully to see.

'I'm quite all right now,' she said.

She held the violets in her hands and by and by she laid them on her knee.

They talked. Wilfrid sat on the other side of the fire leaning forward. Jane thought of the pages in Marcus Aurelius that she was going to show him. But she would not show it to him now; he would stop too long if she did. She hoped Noel Yarde wouldn't come while Wilfrid was here.

But he did. They heard him coming up the stairs. Wilfrid turned his eyes inquiringly to the door and then to Jane. He saw the colour come into Jane's cheeks, and her eyes darken in spite of herself. She got up to greet Noel Yarde, and Wilfrid's violets fell to the floor unnoticed.

'Mr. Yarde has brought some papers for me to sign,' said Jane.

They sat together in the green chairs before the fire and awkwardness fell on them.

'By the way,' said Wilfrid, breaking a silence, 'it was very kind of your father-in-law to write to my mother about her Dacre Mill shares.'

'Did he?' Noel turned a surprised face on Wilfrid.

'Yes, he wrote yesterday. She has some shares—

three hundred or so, and he advises her to sell at once.
It's exceedingly kind of him, because he doesn't know
her, of course. Perhaps he knows she's a widow, with
no money, and he wants to do her a good turn. She's
very grateful.'

' I don't understand . . .' stammered Noel. ' I
thought they . . . Old Briggs said they'd go up
three times higher yet. . . .'

' Mr. Greenwood's just taken over the chairmanship,
or something, hasn't he ? ' asked Wilfrid.

But Noel pursued his own line of thought.

' Are you sure he said sell ? '

' The letter's here.' Wilfrid drew it out of his pocket-
book. ' I was going to thank him for my mother.'

Noel read the letter and handed it back without
comment.

' Would you mind doing nothing at all until I've
inquired into it ? ' he asked Wilfrid. ' I feel sure
there's a mistake.'

' I don't see how there can be,' said Wilfrid.

' There *is* ! ' said Noel sharply. He was disturbed
and alarmed.

Wilfrid was suddenly annoyed by his tone, and infuriated to be in a position to be helped by either of these
men. He was hurt, too, by the sight of the violets
still lying on the floor. He picked them up and laid
them on the table.

' I must go,' he said.

' Don't sell, Thompson,' implored Noel. ' Let me
look into it. I'll let you know to-morrow.'

' Very well,' said Wilfrid. ' Good night.'

He went abruptly, shutting the door to leave them
together. He was filled with bitterness.

It had come to that, had it ? He knew she liked

the fellow, but he hadn't thought she had him in to
see her. What right had he to come to see her?
What relation could he possibly have with Jane that
would bring her happiness?

And she had all but stepped on the violets. . . .

With the old unhappy passion in his heart, Wilfrid
walked on through the damp spring night; on and
on, over the top of Zachary Brow where the cottages
stood in a cold row for all the winds to blow upon;
down into Stoney. It had stopped raining, but the
hedges and trees and the grass gleamed wetly and the
breath of the earth rose visibly under the moon. Wilfrid
came to a halt against a black wall. He leaned his
elbows on it and stared wretchedly before him.

In the silence of the night, he heard a horse chewing
the grass.

On the top of the wall, between his elbows, a small
round cushion of moss caught the moonlight on tiny
oval water-drops held up on threadlike stems.

Wilfrid's eyes fell on it at last.

' The perfect little thing ! The gem ! ' he cried,
bending down to it in delight.

It might have been put there to comfort him.

Each soul has its solace ; Wilfrid found his in such
as this.

CHAPTER TWENTY-THREE

I

JANE was aware that she was being keyed up, day by day, to an intenser life. Her nerves were taut; her blood ran too easily, it seemed, in her veins, rushing up into her cheeks at the slightest provocation ; disgracing her, she felt. Her body was restless and her mind never at ease ; preoccupied always with Noel Yarde. Everything he was and did was of supreme importance. So that when he told her he was playing in a Tennis Tournament she felt she must go and see him play, see him in his own setting, among his own friends.

With a feeling of guilt and embarrassment, she went. She found what she hoped was an obscure seat on the Grand Stand. There was a smell of new wood and canvas mixed with faint confused scents of Coty. All round Jane were the women she knew as customers, wearing the clothes she had sold them. They smiled and nodded to her, but she felt cut off from them. There was an invisible counter between her and them. She had never envied them in any way before ; she had thought their lives, as they lived them, would bore her to death ; but to-day she saw that they had one advantage at least. They could play games. She longed to be able to play tennis as they did ; to be so skilful and quick ;

to be out there on the green courts, absorbed in the game.

Noel Yarde's wife was on the front row of the stand with her mother.

'Why can't her mother let her go about with women of her own age?' thought Jane. 'She hangs round her daughter's neck like a millstone. She's ruining her life. But I don't suppose either of them knows it.'

Sylvia was watching the courts with no great interest. From time to time she opened her bag, took out a little mirror and rearranged the golden flakes of hair that showed under her hat. Her fingers were very deft at this; as if they were well used to doing it. She shut her bag again and looked round at the other women. Jane thought she detected a faint wistfulness in Sylvia's gaze—a lostness.

Ah, there he was! He had come into the centre court to play a single. He was pulling his sweater over his head. There were his arms and his neck. Jane had never seen them before. He looked taller and thinner in his flannels. He hitched his trousers up a little and moved to his place. He gave a rub to his nose with the back of his hand. It was somehow endearing. Jane glanced swiftly at Sylvia to see if she felt this. But Sylvia's blue eyes were as blank as ever.

'Doesn't she take an interest in *anything*?' thought Jane.

Noel Yarde began to serve. Jane was astounded by his speed and strength. She half rose out of her seat, her lips parted. She remembered that she mustn't do that and sat down again. Her eyes darted after him wherever he went; she never looked at the other player.

Goodness, but he was beautiful! She had not

known he was so beautiful as this; his lean hips, his
long stretch of arm and leg, the way his head was set
on his neck. How he played! His shirt clung wetly
to his back. Was he winning? Jane hadn't an idea,
and daren't ask. Her eyes followed him unceasingly.
Now he was going over to the other side—further
away. Oh, why? But she could see his face now;
he made that half-grimace every time he served. He
looked very young and determined. Oh, determined
to death. She almost laughed outright!

He was coming back to this side now—walking face
towards the stand. He looked straight at her. For
the fraction of a second he paused in the hitch he was
giving to his trousers. His eyes deepened and concentrated. He had seen her. He returned to the
game.

Poor Jane! Her calm was shattered. She sat
under the striped canopy, surrounded by excited
spectators, but she hardly dare look on any more.
She knew, suddenly and without doubt, that she loved
him. She loved him. She lowered her eyes in case
anyone should see. When she lifted them, she met
his again. The same deep look. Did he love her?
Was it love that it meant? She sat there, clasping her
cold hands against her knees. Her heart beat so hard
that she felt her body was too thin for it.

When the match was over and Noel Yarde lost for
the moment in his sweater, Jane slipped from the stand
and went home.

II

They knew now, but they made a pretence of not
knowing the next day at the Victoria. They thought
to deceive each other and Wilfrid. They talked, but

over and over again they found themselves falling
silent—coming suddenly into the deep secret consciousness they had of each other.

Wilfrid averted his eyes from them. Their faces
tortured him. He bitterly acknowledged Yarde's
advantages. His good looks, his grace of body due
to playing games from earliest youth.

'I never played anything,' said Wilfrid sourly.

Noel's manner and bearing he put down to public
school.

'I went to the Higher Elementary and left at fourteen.'

Noel was unassuming, even diffident, but he held his
own anywhere without effort.

'You could love him,' admitted Wilfrid.

He even pitied him at times. He could see no
happier issue for Yarde than he could for himself.

But he hated him too. When he saw Yarde come
through the swing doors of the Victoria, rake the room
with his eyes for Jane, and make for her like a man
who has fought through an invisible crowd to get to
her, it was as much as Wilfrid could do not to rush
away from that place of plush and aspidistras, out into
the street, the market, anywhere away from the sight
of those two in love.

But he sat on in his place.

'What about those Dacre shares?' he asked
brusquely, to shatter their radiant isolation.

Noel Yarde started visibly.

'Oh, hold on to them,' he said hurriedly. 'Hold
on to them. I'll let you know when to sell. It was
a mistake.'

That was a euphuism indeed!

He had been to Stanfield the night before to let

Charles Greenwood know he knew of the letter. His father-in-law was considerably startled. He stammered something about it being a mistake; that he had been, as a matter of fact, on the point of writing a second letter to the woman to tell her not to sell after all, but if Noel would let her know through the son, it would be all right.

'Extremely fishy,' was Noel's verdict as he looked at Charles Greenwood.

Greenwood seemed to read his thought, and began on an explanation so minute that Noel was almost convinced that it was genuine. He was anxious to be convinced. He didn't want to think his father-in-law was a scoundrel. He hardly wanted to think about the incident at all. He wanted to think about nothing but Jane. . . .

Jane herself was afraid now of what they had come to, and kept away from the Victoria.

Noel was made desperate. He could manage, he told himself, as long as he saw her, even so little. But when he did not see her, he could not go on.

It was after three days without a sight of her that he posted himself at her side-door towards eleven o'clock at night. He knew all her ways now; he knew she went 'round the Square' for air the last thing at night. He watched her go and now he waited for her return. He leaned against the wall in the dark alley. He was possessed by a tumultuous happiness because he was going to see her; because soon— soon that pale little face would bloom in the dark like a flower, her hand would lie in his, healing him.

'I mustn't startle her, stepping out of the dark suddenly,' he thought, and stood where she should see him.

' Oh . . .' she said, coming upon him. Her hand
flew to her throat.

He had prepared what he was going to say ; papers
to sign and could he come up ; all conventional and
ordinary. But instead of saying it, he took her hand
and burst out :

' Where have you been for three days ? Why do
you do this, Jane ? Why do you keep out of my way ?
Do you do it on purpose ? '

' Hush ! ' murmured Jane. ' Don't talk like that ! '

Her heart beat furiously. She was terrified at
being dragged off the conventional plane.

' Can I come up with you for a minute ? Do let
me. I haven't seen you for such a long time.'

' Oh, you oughtn't to. . . .' It was almost an
appeal to him to help her to refuse. But he did not
hear it.

' Let me come—just for one moment. And I have
a paper for you to sign—really.'

Jane opened the door suddenly. They went up to
her sitting-room. She turned on the lights.

She made an effort to get back to convention and
safety.

' Won't you sit down ? '

They sat in two arm-chairs. Jane tried to prop the
finger-tips of one hand against the finger-tips of the
other, but they shook and would not meet. She
clasped them tightly and looked into the fire. She
did not see that his hands were trembling too.

There was silence in the room. The dying fire
collapsed softly in the grate.

He was gazing at her with all his love in his eyes.
Jane felt that, and with difficulty looked at him in
return. She smiled ; a strange, quavering smile ; an

appeal again to him to help them through this tense moment. He stood up, and unconsciously Jane stood too.

' I suppose I must go.' He, in his turn, clutched at a straw.

' Yes,' said Jane.

But they remained standing, near together. Jane's head was bent, her fingers twisted. She saw his hand move to hers, and shut her eyes. She must move away ; she ought to. Why couldn't she ? Why did she stand there, trembling ?

He put his arms round her and her face lay against his coat. How his heart beat ! Or was it her own ? Her eyes were still downcast ; she couldn't lift them. Neither of them knew how long this strange, silent embrace lasted.

He loosed his arms at last, and she turned away from them at once. Turned her back and stood shaken to the heart. She heard him go ; down the stairs and out into the night.

CHAPTER TWENTY-FOUR

JANE held off now in earnest. She reminded herself sternly of his wife and his son. It must stop now, she told herself, before it got any worse. She did not go to the Victoria, or round the Square at night. She gave him no chance to see her.

She was glad to have a great deal of work on hand. There was all the autumn buying to do. She went to London and spent her days in the wholesale houses. At night she went to the best plays she could pick out. But no problem could seem as great as that in her own life, and no portrayed love distract her from her own. She came away enfevered, rather than allayed.

The nights were the worst. The help of Marcus Aurelius had to be most determinedly evoked to enable her to get to sleep in some sort of temporary Stoic calm. But when she fell asleep at last, her thoughts, released, flew straight to Noel. She dreamed dangerously of him. In reality he had not kissed her, but in dreams she knew the feel of his lips on hers— and so vividly the feel of his shaven cheek against hers that, waking suddenly, she had to turn on the light to convince herself that he was not really there.

The sight of the small, still room, with the sprigged curtains hanging motionless against the bland walls, seemed to her so empty, so lonely, that she turned out the light on it and wept.

Noel Yarde tried, too, to stem the tide. He surprised Sylvia one evening by offering to read to her. He didn't know what to read ; he picked *Emma* at random out of the bookcase. Sylvia was pleased by this attention and smiled like a child through the first page or two. Then her thoughts began to wander, and by and by she got up and went out of the room, quite forgetting that he was reading aloud to her.

The book fell from Noel Yarde's hand. He stared before him.

'Jane . . . Jane . . . Jane . . . Jane. . . .'

Her name hammered in his head and his heart.

Love, although they were apart, grew like a living thing between them, feeding on dreams and thoughts. So that when Noel, at the end of his resistance, came into her flat, they had both travelled far along the same road and faced each other with dilated eyes and shortened breath.

He had come, he said, only to ' put things right.' Thus do lovers deceive themselves.

He shook hands with her, in a fashion nothing short of ridiculous. But as they were both entirely without a sense of humour at this time, it did not matter. He sat down in the arm-chair opposite hers and smoked rapidly.

' I had to come . . . I hope you don't mind. . . . I'm afraid I must have upset you the other night. How long ago was it ? It seems years. Twelve days ago . . . wasn't it ? I know I ought never to have come up that night. I oughtn't to have touched you. Forgive me.'

' No more blame to you than to me . . .' said Jane, very low.

Silence. A tram clanged its way round the market-place.

' You see, I love you,' he said, across the distance between them.

Her eyes answered him.

' God . . .' Noel threw away his cigarette and clenched his hands on the chair.

' And there's nothing for us,' he said.

' I know.'

They sat on, staring into the fire in silence. Another tram went by in the Square.

When he looked up, he saw that she was crying.

With a groan, he knelt by her.

' Jane . . . Jane . . . don't. You'll kill me ! '

He tried to turn her face to his. She pressed away from him. But he was strong and desperate and their lips met in their first kiss.

' Oh, my darling . . .' he cried. ' What shall we do ? '

But now in reality she had his face against hers, and she was filled with happiness and peace.

She pressed backwards from him and looked at him with shining eyes.

' Darling—we can go on. You love me and I love you. It's enough, Noel.'

She caught him up into her exaltation.

' Jane . . . you're so wonderful ! '

He wrapped her more closely in his arms. Her body was pliant against his. Love taught her, in one moment, ways she had never known—words she had never used before.

' Nothing for us, you said ! But there's love, my

dearest. You must go on doing your duty. We can't go any further—but as long as we know we love each other, we can do what we have to do,' she told him.

Holding her in his arms, scanning her radiant face, he believed her.

'We must play the game. We will, Noel. We mustn't even kiss again.'

'Oh, Jane!' He pressed his face into her neck.

'No, my darling one. . . .' She pressed his head closer with her hands.

'But I'll go back to the Victoria,' she said. 'We'll be able to see each other—and all the time you'll know I love you and I'll know you love me.'

'Oh, Noel. . . .'

'Oh, my beautiful,' he said, looking at her gravely. 'You're right. It is enough to be on the earth together.'

He kissed her hands, pressed them to his face, and then put them away from him with resolution.

He came back again to enfold her once more, and press his lips to hers again and again.

'Go now,' she whispered, pushing him gently away. She couldn't bear too much.

'Yes,' he said. He went to the door, then turned to look at her. She stood with her hands still at her throat where he had kissed her, her face transfigured.

'Good-bye.'

'Good-bye.'

He went down the stairs like a man in an ecstasy.

s

CHAPTER TWENTY-FIVE

I

BUT though they were strong, they were not strong enough. Little by little they gave ground.

First they must never kiss. So long as they knew each loved the other, they need not kiss.

Then they must kiss ; they could not keep from it. But it did not hurt anyone.

Then they must see each other, be together sometimes. It would be all right so long as they saw each other sometimes. That was all they wanted.

II

They were swept out into the full stream of love. They tried to clutch at the bank, thinking to save themselves, but they were whirled out further and further, until they at last could no longer ignore the desperation of their plight.

They met in the country ; in the stony lanes and the black woods as far from Tidsley as they could get. Spring was hanging out her pretty signs, but they hardly noticed the lambs'-tails lose their winter stiffness and dangle loose and golden on the willows, or the first celandines bloom like stars low under the hedges. They walked with wan faces or stopped to clasp each other despairingly. Their talk was now always the same.

'We can't go on like this. You know we can't, Jane. Life without you is nothing.'

He talked about his marriage.

'A failure from the beginning. I knew almost at once. I can't explain why. I don't blame Sylvia. She gets no more out of me than I get out of her. We have no point of contact. Never had. Our life together is simply negative. We never quarrel. There's not as much even as that between us.'

Jane listened. She tried to beat down the fierce exultation in her heart. She mustn't be so glad that he had found nothing apart from her. It was disgusting to be so glad. . . .

'I'm thirty-five,' he went on. 'I might go on for another forty years. I can't face it, Jane. Not now. I might have gone drubbing through year after year if I hadn't loved you. I didn't know, before I loved you, that there was anything different. My darling, I had the poorest expectations of life before I knew you. Isn't it strange?'

He halted and caught her in his arms, looking down at her as if he could never look enough. Her hair was dewy in the mist, and her skin fresh and cool under his lips.

'Oh, why is it all so difficult?' cried Jane, in sudden despair. 'Why couldn't we have been like other people—with everything nice and ordinary, getting engaged and married and growing old together? Why? Why, Noel?'

'Oh, my dear . . .' He shut his eyes and sighed sharply.

They walked on, the stones rolling under their heedless feet.

'Sylvia . . .' said Jane, slowly, feeling for her

words, ' I don't think so much about. I suppose I
ought to, but I don't. It would hurt her to lose you,
but it would hurt you to lose me. I weigh your hurt
against hers, and of course I care more about yours.
If only one has to be happy I'd rather it was you. But
your son, Noel. I simply can't bear the thought of
hurting him.'

They went on in silence.

' It's strange,' Noel began again. ' I must be
devoid of paternal feeling. It's been left out of my
composition. I don't remember, half the time, that
I have a son. I hardly ever see him. They're always
busy in the nursery with him when I leave in the morning, and when I go home at night he's asleep. And
the nurse, quite rightly, thinks it's bad for me to turn
the light on to look at him then. It will go on like
that until he goes to school, I suppose. Then he'll go
away to some public school and on to Cambridge.
Then he'll strike out for himself. He'll live a life of
his own. I shall hardly have a hand in it at all.
Have I to stand about here, being a background for
him, refusing life for myself?

' He'll have plenty of money, you know. It's not
as if he or Sylvia were dependent on me, or
needed me in any way, except as a domestic addition. . . .

' My life's flat and heavy. I never look forward
because a future like the present doesn't interest me.
I don't take any interest in my work ; for one thing
it doesn't matter whether I do or not, and for another
I dislike law. There's nothing at home for me. I
hate going home. . . .'

The exultation died in Jane's heart ; she was filled
with pity for him. His life seemed to have been such

a poor thing ; so lacking. Even if she felt, vaguely, that he could have made something better of it, it only made her feel that he needed her to love him, to help him to live.

She reached up to put her arms round his neck and kiss him with a passion of tenderness.

' My poor lost boy . . .' she murmured. ' Oh, Noel, I love you. . . .'

He crushed her to him.

' Let's break away from it all, Jane ! Let's start again. Let's be together, my darling. I want you so. I can't live without you. Oh, Jane, we can't miss each other. We can't let each other go. This is the best life has to offer—do you realize that ? '

Jane submitted to his kisses in silence. They walked on again, hand gripping hand.

' Let's go to South Africa, or somewhere, and hack out a new life. We'll have to go through a lot of mud. But I'll keep you out of it as much as possible. I'll put it openly to Sylvia and the Greenwoods before I go. I'll not sneak away. It only needs courage, dear.'

' Courage to hurt other people,' said Jane. She felt wretched yet helpless.

' It won't hurt them as much as it would hurt us if we went on without each other.'

They argued. They considered from every point of view. But stronger than any argument or considera-tion was their love, growing from day to day, consum-ing them entirely.

III

Mrs. Briggs came to see Jane. She sat on the edge of a chair, her face puckered with anxiety. She did not notice Jane's pallor, or the effort she made to listen. She burst out with her trouble at once.

'Eh, I am worried about Albert. I don't know whatever's 'appened to 'im. For the last two days 'e's acted so strange I 'ardly know 'im. 'E won't eat anything. I can't tempt 'im with nothing. 'E won't sit in the same room as anybody else, and when I go in to where 'e is, I find 'im staring in a terrible funny way, as if 'e'd 'ad a stroke, or something. I daresn't ask 'im what's the matter. I 'ear 'im walking about 'alf the night ; up and down ; up and down. Eh, love, I'm bothered. Whatever can it be ? What can it be ? '

' Cotton's so bad,' said Jane. ' Perhaps that's it.'

' I on'y wish it were that and nothing else,' said Mrs. Briggs, wiping her eyes. ' But surely 'e wouldn't take on like that about losing money ? They're all losing money, I'm told. Buttertubs 'as got half its looms idle this week. But I don't 'ear tell of Greenwood's mills doing badly. I can't think it's that, love.'

Jane tried again to find a reason for Albert Briggs's strange behaviour. But in an undercurrent of thought she was wondering how good, simple-hearted Mrs. Briggs would take her going away with Noel. She would have to tell her before she went ; it would be awful. Mrs. Briggs would be shocked, uncomprehending. She'd be hurt, too. It seemed a dreadful way to behave to Mrs. Briggs when she'd been so good to her. Jane looked at her friend's face with such sadness that it penetrated Mrs. Briggs's anxiety. She attributed it wrongly.

' Nay, don't you take on about it, love. It's nothing to do with you. And of course it *might* turn out to be

nothing but bad business. Don't look like that, love.
Come and give me a kiss. I must be going. I want
to be at 'ome when Albert comes in.'

Jane took her downstairs, her hand warm under
Mrs. Briggs's arm. She closed the door on her and
came back to her chair. She sighed and pressed her
hands over her eyes.

What a relief it would be to get away . . . to have
burnt your boats at last !

IV

The pattern of life, once compact and simple, was
breaking up ; a disintegration had set in.

Wilfrid came to her flat, haggard but firm-lipped.

'I've come to say good-bye,' he began abruptly.

'Good-bye ? Where are you going to ? ' cried Jane,
startled out of the preoccupation that nowadays enwrapped her.

'To London.'

'To live with Sycamore ? '

'I don't know. But I'm going,' said Wilfrid, staring
at her with burning eyes. 'I'm getting out of here.
My mother has sold those Dacre shares. Yes, on
Yarde's advice we've sold them for enough money
for me to get out of Yarde's way. Funny, isn't it ?
One of life's little ironies, isn't it ? '

'Wilfrid . . .' faltered Jane, paling.

'Oh, I can't stand any more,' cried Wilfrid, jerking
his head backwards. 'I don't blame you much.
Only I think you might have left me alone
after the War, when I tried to keep out of your
way.'

'I thought you didn't care any more then,' she
protested. 'I never wanted to hurt you, Wilfrid.

You've always been my best friend. Why should I want to hurt you ? '

' Well—I don't know. . . .' He spoke at random in his despair ; he said anything. ' But I can't stand seeing Yarde . . . You love him, don't you ? You can't say you don't love him ? '

Jane was silent.

' There you are, you see ! ' he accused her. ' You love him ! D'you think I haven't seen it coming all these weeks ? You remember Blake, I suppose . . .

> " A traveller came by
> Silently, invisibly,
> He took her with a sigh."

' It's been just like that, hasn't it ? I knew it would be. I've been a damned fool. I've loved you too much always. Well, I'll remove myself now and you and Yarde can go on—to what ? Ah, well. . . . I won't inquire. Good-bye.'

He strode out of the room and closed the door firmly after him. Jane stood trembling, staring at the door. It opened again.

' Jane,' he said, more calmly, but breathing hard as if he had been running, ' if ever you want me, write to this address. See—I thought I could cut clean off from you—but here I am leaving this thread ; and I shall go on hoping you'll pull on it some day, I suppose. Don't despise me too much. Good-bye.'

He put a piece of paper down on the table near him.

Jane took a step towards him.

' Wilfrid . . .'

' No,' he said in refusal.

He closed the door again and ran swiftly down the stairs.

She wept because she hurt him, but she was glad
he had gone.   Far better that he should leave than be
left ; he would suffer less that way.   Perhaps never
know that she had gone.

CHAPTER TWENTY-SIX

WHEN they had decided to go, they were calmer. As other lovers waited for marriage, so they could wait for each other.

They arranged that Jane was to sell her business and to go away ; then Noel was to sell his practice, wind up his affairs, tell the Greenwoods and his wife, and follow Jane. It was all arranged.

Jane took the first step. She began, wondering at herself, to cut the ground from under her feet. Venner's had many times suggested that they should buy her business and she had refused their offers with gay scorn. But now she intimated to them that she was prepared to consider it. They immediately, with concealed eagerness, jumped at it. Mr. Belton himself came down to talk things over and incidentally, by putting up at the White Hart for a few days, find out all he could about the business and the town itself. He went away well satisfied, but puzzled. Why anyone should want to part with such a little gold-mine as that shop, he couldn't understand. He had been suspicious at first as to its finances, but he had been obliged to admit that his suspicions had no foundation.

'You never can tell with women,' he said to himself. 'They reckon they're as good business men as us. She is, I admit. But they're not sound. Let them get a fancy into their heads and they'll chuck everything

up, and go back on everything they've maintained
before. Well, well . . . good thing for us men,
sometimes ! '

The agreement arrived. Jane sat at her table in
the window high above the town and read it through.
It gave her a fierce pang to have this parting with her
shop set out in unmistakable terms.

And how strange to be handing over the destinies
of Lily and Bob, Miss Sutton, Susie, Mrs. Megg and
the others to strangers ! She had arranged, minutely,
with Venner's that they were all to be kept on until
they failed to please the new manager. It looked safe
for them, since Venner's had declared themselves completely satisfied with the way she had run the establishment. But would anybody see that Susie was dosed
with cod-liver oil in the winter ? And would anybody insist on getting a cheerful word out of Mrs.
Megg from time to time ? Would anybody keep Bob
straight ? Although he seemed all right. He hadn't
lapsed once from the straight and narrow path of
the good lorry driver since he had been under her
roof.

She had always thought she lived by herself and for
herself, but now it appeared that several people
depended on her for fair-dealing and some happiness.

She sat at the table, looking out over the town. It
lay huddled blackly under the pale sky. It was an
ugly place, a small place, a dirty place—and yet it
meant a great deal to her. She knew it in all its
aspects. She knew the streets, the shops, the market,
and the market people ; the tram-men, the postmen,
the policemen. The clang of the tram-bells, the tones
of the church bells, the different mill-hooters—Buttertubs, and Primrose and Stikes and all of them. She

knew the men in the offices and the shops ; the young
girls and the mothers of families. She knew the High
School hats and the Grammar School caps. And the
Park and the scanty open spaces, and the hills beyond
and the woods. What other place would she ever
know so well again ?

No other place. Noel and she would be wanderers
on the face of the earth. Outcasts. Jane knew she
was dreadfully respectable at heart ; she knew she
would suffer.

No home. No children. What a bitter prospect !
No children.

' But I would rather have you, my darling . . .'
she said gravely, having thought it all out.

She folded up the agreement. She would not sign
it until Noel had seen it. She put it away into the
desk, but the strangeness it had brought with it persisted. She felt she belonged no more to the flat or
the shop. She was already gone in spirit, projecting
herself into the future where she would be with Noel,
and no longer concerned with what went on in the
present.

She wrote again to Mrs. Rhodes about her unpaid
account, threatening her with a solicitor's letter ; but
she would be gone before the time came to carry out
the threat. She interviewed the travellers and ordered
the winter goods, but she would be gone before they
were delivered.

No one, neither customer, nor Miss Sutton, Susie,
Lily, Bob, seemed to matter any more, nor even to be
quite real. She lived in the isolation of a deep, warm
dream. Troubled at times very roughly, but never
completely broken. Not even by the appearance of
Noel's child in her salon.

She was standing idly in the middle of the empty room when she heard a small high voice counting :

' One, two, sree, five, six, ten, eight, sirteen . . .' and low down in the doorway appeared a round felt hat, above a pair of wide blue eyes. The child stood and stared at Jane and the room. He attempted to clasp his hands across himself.

' Hullo,' he observed.

' Hullo,' said the unsuspecting and enchanted Jane. ' How did you get here ? '

' Up the steps. Mummy's coming.'

' Is she ? '

' Yes, in a minute. She's going to buy a new dress. Can she have that one ? '

' Yes, if she wants it.'

' Can she have that one too ? ' he inquired, advancing. ' And this one . . . and this one . . . and that one . . .'

He ran from one dress to another, making a game for himself. Jane could not resist the temptation to catch him as he passed her, but he struggled free, his eyes fixed on the dress he wanted to touch next.

' There's Mummy,' he shrieked, rushing to Sylvia Yarde in the doorway.

Jane smiled to cover the violence of the emotion that beset her when she realized that this was Noel's child.

' Don't pull my coat like that, Toby. No, don't . . . let go ! I shan't bring you out again without Nurse if you aren't good.'

' I are good,' said the child, standing with his legs defiantly apart. The next minute, however, he hung his head and grimaced to keep back the tears. He made a silent recovery and leant against the legs of a chair while his mother told Jane what she wanted.

Jane ushered her into a fitting-room.

'One moment . . .' she murmured, and hurried away. She sent Miss Sutton to attend to the customer and fled upstairs to her room.

She closed the door and knelt on the floor by the arm-chair. She pressed her hands against her eyes. That baby . . . to take his father from him . . . how could she do it?

If only she had never seen the child! She would never be able to forget him now. She would never be able to forget this son of Noel's whom she had bereft of his father.

'It's terrible . . . all this. . . . No wonder people keep to their marriages; it's so hideous getting out of them.'

The greenish light thrown upwards from the lamp in the street shone on the ceiling, leaving the base of the room in gloom. Jane crouched low on the floor. It was like being at the bottom of a pool. She felt as cut off from all warmth and contact as if she were.

She moved at last and turned on the lights. She shivered slightly with something like fear of herself. Because, in spite of her bitter foretaste of remorse, her decision to go with Noel remained unshaken.

CHAPTER TWENTY-SEVEN

I

TOWARDS half-past five of the afternoon, Varley came into Noel's office to announce a client.

'Mr. Albert Briggs, sir, of Greenwood and Briggs.' Varley coughed to excuse himself. This information might possibly be considered superfluous to the son-in-law of the senior partner of that firm.

'Why does he come at this time?' said Noel testily. He had been watching the minutes on the slow face of the clock, waiting for it to be six o'clock so that he could go to see Jane. She had said on the telephone that he could go at six, and all day he had been in a madness of impatience, longing for the sight of her, feverish, worn with longing as only a lover can be. And now old Briggs was here, delaying him. . . .

'Show him in,' he said to Varley, as if it was Varley's fault Briggs had come, 'but you come in at five to six and remind me of my appointment, and don't you forget.'

Varley looked aggrieved; as if he ever forgot anything. Mr. Noel might give him his due.

Albert Briggs came into the office, and Noel, disguising his impatience, advanced to take his hand. He had hardly time to remember that Jane had said Briggs's hand was like a pound of pale sausages,

before he sobered into the reflection that something
was wrong with the man.

'Sit down, sir, will you?'

Albert Briggs sat down heavily by the desk and
startled Noel further by covering his face with his hands.

'What is it? Are you ill?' burst out Noel, at his
side in an instant.

'Nay . . .' Mr. Briggs answered from his hands.
'I'm not ill.'

'Something pretty bad,' thought Noel in silence.
'Poor chap.'

'Eh, lad.' Mr. Briggs looked up haggardly. Noel
noticed that he had reverted to the Lancashire speech
he had tried so hard to throw off. 'Lad, I'm here on
a bad business. . . .'

He got up from his chair unsteadily and put his
hands on Noel's shoulders.

'And I'm sorry to tell you, boy, it'll hit you pretty
near as hard as it's hit me. But you're a young chap.
Your life's before you. You'll get over it. But I'm
done for.'

'Hit me! What d'you mean?' Noel gripped the
wrists on his shoulders and stared into the small, un-
utterably wretched eyes of Albert Briggs. 'What's
the matter?' he asked again on a sharp note. Already
some chill warning crept to his heart.

'Can anybody overhear us?' Albert Briggs looked
round nervously. 'Don't let anybody hear us. They'll
all know soon enough, Just see that there's nobody
about.'

Noel, sick with misgiving, hurried out to tell Varley
he was on no account to be disturbed, and hurried in
again, locking the door behind him.

'Now then . . . what is it?' he asked urgently.

'Anything to do with my . . . with old Greenwood?
Not dead, is he?'

'Dead,' sneered Albert Briggs, 'I wish to God he
was dead. I'd shoot him with my own hand, if it
'ud do any good. But it won't.'

'Come on, man,' cried Noel, striking the desk with
his fist. 'What is it?'

Albert Briggs leaned forward across the desk.

'He's done the Income Tax people out of something
like a hundred thousand pounds; he's made false
returns for more than twenty years—without me getting a smell of it. I've never suspected a thing. I've
been the bloodiest fool as ever walked the earth—
I've trusted him like my own brother. . . .'

Noel put out a hand to stop his talk.

'What did you say? What's he done . . . do you
say?' He was entirely taken up with trying to grasp
the significance of Albert Briggs's first words.

'He's going to be arrested, I tell you. . . . It
can't be hushed up. There might have been a chance
once—but he's gone on lying and falsifying the books
worse than ever. He's got their backs up all right now.
There are people down from London already. He'll
go to gaol all right, and me too probably—and I never
knew a word about it. Never such an idea come into
my head. It's him and Barker did it all together.
More damned fool me! I saw them as thick as thieves
together—and I never suspected a thing. Chaps'll
laugh at me all right. My name 'ull be a byword on
'Change. They'll say I deserve to go to gaol for being
such a bloody simpleton. But what about my poor
wife? How'll she stand it? And what about your
wife and your son? Nice grandpa for him, isn't it?'
Albert Briggs laughed bitterly.

The clock on the wall struck six unnoticed.

' My God . . .' whispered Noel.

' And what in the name of hell has he done it for ? '
went on Briggs savagely. ' We've done fine these last
twenty years. He's worth two hundred and fifty
thousand if he's worth a penny. It's been for sheer
crookedness and love of lies as he's done it, and
may God punish him for it. He's brought us all
down. Me and my lot and you and yours—innocent
folk. . . .'

Albert Briggs choked back a sob.

' Can't hold my head up again—even if I get
off. . . . My poor wife . . . and my boy. . . .'

Noel was completely silent. His silence penetrated
Albert Briggs's preoccupation. He put his fat hand on
the bent head.

' Come, lad, don't take on too hard. Your name'll
come out of this all right. Your father was the most
respected man in the town. It's your name your
son'll bear, and it's up to you now to protect your wife
and build up your own position. I warn you all
Greenwood's money 'ull be needed to pay the fine and
defend him in the case, and even then he'll go to gaol
as far as I can find out. They're after him all right.
Nay, your position's better than mine. I'll never get
a job again. Who'll employ a fool ? And cotton's
bad and going to be worse. I'm done for. And all
because I trusted a scoundrel. Done me out of thousands, too. Defrauded me out of my proper share
. . . and yet nobody'll believe I knew nothing about
it. . . .'

Varley knocked on the door and said discreetly
through the crack :

' Shall I wait, sir ? '

'No, go home, Varley . . .' said Noel in a strange, thick voice.

The fire went out, leaving the room chill. They did not notice it. They sat on in their places, each preoccupied with his own sharp problems, Albert Briggs throwing in more detailed information as it occurred to him.

Noel was roused at last by the booming of the market clock.

'Nine o'clock? It can't be. . . .'

'It is,' said Albert Briggs, moving stiffly. 'Well, we'd best get home to our wives, poor things.'

But it was not of his wife that Noel was thinking. Jane had been waiting for him three hours— and with what dreadful news he was now to meet her.

He groaned aloud.

'Don't, lad,' implored Albert Briggs. 'Bear up. Save yourself. There's a terrible lot more to come.'

II

Jane had waited three hours for Noel. She hated waiting at all times ; she waited badly, going through the whole gamut of impatience, resentment, anxiety and back again. She had given him up and was becalmed in despair, in the arm-chair, the agreement papers for the sale of her shop in her lap, when she heard his ring ; three short pressures on the bell of her side-door. She flew down the stairs.

'Oh, Noel, I thought you were never coming ! '

He merely gripped her hand, but she knew at once that something had happened.

'What is it ? ' she whispered on the stairs.

He moved his head, dumbly.

Jane shut the sitting-room door and stood with her hands clasped at her heart.

' Noel—tell me ! '

He didn't know how to begin, it seemed.

' What is it ?   Noel ? '

He put his arms round her, leaning his head on hers, as if he needed her to support and help him. Jane put her hands under his shoulders in a passion of tenderness and fear.

' Jane,' he began. ' Old Greenwood . . . he's been cheating the Income Tax people. It's very serious. He'll go to gaol ; he'll be tried at the Assizes. . . .'

Jane dropped her hands. She pushed Noel away from her, peering into his face.

' Noel . . . what ? '

He said it again, more clearly, more fully, more despairingly.

' Noel ! '

Other words failed her. She sat down in the arm-chair, her lips parted, her eyes gazing at him uncomprehendingly. Her mind ran about like an ant, picking this bit up, that bit up, piecing information together. Noel was silent, waiting for her to grasp the full significance of what had happened.

He had not long to wait. He saw realization dawning in her eyes—and fear.

' Oh, Noel—it means that you and I . . . It means you can't come with me ! '

She threw out her hands as if she were falling somewhere deep and sudden. He caught her and held her close, trying to comfort her.

' Does it mean that ? Does it ? ' She spoke desperately, urgently, pulling at his collar.

He pressed his face against hers.

'We can't tell what it means yet, my darling. But I'm afraid, I'm afraid, Jane!'

Jane stood silently in his arms. Her hands dropped slowly from his collar.

'There's no question about it,' she said, turning away. 'You can't leave your wife and child now. I see that. I see it all. . . .'

He tried to draw her near again. He felt an extreme need to hold her close. But she was making a great effort to stand the blow that had fallen, and must do it alone. She put off his hands.

He was profoundly hurt.

'Jane—don't treat me like this! As if it's my fault.'

'Fault?' echoed Jane dully. 'Oh no. But hadn't you better go home?'

She wanted so much to be alone.

Noel made an inarticulate sound. Everything was failing him—even Jane.

He leaned on the mantelpiece, turning his head away, his hand covering his mouth. The situation was too much for him; too many thoughts, conflicting ideas of duty, love for Jane, anxiety to get alone and think, schemes for ways out, stuffed his head and made him helpless.

Jane turned her head and looked at him. His attitude, his fingers drumming on his cheek, moved her dreadfully. She went to him, feeling as if her heart had actually broken within her. She lifted his arms from the mantelpiece to herself.

'Oh, my darling . . . my darling . . .'

They enwrapped each other despairingly. A sob shook Noel.

'Oh, Jane . . .'

Jane made a violent effort at recovery. She dared not be swept away by this storm.

'No, Noel . . . don't let's give way. Don't. You're too tired. We'd never stop. Don't, don't, Noel.'

She pushed him into the arm-chair and knelt beside him. She pressed her hands over her aching lips.

'See, Noel. See, darling. I'm all right now. And so are you. Let's be calm.'

She forced down the welling misery in her heart. Time enough for that. All time. . . .

She held Noel's hand, pressing it to her cheek.

'I can't leave Sylvia and Peter in this mess. It's unthinkable. I'm chained for life. I've got such a job thrust on me as I never thought of, I can tell you. . . .'

And Jane saw, with pangs of love and jealousy, that he was already squaring his shoulders to meet it.

For three hours he had faced a future without her, and by the almost pitiful adaptation of the human being, he was already used to the idea.

'Quite gone from me already,' thought Jane, her eyes fixed on his face. 'Even his thoughts. . . .'

She persuaded him at last to go home. It was becoming more and more necessary to her to be alone; pressing on her like a pain. She felt, if he stayed longer, she would cry out:

'What about me? What about me? What about me?'

Let her get him away.

She found the hat he had thrown down. She kissed him quickly, with no lingering. He thought again how strange she was and went downstairs puzzled.

But before she had shut the door on him, his thoughts returned to his own urgent problems. How to tell Sylvia now. . . .

Jane went back up the stairs and locked her door. She threw herself down by the arm-chair again. Now she could weep. Now she could give way. But no tears came ; no relief. She knelt there in stiff calm.

' Well . . .' she said, getting up at last. ' I'm alone again. Nothing new in that.'

She leaned on the mantelpiece where he had leant.

The gold and shagreen clock he had given her struck midnight.

Jane sighed. She must go to bed. To-morrow would come, and she must be ready for it.

Mechanically she shook up the cushions and opened the windows. She turned out the lights and went into her bedroom. She undressed and got into bed. She abandoned herself to the dark.

She soon turned on the light again. Impossible to lie there with that torment of thought.

Not going. Noel was not going with her. She had lost him. Lost him. He was Sylvia's husband and his son's father now for always. Never hers.

A rage of jealousy of Sylvia filled her. A fool like that to have him for ever . . .! He would go home to her every day and take up the habits of marriage again with her. Jane pressed that sharp thorn further in and winced intolerably. Yes—he would. Sleep with her. Give her more children.

Oh, it was unbearable ! She turned over and groaned into her pillow. She felt sick at what she forced herself to see.

' I can't stand it. I can't stand it,' she cried, leaping out of bed.

She walked up and down between the bedroom and the sitting-room, wringing her hands and weeping with a distorted face.

She got back into bed and pulled the sheets over her body.

Oh, God—what dreadfulness filled her ! What awful desires and thoughts !

What was the good of this virtue—these high denials ? Why hadn't she taken him when she could have had him ? Gone—without any soft considerations ? It had been idiotic of them to think it made what they planned to do any better by telling other people about it. Silly, self-deceiving fools they had been ! Worthy. They wanted each other madly, terribly—and they had stayed to arrange business matters. Served them right, then ; they were baulked.

She got out of bed again and went to crouch over the dying fire.

'What shall I do ? What shall I do ? ' she whispered.

She stared at the rusty ash.

What was there to do ? What would life be without Noel ?

'I can't bear it . . .' she whimpered.

All her body shivered under her thin night-gown.

Mechanically she reached under the chair for the agreement papers she had let fall when she heard Noel's ring.

Some of the grim bitterness she had felt earlier returned to her.

'I might have sold out,' she said, with a twist of her lip. 'And a nice hole I'd have been in then.'

She put the papers back into her desk, and sighed again.

' I must get to sleep. Somehow I must get to sleep. . . .'

She picked up her Marcus Aurelius and went back to bed. She turned over the pages.

' For nowhere either with more quiet or more freedom from trouble does a man retire than into his own soul. . . .'

Of course, it was all rot !

' For nowhere either with more quiet or more freedom from trouble does a man retire than into his own soul. . . .'

She read the words aloud, saying them over like a charm, making herself follow them.

Lost . . . lost . . . lost him.

The book fell from the bed.

This love . . . this wonder . . . over.

There was nothing for her now. She could never share him with Sylvia. Never share. . . .

She reached again for the book.

' For nowhere with more quiet or more freedom from trouble does a man retire . . .'

' Oh, poor boy . . . poor boy ! How awful for him, too ! '

Tears flooded her aching eyes. She held the book over her face and wept. She wept until she was worn out, and the dawn breaking over the roof of the Free Library found her asleep with stained cheeks and the copy of Marcus Aurelius still in her hand.

CHAPTER TWENTY-EIGHT

I

THEN followed strange heavy days in which she seemed to stand in complete darkness, seeing nothing at first, but through which she began to make out what lay before her.

Noel came in again, distraught with anxiety and fatigue. He moved restlessly about her room, talking rapidly.

'It will all be out soon. God! You've never seen such a tissue of lies. And he goes on with them! He goes on with them! The poor fool can't be made to understand that the game's up. He's driving Briggs mad—and me too. And I haven't told Sylvia yet. I daren't tell her. I feel I can't stand any more at present.'

Jane forgot herself when he was with her. She was filled with pity for him. She listened to him and tried to help him as best she could. She would have pressed his tired head to her breast and soothed him, but he gave her no chance. He was too restless, too preoccupied for any such ministrations of love.

He went and she was left alone again to face her own desolation. She sat far into the night, staring at it.

The next day, Mrs. Sykes came in with the first intimation that the news was out. She was so excited that she called Jane 'my dear.'

' My dear . . .' she began, with shining eyes, ' I've
heard the most astounding thing. You'll never
believe it. The most astounding thing ! Mr. Greenwood—you know, *the* Greenwoods—he's going to be
arrested for cheating about his Income Tax. I said
to my husband, well, I said, doesn't everybody ? But
this is for hundreds of thousands it appears. That is
going too far, isn't it ? Rather much, isn't it ? One
moment, the hook has caught on my lace ! But, my
dear Miss Carter, aren't you astounded ? A J.P.,
three times mayor, and so very strait-laced. But
my husband says they're always the worst. What a
blow for Mrs. Greenwood ! She'll have to lower her
head a little now—and her voice, won't she ? And the
daughter—so spoilt and pampered ; nobody good
enough for her. How will she like it ? I'm terribly
sorry for her husband—a nice boy, Noel Yarde—far
too good for that girl, I always thought. Oh, is that
Mrs. Temple's voice ? Molly, is that you ? I say—
have you heard about old Greenwood ? Oh, my
dear. . . . Come in. . . .'

The news spread. Tidsley was a-seethe. No event
of such delicious excitement had happened in the town
since William Farrar kidnapped his own wife in 1890.
This affair was so magnificent ; no tuppenny-ha'penny
little townsman—but Greenwood, Greenwood himself, the richest man in Tidsley, and he'd swindled
the Government on such a princely scale and been at
it for a score of years. Tidsley was secretly proud ;
if blot there was to be, let it be a decent-sized one.

Everybody was pricked into new life. People spoke
to each other who had never spoken before. Mr.
Chadwick spoke to Jane.

She had been driven out into the streets by her own

restlessness and met him just after he had heard the news. He was rushing up to Fenwick's, without a hat, and almost ran into her arms.

'Well,' he cried out, 'have you ever heard of such a thing as this? MR. GREENWOOD! MISTER GREENWOOD! . . . Miss Carter, you could knock me down with a feather. With a feather!' he repeated solemnly. 'It just shows how you can be taken in.' Some recollection of how he had been taken in by her seemed to pierce his present amazement, because he bowed with sudden stiffness and hurried on.

Jane went back to the shop. They were very busy in the fitting-rooms, said Miss Sutton. Everybody seemed to have come in at once.

Jane, pressing her hands over her eyes—they felt like stones in her head from lack of sleep—assumed a conventionally placid mask and went to help.

How trivial to her now seemed Mrs. Mallett's preoccupation with a white evening frock!

'Make it tighter, will you?' said Mrs. Mallett, pulling the dress close across her body. 'I always wear my clothes very tight.'

She turned about and surveyed herself with passion in the glass walls of the cubicle.

Jane gave instructions to little Miss Pepper, who knelt on the floor with pins.

'Here . . . and here. . . .'

There was a shriek from the salon itself.

'I say . . . old Greenwood's going down the street!'

With one accord the cubicle doors flew open and the occupants, in various stages of undress, precipitated themselves to the windows. . . .

' Where?   Where? . . .'

' There, by the Arcade. . . .'

' Good heavens ! '

' How dare the man show himself ? '

' He's got a little bag ! '

' Full of lies, probably ! '

' Or bullion for the Government ! '

' They wouldn't have it now ! '

Joany Sherwood was in her petticoat, and Sheila Penn half in and half out of a red frock ; Mrs. Mallett held lace across her breast—Aphrodite trailing foam —but portly Mrs. Smith had been in such haste to see Greenwood that she had omitted to pull down her dress at the back, and though from the front she was more clad than any, from the back she presented the grotesque spectacle of a pair of legs clothed in cambric knickers of antique cut and needlework frills. But as attention was concentrated on Mr. Greenwood she was, for the moment, safe.

' I'm so sorry for Sylvia. . . .'

' Are you?   Do you think she will feel it ?   Does she ever feel anything ? '

' Mrs. Greenwood is too wonderful.   She behaves as if the Government were the criminal party and will find itself in gaol before long.'

' I know !   I met her this morning, and was going to bow and pass on because I thought she might feel uncomfortable, but she bore down on me, shouting louder than ever, and reminded me that I'd promised to get my tickets for the Nurses' Bazaar from her.'

Mr. Greenwood had gone from sight, and the excitement died.   They turned from the windows to the business of clothes.   And as the flick of a white scut sends rabbits to their burrows so did the back view of Mrs. Smith send customers and assistants, with one accord, scuttling to cover. The air was heavy with stifled intakes of breath, and faint squeals of distress from Joany Sherwood's box.

'Allow me,' said a discreet assistant as the unconscious Mrs. Smith was preparing to leave the premises.

II

The day Charles Greenwood was arrested, Jane went to see Mrs. Briggs. She was ashamed to have so long forgotten her.

She found Mrs. Briggs in her rocking chair and Albert Briggs staring out of the window as if he had been doing it for a long time. At the sight of Jane, Mrs. Briggs jumped up with as much alacrity as her years would allow and ran forward.

'Well . . . love! Well, love! I am glad to see you. Come in. Albert, now, you don't mind Janey being here. Don't go out of the room, Albert.' She intercepted her husband's passage to the door and got him to the fireplace. 'Sit you down here, and don't be so foolish, man. Sit here, Janey.' She managed them both into place and sat down herself between them.

'Of course you've heard,' she began significantly to Jane.

'Yes,' said Jane.

'You'll have been wondering why I didn't let you know myself,' said Mrs. Briggs, 'but I've had all my time taken up, love.' She looked anxiously towards her husband.

'Oh yes . . .' said Jane again.

She was embarrassed, nay—moved by the sight of Albert Briggs. He was nothing but a shadow of his old self; all his brisk prosperity gone, the shine gone out of him, his ruddy cheeks pallid and fallen in, even his clothes hanging on him. His eyes were haggard.

'Well, they've arrested him,' he said suddenly in a hoarse voice, looking at Jane with a mixture of humility and appeal. 'Marvel to me they didn't arrest me too. I suppose everybody expected them to.'

'Albert love,' said Mrs. Briggs, leaning over to put her hand on his and speaking as if she were again taking up a long argument, 'you're being downright silly. What should they arrest an honest man for? You're an honest man and everybody knows you're an honest man. You've had good proof of that to-day. They've arrested them as is guilty—Mr. Greenwood and that Barker. You can rest easy a bit now. Rest easy, Albert love, do.'

He turned his wretched eyes on her and his face relaxed a little. He lifted his hand from under hers to press it in his own.

'Eh, Mother,' he sighed, 'I'm wearing you out, aren't I? You're a grand little comforter, though. I don't know whatever I should have done without you. But I'm a ruined man, Miss Carter,' he burst out again. 'Ruined.'

'Now, Albert . . .' broke in Mrs. Briggs.

But he went on:

'Ruined. Every penny we have 'ull go to pay that fine. The partnership's responsible for liabilities incurred by a partner. And I was a partner!' He laughed grotesquely, shaking his body silently. 'I was a partner! Or rather I was the danged fool that left my money in the business—on'y took "drawings," if you know what that means. Consequence is that there's thousands owing to me that'll go to pay this fine. Round about three hundred thousand pounds it'll be, you'll see. So 'ere I am at my age, landed without a penny and without a job, with no home to take my wife to, and my son ruined with me—in the same mill too. Nice mess I've landed them in, haven't I ? '

Jane was aghast. She had not realized that the Briggses were involved like this. She was ashamed of herself for not having known.

' Oh—will it really all have to go ? ' she cried, seizing Mrs. Briggs's hand.

' All,' shouted Albert.

' But it's not fair. You've done nothing. Why should you suffer for what Greenwood has done ? It's cruel. . . .'

' It's the Law,' said Albert Briggs grimly. ' If I'm such a danged fool as to mix myself up with liars and cheats, the Law'll make me pay—and I don't blame it, either. Marvel I've got off without going to gaol, I say.'

Jane gazed into their faces, dumb with alarm and amazement.

' Will it all have to go ? ' she asked Mrs. Briggs again.

' Yes, it'll all go,' said Mrs. Briggs. ' Albert's right. We've not got a penny.'

' No—you can't say that,' said Jane suddenly. ' What about that thousand due to you out of my business ? '

Mrs. Briggs and Albert stared at her, their mouths alike fallen open.

' You've got that thousand, you know. And it's yours, Mrs. Briggs ; they can't claim that.'

Mrs. Briggs with some difficulty found her voice.

' You don't mean to say . . .' she began.

' Eh, well,' she began again, gazing wonderingly at
Albert, ' I don't know what's happened to me these
last few days, but would you believe me, I'd forgotten
I'd ever lent you any—and what's more, I'd clean forgot
as I've got one hundred and thirteen pounds in the
Savings Bank at this moment. Well, 'ave you ever
known me to be such a simpleton as to forget that?
A thousand! You don't mean to say I've got a
thousand? Nay, come, love, you're putting it up to
please me.'

' Indeed, I'm not,' protested Jane. ' It's a thousand
if it's a penny, and you can realize it now if you like.'

' Well . . .' gasped Mrs. Briggs.

' What? What're you talking about? What thousand?' urged Albert Briggs.

' Mrs. Briggs lent me a hundred and fifty pounds
when I set up for myself. She put it back into the
business with her profits year after year and now it's
a thousand. You can go into it all. You'll find
that's what's due to her. I know, because I have just
been into it all.'

Albert Briggs turned to gape incredulously at his
wife.

' Mother!' he cried.

She was red in the face and confused between
apologies and pride.

' Well, Albert . . . you see, I 'ad too much 'ouse-
keeping money. I couldn't use it, so I put it by, and
when Jane 'ere needed a bit of money, I lent it to her.
I didn't tell you, love. It was no good bothering you.
But you see how lovely it's come out. Eh, it's a god-
send.' Mrs. Briggs clasped her hands ecstatically.
' Fancy a thousand pounds turning up like that!

U

Nay, love, are you *sure* you're not making it out to be
more to please me?'

She peered into Jane's face, seeking the truth.

'I'm not! I'm not!' Jane protested. 'I'm so glad
it should have turned out so well for you. You've
been so good to me. It makes me so happy to think
the money's done well enough in my hands to help
you now.'

On mutual impulse, she and Mrs. Briggs kissed
heartily.

'Eh, bless you!' said Mrs. Briggs damply. 'To
think . . . well.'

She went to Albert and pressed her face against his.

'To think I should be able to bring out enough
money to get a little 'ome together,' she said, 'and
keep us going. . . .'

Albert Briggs stood up and put his arms round her.

'Well, Mother,' he said, 'you've flabbergasted me!
Fancy you going about in your little quiet way making
money while I've been losing it! Eh, you are a deep
one!'

The first smile for weeks appeared on Albert Briggs's
ravaged face.

'Am I?' Mrs. Briggs looked up at him, her face
puckering delightedly.

'You are an' all!' he said, squeezing her shoulders.
'But seriously, Miss Carter,'—he turned to Jane,
whom they seemed to have forgotten for the moment—
'this means a lot to me, if it's really so. It'll keep
ruin from us. It'll keep us on our feet, and help my
son, too, until we can get other jobs. That is, if I
ever get another job.'

'Now then,' scolded Mrs. Briggs. 'Don't talk silly,
Albert. Of course you'll get another job. They'll

jump at you. Best cotton man in the town. You know you are. You'll make plenty of money yet. Not that I care if you don't, to tell the truth. Let me get us into one of those little Corporation 'ouses, parlour type, you know, and let me get to me own work without any of these starchy maids, and I won't want to move again for the rest of me life. And you won't need to be ashamed of living in a Corporation 'ouse, neither, Albert,' she told him. 'They're very nice people living in them, retired folk, and such-like. The Corporation 'ouses was built for working-men, I know, but you don't need to be afraid, they've never got into them. You'll still be among the better-end, Albert.'

'Pah!' burst out Albert. 'I've had enough of the better-end as you call them. I've had my lesson. Give me my own kind. Give me honest plain folk as you know where you are with.'

He remembered the slow, silly walks with Mrs. Greenwood up the Road, and blushed.

'Well,' said Mrs. Briggs briskly, 'I'm going to 'ave a cup of tea now I've got a thousand pound be'ind me. D'you know, Janey, 'e's 'ardly let us eat anything since this business came out? 'E says we're not entitled to a penny we spend. 'Ave you ever? Well, I'm going to 'ave me tea now, and what's more I shall send Polly out for a bit of tripe. Take your 'at off, love. Nay—now you must stay and tell us a bit more about this wonderful thousand.'

CHAPTER TWENTY-NINE

I

NOEL came into the room where Jane had been sitting for a time she had lost count of. He was very tired, with lines of fatigue round his eyes, and a new, stern set to his mouth. He sat on a low stool at her feet and leaned his elbows on the arm of her chair.

She smoothed his forehead, with all her love in her fingers. She longed to talk to him about the problem that faced her, but dared not add to his anxieties. If only he would ask her what she was going to do. . . . She was waiting for that.

'I've managed to get Sir Charles Transom for the defence, and Kearns and Wilmot, but of course there's not the slightest hope,' he said wearily. 'Not the slightest.'

He was lost again in dismal conjecture. But he moved his head under her hand as if he liked the touch of it, and she kept on stroking his temples and his eyelids.

'Three weeks to-morrow, the trial,' he went on. 'God! The work to be done before then—and all for nothing.'

He raised his head to look at her.

'Isn't it incredible—incredible—that this should have happened to us?' he said. 'Old Greenwood working like a mole in the earth all the time we were making plans for happiness? I'm done for, you know, Jane. I'm here for life. They all depend on me now. In all sorts of ways. I had to send the nurse away yesterday. I found her at the end of Hill Rise with about six other women and prams, all gossiping about the case, with Toby hanging on every word. That sort of woman isn't fit to look after my son. So I sent her off. She said she was glad to get out of such a family.' He laughed shortly. ' I shan't get another. Sylvia must look after Toby. But I have to do a good deal for him myself. He's rather hard to manage at present. He won't let anybody put him to bed but me, the little beggar !'

The look of pride in Noel's eyes gave Jane an extraordinary pang. She averted her face so that he should not see.

' Toby's such a jolly little chap. Isn't it rotten luck for him that this should have happened?'

' Awful,' said Jane, in a strange voice.

Noel moved until his head rested against her knee. ' What peace I feel when I'm with you, Jane. . . .'

' Do you, my darling?'

She put her hand on his head again, and they were silent. When she looked down at him in a little while, he was asleep.

Then all the pain in Jane began to stir. To move and break the control she had forced on it as if it were alive within her. She cried out under it, then bit her lips together in case she should waken Noel. He did not wake. She put up her free hand to wipe off the tears that ran down her cheeks, in case they should fall on his sleeping face. She sobbed very carefully, so that he should not feel the tremors of her body.

She would have to go. She would have to leave him. There was no place in his life for her now.

The weakness and vagueness of the last few days cleared away. She saw sharply that the only thing left open to her was to go away and leave Noel to his duty. To leave him free to do his stern task. If she stayed, he could not do it ; she knew that.

Now, at this time, his desire for her was submerged by pressing anxiety ; she was almost crowded out of his thoughts at present. But when this crisis was over, weeks ahead, when he was settled down into his daily round, he would want her again. If she stayed within reach, within sight, Noel would inevitably turn to her. She would draw him off from his wife and his son in spite of herself. Jane knew herself ; she knew that she went so hard for what she wanted that she almost always got it in the end. But here it must not be. She must go. Simply get out of Noel's way.

It must be all or nothing in love. And since it could not be all, it was nothing.

'Nothing,' she said aloud to Noel.

But he was asleep.

Desolation engulfed her.

'Oh, God ! Oh, Noel ! . . .'

No good calling to anyone. She was alone. She went down into depths she had never known.

She sat in the green chair, her fingers slack on his hair, tears stiff on her cheeks, all her thoughts vague and terrible.

The windows of the room were wide open to the spring night, and the noises of the town were muted.

She leaned forward suddenly in passionate contemplation of his face. Let her learn it by heart, because she would perhaps never see it again.

She bent over him, until she felt his breath come and go against her cheek. Oh, intolerably dear . . .

He moved and turned his face inwards to her breast.

'Oh, Jane . . .' he murmured. 'Is it you . . . here?'

She felt his lips through the thin stuff of her dress, and held him closer in an agony of love.

Suddenly he sat up.

'What time is it? Did I go to sleep? Have I slept long? Damn it all—wasting the precious time I have with you! Why did you let me, Jane? Is it half-past? I have to meet Briggs with Kearns at half-past. Oh, my dear—always leaving you.'

He got up wearily and looked round for his hat.

'I do hope I shall get in again this week. Oh, isn't it all damnable, Jane? I'm so tied up and involved and so dead sick of it all. But I've got to go through with it.'

'I know,' said Jane.

He took her in his arms, and she stayed there in silence. The last time. The last, last time . . . and he didn't know it.

'Good-bye, my dearest.'

'Good-bye, Noel.'

'Don't think, if I don't come, that I am forgetting, or anything like that, will you?' he begged.

'No,' said Jane. 'We must both do what we have to. I know that.'

'Good-bye, then, darling one.'

'Good-bye.'

She could hardly bear his kiss, but he came back from the door to kiss her again. Once more, and then he was gone. Gone.

Jane, her eyes fixed, listened. Far away down the
stairs the side-door closed, and in the street below his
footsteps died away.

II

She got up at last from where she had thrown herself by the chair. She went to the windows and leaned
there looking out. The town lay huddled blackly
under the lamps, silent, save for the occasional rumble
of a lorry travelling in the night.

Her eyes wandered to the woody heights. Noel
slept somewhere there with his wife and his son. And
Mrs. Briggs contentedly with her Albert. They would
go on without her.

What could she say to Noel? She must write; not
see him again. A letter would hurt less. The blow
would be halved if she was gone before he realized it.

She wandered about her rooms, moving things here
and there, talking unhappily to herself.

She opened the door and went down the stairs.
She wanted to get into the air, away from this room
where she was so unhappy. She went out into the
market-place, where night after night for years she
had walked round and round. She walked round and
round now under the lamps, coming into the pools
of light with her pale face and wrung hands, passing
into the shadows, and emerging again; round and
round.

She came to an abrupt halt. She had almost run
into a man. She looked at him without seeing him,
and would have passed on. But he did not move
aside. She looked at him again, and came out of her
preoccupation sufficiently to recognize him.

'Oh . . .' she said in a bewildered way. 'Wilfrid?'

' Yes, Jane—again,' said Wilfrid. ' I'm over just now, and I wanted to see you.'

She had forgotten he had ever gone away. She asked none of the questions he had been afraid of. He was afraid of having to admit that he had come specially to see her when he heard of the Greenwood case.

' Can I come up, Jane ? '

' Oh, I '—she looked round the market-place in distress—' I'm so tired.'

' I can see that,' he said gravely. ' But I do want to talk to you. Just for a moment.'

Jane turned abruptly and went through her door. She was past talking. She had no curiosity as to what Wilfrid would say. It was just another thing to be borne.

He followed her into the sitting-room, where all the lights were burning as she had left them.

He pulled a chair to the fire.

' Sit here, Jane.'

She did as she was told. He closed the door and came to sit opposite her.

' What are you going to do, Jane ? ' he asked.

' Going to do ? ' repeated Jane wanly. ' I'm going away. I'm leaving the shop and Tidsley and—and everything. The agreement is drawn up. I was going before . . . but now . . . I'm going just the same. . . .' Her voice trailed lamely off into silence.

Wilfrid's eyes filled with tears. She was so badly hurt. As hurt as he had been. And there was nothing he could do to comfort her. Except be there ; be with her. Even though she disliked it. He looked away from her. He felt he ought not to be a witness to this suffering.

The plans he had come with seemed futile ; too small to offer.

She sat on in the chair, still and pale.

'What did you come for, Wilfrid ? ' she said at last, remembering him with an effort.

He did not answer, wondering how he was going to put it.

She waited ; but without interest.

'Well . . .' he began, and paused. Then he plunged into it. 'Jane, I guessed something like this would face you. I even guessed what you would do. Yes, isn't it strange I should know you so well ? But, after all, it's a long time. Ten years, about, you and I have been friends. That's why I do hope you'll forgive me if I seem to be thrusting myself on you now.'

He spoke with such eager persuasion that Jane was moved out of her self-absorption. She looked at him for the first time as if she saw him.

'I thought you'd want to get out of here,' he went on. 'And I know you've got no people. I thought you'd feel . . .' He faltered, overcome by a wretched embarrassment. He shook it off. 'Jane, I know you're alone,' he continued more firmly. 'You have to make a fresh start. It's dreadfully hard when you don't care whether you make a start or not. Don't be alone. Come to London, and get another shop going as quickly as possible. I'll be there and I'll be able to be with you, and go about just as we used to— d'you remember the old days ? Plunge into life again, Jane—at once. It's the only way. Specially for you. Come to London, Jane.'

He ended on a desperate pleading note.

Jane put out her hand and took his. She did not speak, but smiled waveringly at him.

He was encouraged. He leaned forward, holding her hand in his, and poured out plans and ways and means.

' You say you must go somewhere, Jane,' he finished. ' It might just as well be London.'

London ! The home of the homeless !

' I think I always meant to go to London,' she said at last.

She didn't say she didn't care where she went ; he was so eager.

' There's so much to see. Every time I see anything —you know—*our* sort of thing, I wish you were there to see it too. I found that memorial in Westminster cloisters the other day ; that one about rendering an unspotted soul to God in spite of the small-pox. You told me about it. Do you remember ? '

' I copied it out on a post-card to send to you during the War,' said Jane, following him with an effort.

' But you didn't send it,' he said.

' No,' said Jane.

She remembered the withdrawal of Wilfrid during the War. And afterwards—when she had drawn so close to him. How strange life was with its ebbings and flowings, its fluctuations, its inexplicable movements towards and away from . . .

' Well . . .' she said, getting up from her chair. ' I'll go to London. I suppose I should have gone anyhow, but you've helped me to make up my mind. And you're so good, Wilfrid, to have come to help me. So good . . . always. . . .'

She wanted to cry. But she pressed her fingers to her lips and hurried to the desk.

' Here's Venner's agreement,' she said quickly. ' Let's get it signed. You can witness it.'

She smoothed out the paper with trembling hands. She took up her pen and wrote her name without pause.

Then she looked in a lost way at Wilfrid.

' What an end ! ' she cried.

He caught her hand in his, firmly, warmly.

' My dear . . . it's not an end,' he said.

If you have enjoyed this Persephone book why not telephone or write to us for a free copy of the *Persephone Catalogue* and the current *Persephone Biannually*? All Persephone books ordered from us cost £12 or three for £30 plus £2 postage per book.

PERSEPHONE BOOKS LTD
59 Lamb's Conduit Street
London WC1N 3NB

Telephone: 020 7242 9292
sales@persephonebooks.co.uk
www.persephonebooks.co.uk